Leif Andersson knows a lot of things. How to hunt terrorists, where to hide from his neurotic, overbearing sisters, when to make a reasonable judgement call, and why he's never settled down with a woman. When a SEAL base opens in the small, coastal town of Bronze Bay, Florida, Leif knows it's the perfect situation to shake things up after years of fighting a monotonous, global war. A simple place, to build a simple life turns out to be anything but when he meets and falls in love with her.

Dementia stole Malena Winterset's mother. It also took her father. He abandoned them both a decade ago when the mental illness grew to be more than he could bear. As the primary caretaker for her mother, Malena spends her days planning parties and working at the Bronze Bay General Store. Her nights are spent at home, wishing for something more. When a SEAL base opens, a new, handsome face in town makes his presence known, but his affections come with rules.

1.) Two forms of birth control

2.) Never leave stuff at his place

3.) Be content to never meet his family

4.) Don't fall in love with him

When the unthinkable happens, and three of the rules are shockingly, and accidentally broken, lives are changed forever.

At least Malena never left her toothbrush in his bathroom…
ok

PRAISE FOR RACHEL ROBINSON NOVELS

"Rachel Robinson knows SEALs better than SEALs know themselves."

Natasha Madison, Bestselling Author

"INTOXICATING. Absolutely consuming! What a ride. And it's such a different story! It really is. I just loved it."

Angie, Angie's Dreamy Reads

"Rachel Robinson has penned a flawless story of pain and heartache, damaged pasts and uncertain futures mixed with soul searing heat, all consuming love and breathtaking beauty. Black and White Flowers is a stunning novel worth an infinite amount of stars."

Sophie, Bookalicious Babes Blog

"Achingly beautiful. This book will haunt you in the very best way."

J.L. Berg, *USA Today* bestselling author

"In Life Plus One, Rachel Robinson delivers a captivating romance with characters you easily fall in love with. Harper and Ben's story is a heart breaking love story I never wanted to end. Her best yet!"

Josephine Brierley, Author of *Delicate Lies*

"I loved this book so much that I want to shout it from the roof tops. A beautifully written love story that will keep you wanting more."

New York Times Bestselling Author, Aurora Rose Reynolds

TITLES BY RACHEL ROBINSON

CONTEMPORARY ROMANCE
CRAZY GOOD SERIES
CRAZY GOOD
SET IN STONE
TIME AND SPACE

THE REAL SEAL SERIES
BLACK AND WHITE FLOWERS
HERO HAIR
LIFE PLUS ONE

THE BRONZE BAY SEALS
KEEPING IT

ROMANTIC COMEDY
FROG HOG NOVELLAS
Frog Hog – Valen and Hutch

EROTIC ROMANCE
THE DOM GAMES

Visit Rachel Robinson online
www.racheljrobinson.com
facebook.com/racheljeanrobinson

A NAVY SEAL AND SECRET BABY ROMANCE

tossing it

INTERNATIONAL BESTSELLING AUTHOR
RACHEL ROBINSON

Copyright © 2018 Rachel Robinson

All rights reserved.

Cover design by Allison Martin at MakeReady Designs
Cover Images by Lindee Robinson Photography
Cover Models: Jeff Kline & Angel LaCoursiere
Edited by J. Wells
Proofread by Ellie McLove at Gray Ink
Formatted by C.P. Smith

Without limiting the rights under copyright reserved above, no part of this publication may be reproduced, stored in or introduced into a retrieval system, or transmitted in any form, or by any means (electronic, mechanical, photocopying, recording, or otherwise) without the prior written permission of the above author of this book. This is a work of fiction. Names, characters, places, brands, media, and incidents are either the product of the author's imagination or are used fictitiously. Any resemblance to actual persons living or dead, locales, or events is entirely coincidental.

For anyone who has ever kept a secret.

tossing it

Prologue

Malena

Present day . . .

Even though they sell them at the General Store, you can't really buy them there. No one does. You'd be the talk of the town. The last time I glanced at the fully stocked shelf was when I dusted the boxes during a bi-annual store cleaning. Instead, like all of the terrified women that came before me, I sit on this table. The cold metal brushing my bare calves, the crumpled paper gown rustling anytime I move my arms, waiting for Doc Taylor. He is one of the only people bound to secrecy in Bronze Bay—the solitary resident who has never spoken a sordid secret, or passed gossip like it's his job. Probably because it's against the law. Thank God.

The old wooden door creaks open, and I hold my breath. Doc pushes his reading glasses up his nose using the manila file folder that contains my fate. His face gives nothing away, a practiced stoicism that comes from doing this hundreds, hell, probably even thousands of times before. The paper wrapping my body makes a crunching noise, and I stifle the irritation. *This is part of the experience, Malena, I remind myself. You deal with it.*

"Ms. Winterset," he croaks, the deep wrinkles on his forehead creasing further. "Looks like I have some news for you."

Sweating is normal in Florida. It's hot as hell, and it's just like breathing. There's a vent blowing air conditioning right on me, and I'm naked under this paper "gown," so I blame the puddles in my armpits and behind my knees on pure, unfiltered stress. "Yes. Good or bad, Doc. Don't keep me waiting here. I'm dying. You're killing me."

He chuckles, the throaty noise easing my nerves a touch. Wait. I bet that's another skill in his arsenal. I clear my throat as he sits on the round stool in the corner, propping one elbow on the desk beside him. "Malena, you already know what this file says. You marked down on the paperwork that your monthly cycle is two months late," Doc says calmly, then he smiles. "You're pregnant!"

My heart sinks. I'm not stupid, no, don't assume that. I am a woman who can't possibly be with child. I recall all of the negative pregnancy tests over the course of our marriage and shake my head again. All of that time trying to have a baby and not being able to give him what he wanted. While I know my period is late, I still held out hope my cycle was off and it had forced me to skip a period…or two. I hang my head as hot shame and disbelief wash over my body like a hoard of fire ants. I can't pass on my genes, *her genes,* to anyone. I definitely can't do it alone. My breaths come quicker as I conclude my initial reaction. Terrifying, horrified, panic. "No. No. This can't be happening. How sure are you? This isn't in my plan. Remember? They said I was unable to conceive. My uterus. The hormones. You have the paperwork. Look at it," I say, pointing to my thick file.

Doc taps the front of the file with his knuckles. "They can make mistakes. It wasn't a solid diagnosis, either. It was an educated guess." He shrugs. I flounder with my thoughts. My past. "I made you keep on that gown so we could sneak a little ultrasound in today. I had reception clear my schedule for the next hour. You're twelve weeks pregnant. We can do an ultrasound. Would you like to see your baby?" He perceives the panic on my face, and wheels his stool closer and stands next to me. "It's going to be okay, Ms. Winterset. You're not the first woman to get pregnant outside of wedlock in Bronze Bay, and you won't be the last. Let's have a look, shall we?" If it were only that simple. If the man who impregnated me by some miraculous deed wasn't adamantly against family and babies.

I feel full at the new knowledge and I press both hands against my lower stomach as the gown makes another awful crinkling sound. "I can't take care of a baby. I can't do it. What can we do if I can't do this? If I can't have this baby?" It's impossible to meet his eyes as I plead for

tossing it

options. I've known him since I moved to Bronze Bay as a small child. I see him at town functions and every time I have a bad cold or twisted ankle. He's watched me grow up. This man treated my mom for years before her case of dementia became too much for a small town general practitioner to handle. Eventually, she saw doctors who make house calls because taking her out of the house became too much of a risk. She forgets where she's at and who I am. She forgets that my father abandoned us a decade ago and starts screaming for him, like I've stolen her from some ideal life. My stomach flips. "If I can't do it?" I ask again.

Doc pretends he doesn't hear me. I'm not sure if that's his response to my harried plea, or if it's his way of deterring me from saying anything further on the subject. He tells me to lay back, and I do, sniffling a bit as I go. The silence as he readies the small machine tells me he's thinking about Betty Winterset. "How is your mama doing?" he asks.

"About the same. They have her stabilized at Garden Breeze. It's good for her. She seems very happy," I reply. A nurse slips into the room and tries to keep her gaze away from mine, watching the doctor squirt some sort of warm gel on my stomach. The thought of my mother distracts me, and I think that's what he wanted to accomplish. It became too much for me and her nurse, the woman who was there any time I wasn't because she couldn't be by herself. My mom requires a full-time caretaker. It was hard to watch her slip away a little at a time. It must have been even harder on my father, because that bastard took off as soon as her diagnosis rendered her useless.

A baby? I can't handle that. The bravest person on

the planet would balk at this, I'm sure of it. I saw what happens when a family is torn apart, and I'm not willing to force any children into my messed-up life.

Doc is talking about her condition as his hand with the small wand moves over my lower stomach. When he presses harder, and pauses, I look at the fuzzy black and white screen. I know what it is immediately. I see the goblin looking head and the slip of a body. It moves around on the oblong shape, directly in the middle. It shimmies and bobs as if it's taunting me.

"Oh, my God," I gasp, tears welling in my eyes. Some moments will always be singed in your mind regardless if they are good or bad. The view of the wiggly tadpole body that currently resides in my supposedly barren uterus is a moment I'll never forget. I close my eyes, but the image is burned on the insides of my eyelids.

"It's a beautiful miracle," Doc says. "Now shush," he chides. The faint ba-bum-ba-bum-ba-bum echoes in the room. "That's the heartbeat." He points out the heart as he ups the volume on the whooshing noise. Years ago, I would have sold my soul to have this moment with Dylan sitting next to me, his hand in mine, both of our eyes transfixed by what we made. What he wanted so desperately. Love isn't enough sometimes. Dylan left at my insistence and God knows where he's at now, or why I'm rehashing old wounds in my time of crisis. He wanted kids and I couldn't give them to him. Now I'm carrying the child of a man who rejoiced at the idea of my inability to start a family.

My gaze strays from the screen to the nurse. Her eyes lock on mine. "Your boyfriend will be so happy," she says, a comforting smile on her lips. Doc Taylor's wife

tossing it

has been his nurse the entire time his practice has been open. I know she means comfort in her words, but fear is all that is bubbling out of me at this moment. I try to return her smile in equal measure but know that I fall woefully short.

I look away from her and focus on the monitor and the constant noise coming from it. I cling to that noise and know what I must do. Doc is taking measurements and reassuring me of a healthy pregnancy even though I've yet to receive prenatal care. He mentions the OB in the next town over and tells his wife to schedule me an appointment and directs her to order some bloodwork before the appointment.

"I'll print this photo out for you to show the proud daddy."

I haven't felt sick for twelve weeks, but for the first time, I feel like I might vomit. The contents of my stomach swirling as the nausea hits. I snatch the photo from his hands as I sit up.

Hanging my head, I try to control the knots welling in my stomach, the black and white photo clenched in one hand. "I can't believe this," I mutter. *This is what it feels like to lose control over your life. This. Right here and now.*

"Malena," Doc says, breaking the professional atmosphere. "It is going to be okay. No one is ever truly ready for parenthood. You just do it. You have changed and adapted to far harder things." He nods. "You'll be a fantastic mother."

Shaking my head, a tremor of a chill shoots up my spine. "That's the difference between everyone else and me. I can't do it. Not well," I say. Doc nods sweetly at his wife and she leaves the room, taking my dirty secret with her.

"You can do it well. It's a shock. A blessing. I'll be here for you," he says. "Bronze Bay will be here for you. You aren't alone." Doc assumes my hesitance is because of the father of my baby, or the lack thereof. Well, obviously, Leif doesn't want anything to do with the predicament I'm in, but surely he'll be there for me in whatever form that means for him. He is a kind man to the core. A generous, beautiful man. The only reason my mother is in a top-notch facility. A monthly support check? A pop in once a year for a birthday party? Doc Taylor goes on trying to assure me, and comfort me. He tells me a story about when his son was a baby and I know I'm supposed to smile or laugh, but I can't. Now I'm thinking about Leif. And that's a heartache that brings me to my knees.

My baby isn't being born into a loving family. It would arrive right smack dab in the middle of a nightmare. I thank the doctor and he leaves so I can dress and collect my purse from a chair across the room.

I fix my hair in the mirror above the small sink and slick a coat of lip gloss along my bottom lip and rub my top lip against it. I school the tears threatening to break free, and exit the room, accept the appointment card thrust into my hand, and step into the salty breeze of a Bronze Bay afternoon. I start up my car, check my emails on my phone, and head to my mother. If nothing else, her presence will bring me comfort.

I tilt my chin up and drive toward the ocean, my mind on the percentages of false infertility diagnoses. And the decision I just made about my future. About *our* future.

Chapter One

Leif

Sweat drips off my chin. I pump the bar up and down once more—my arms shaking from exertion. Sutter throws down weight next to me and grunts. I do one more bench press, lock the bar in place, and then hop to my feet. With my hands on my hips, I suck in several large gulps of air while my friend does the same. "What's on the agenda today?" Sutter asks.

I raise and lower my shoulders. Fact of the matter is, it's been slow around our base here at Bronze Bay these days. After the terrorist attacks that spanned our whole world, we opened up smaller SEAL bases outside of the ones in San Diego, Virginia Beach, and Hawaii. Now we are spread out across the United States. We have quicker reaction times when SEALs are needed. When we're not needed, we're hitting the gym and practicing the skill sets that make us the most lethal force on planet earth. "Want to go shoot at the range?" I ask. "Tahoe went over

tossing it

to the airport again. Hopefully we'll be skydiving soon."

Sutter nods, wiping the sweat off his face with a towel. "Fuck yeah, man. I want to get up in the air as soon as possible. I'm going to grab lunch at the diner and then meet you at the range after? What do you want to shoot today?" Sutter is a sniper, so he's going to blow me out of the water no matter what we're shooting. He knows that and he is only asking to rub it in later that it was my choice and he still shot better.

"Pick your poison," I say. Smiling, he leaves the weight room and hits the showers, knowing I'm no competition. My cell phone rings on the bench in front of the mirror and I roll my eyes. It's a ringer assigned to one of my sisters. The more annoying one. The decision to let voicemail grab it is easy. My sisters made my choice to leave Virginia Beach and move to Bronze Bay uncomplicated. Overbearing, loud, calculating in the name of sibling love, and utterly infuriating are the qualities attached to my sisters, Eva and Celia. My mom used to be able to control them when we were kids, but now all bets are off. They show up at my apartment and overstay their welcome. It doesn't help matters that I am the baby brother. A grown ass adult male doesn't want his sisters meddling, but they don't believe me when I tell them. Like it's so farfetched, I have to be joking.

When Eva married a nice, quiet man, I assumed the eldest sibling would be a monkey off my back. I had a vision of her riding into the sunset on horseback, never looking back. In reality, her stallion is a white sedan that sits in front of my house multiple times during the week. That nice quiet man is also a busy man who leaves Eva to her own devices much of the time. He's also the reason they moved twenty minutes away to take a job so my sister could live next to family. His absence only made less intense by my immediate presence. My meals are cooked and prepped for me every Friday night, and it's a nice gesture, but I'd much rather starve than have to endure the conversations that accompany the cooking. Eva asks if I've had any dates. Celia, who now lives a little farther away than Eva, visits a touch less but wants details—names, and descriptions of the women I've seen around town when she is here. When they're together, they stalk around the quiet town of Bronze Bay to scope out prospects for me. At least twice, they've returned with the names and phone numbers of women they've met and deemed appropriate for me to take on a date.

For most of my life, I've been wrapped up in war and everything that means. Deployments, training, work up cycles when I'm away more than I'm home, missions to gain Intel, missions to kill bad guys. If it's in the same vein as war or has anything to do with it, chances are, I've been up to my eyeballs in it. Being a SEAL is something that fell into my lap. Unlike a lot of my brothers, it wasn't something I'd always dreamed of. It was a choice I made because of the climate of our world. Make a difference, my mother said when I was contemplating my future after high school. The military was appealing because I could get away from the tight love-noose my family created. The Navy was even more appealing because they couldn't follow me into the ocean, right? Becoming

tossing it

a SEAL was something I knew would definitely give me an edge. I could make a difference and score chicks whenever I had the chance. With lots of work and a little luck, I made it through training.

My cell notifies me of a voicemail, and I grunt out of frustration. No one leaves voicemails these days. No one. Not unless it's a spambot politician call, or my sisters demanding my attention. Scooping up my towel and phone, I hit the shower. A few of my brothers are exiting as I enter, and I nod at them and give them the plans for the day. It's nice to have such a lax agenda after years of a punishing, demanding schedule that left most of us browbeat. Some of the SEALs that staff this base are here because they need a rest from the breakneck deployment pace, others are here because it's more conducive to a family life and they need a change to help facilitate that. Some men have been sent here even though they don't think they need a break. Those are the ones I have to watch out for. They don't want to be here, and they'll burn it all to the ground because of it. Sutter went on a sex spree so savage I was hearing about it for a month after. Small towns don't offer secrecy in any amount.

Everyone talks. It's exactly as horrible as you'd expect. The old women click their tongues when we walk by, upset we took over their land, and part of their beach. The local diner is a hotbed of hearsay. Within a few weeks of moving here, I knew more about the residents of Bronze Bay, Florida than I ever knew about my best friends back home; including the fact Irene McAllister's curtains matched her carpet. The slow pace of life mixed with the location—far away from any large cities, force gossip like the gospel. That's not something I signed up for when I became a SEAL. Typically, we are a close-knit community with many secrets. This is a whole new experience in every way. One I love and loathe in equal measure. Do I miss the thrill? The heart in my throat feeling when I'm rounding a corner about to fight fire with fire? Yes. Idle hands, idle minds, and all that. This beach town doesn't provide much thrill, and the monotony of the daily grind wears on me, but I know I'm serving a purpose and one day my reason for residing in Bronze Bay will come to light. If anything, I am a motherfucking team player.

I let the voicemail from Eva play on speaker while I shower—the shrill ring of her voice alerting me and anyone in listening distance that she's upset I didn't pick up her call. She tells me she's coming over after work today and wants to talk about the details of our mother's birthday.

"Great," I mutter, soaping my body.

"You should have answered it," Aidan replies, his body hidden by a wall. "You could have thwarted her attempts to rule your life." Aidan is the king of comedy. He makes jokes or inserts humor any chance he gets. He also inserts his dick into anything in female form, anytime, any chance he gets. It gets him into trouble. He's a good operator. A damn good one. When it's time to work, he's the one I want covering my back. I wouldn't trust him with a girl for all the money in the world.

"I know," I growl. "They're ruining my life. We can

tossing it

plan something for Mom's birthday over the phone. I don't get her need to be in my business constantly." It's not just my opinion, everyone around me agrees my sisters are over the top.

"It's not normal," Aidan chirps, rounding the corner dragging a white towel over his head. We talk a little bit about how his family stays out of his way. He doesn't have annoying sisters or my troubles of breaking free of his family's clutches. If I were to tell them both to fuck off, I think that would drive them to hound me even more than they already do. At the end of the day, they're all I have. I've had several romantic relationships. None of them ever lasted more than a few months. My schedule combined with their need for attention wasn't something that ever worked out. I've been called cocky, self-centered, altruistic, and cynical. I've been called heartless, cold, smug, and inconsiderate. I can't confirm or deny if there's truth to any of it. I've never been attached long enough to self-evaluate. Moving on is what I'm good at.

When Aidan brings up the fact my sisters are meddling with my sex life, I have to defend myself. "Listen. They thought me being reassigned to Bronze Bay meant I was going to settle down in all ways. They're disappointed I haven't yet. I can't be sure if they really would be happy with any woman I chose. You have to admit the fact that everyone talks, and it seems everyone is friends here, halts a lot of our sex lives. I'm not like you, I'm not opposed to finding a girlfriend per se, because that would be sort of mandated if I don't want to get Bay blacklisted, but it would come with so many strings, I'd trip up even the best of candidates."

Aidan laughs. "Candidate? This isn't BUD/s man." It would be easier if it were.

I crank off the water. "It's not, but I might as well treat it as such. It's a small town. Can't afford to not screen well." The thought of having a girlfriend is utterly terrifying. I've got a long-term relationship with my job. That shows I'm commitment worthy, right?

"Good luck with that. I'll just continue my underground app trolling. Did you see the chick Tahoe's talking to?"

Drying off, I throw on a pair of shorts and a T-shirt, and slide into my flip-flops. "I'd stay away from her, man. That one has his name written all over her." Tahoe is fucking smitten. We all know it, but we're waiting for him to finally admit it to himself. Let him live with the turmoil a little while longer.

Aidan scoffs. "Whatever. He hasn't said anything to let me know otherwise, so I'll do what I want." There is the true Aidan. Rolling my eyes, I grab my bag and scold him over my shoulder. He waves me off, that challenging look in his eye. Tahoe is going to crush him. Aidan will undoubtedly earn it.

The gun range is a decent practice session. Keeping up with my skills feels good. It reminds me that I am, in fact, a SEAL regardless of where I'm situated geographically.

tossing it

Sutter kicks my ass via three different weapons, but it's okay because I *almost* won once which makes him grumpy. We close the day with a meeting, which is an informal occasion—a bunch of dudes in civilian clothing sitting around a conference table. The updates stream into our system as we're briefed on what's going on in the world. Terrorist quads lurk everywhere, but they've stayed in hiding because we've gotten so good at rooting them out. For the first time in a long time, we can breathe a little easier—take our time in deciding our next course of action.

Civilians have no clue what really goes on in the name of keeping America safe. It's easier that way. There would be panic and disbelief, conspiracy theories and outrage. Instead, our military has created a false sense of security—increasing our presence around the United States. Reports of incidents aren't shared as effortlessly as they were at the beginning of the war. To preserve the sense that we have everything under control, it's now a weekly recap that spews from the mouths of reporters late at night. We're confirming reports of such incidents right now.

The email flashes on the large overhead screen. "That one looks good. Send it on." Someone brushes past me, in a hurry to wrap and get out of here for the weekend. The email is forwarded on and the last one pops up as I speed read expecting more of the usual. It's not. It's the name of a bad guy we've been going after for years. A name of a guy I personally missed by the hair on his chinny-chin-chin. The sole name on my list of bad guys I must dispose of before I die. He's up to no good again, trying to recruit more sinister assholes to keep me gainfully employed. I nod at the guy working the laptop. "Email me that one. I'll come back later tonight to finish up. Let's get out of here." The guys know the name—and my feelings about the fact he's still at large.

Adrenaline hits me, my fists clenching by my sides as I remember the last mission I was on. Nothing compares to the thrill of the chase and the close call that inevitably follows. They're all close calls in one form or another. It's why there's no room for errors on the Teams. Every mission is a no-fail mission. Before we leave for an operation, we're confident we'll be successful. That mindset trickles into my everyday life, but I'm acutely aware of the difference. Bronze Bay has taught me that.

Even if it's hard to admit, the slow pace of life and the sleepy beach town has done wonders to detoxify my mind. I can ride my bicycle or moped most places. There's plenty of water to wakeboard, fish, and boat. There's time for me to have a life outside of the grind for the first time in a long ass time. From the day I graduated BUD/s to the day I landed in Bronze Bay, life has been one seamless work cycle with little blips of non-work experiences. I love my job. I loved being busy and making a difference, but there's also something to be said about calm. I ride home on my shiny black moped on a deserted road. The scent of saltwater and sand clinging to every breath I take. Yes, it is indeed a love-hate relationship.

I see Eva's car pulling into her usual spot as soon as I

turn into my small apartment complex that faces the bay. There are four large units, and we share a dock and a little slip of beach. Old Mr. Olsen is sitting in his lounge chair on his porch when I walk by. He tips his worn-out straw hat as I approach. "It's a beautiful day, son. Stop and smell that breeze?" he chirps, voice hoarse from years of chain-smoking Marlboro Reds. He stopped a couple years ago when his pesky cough turned out to be cancer, or so he's told me. Sometimes I smell cigarette smoke early in the morning, and I know I'm not imagining it.

"All the way home, Mr. Olsen," I reply, holding up my dorky helmet. If I'm going to die, I better be shot through the heart or blown to pieces. I refuse to be road kill in this town. That's a hard line in the sand for me. Safety in all non-hazardous areas of my life, and caution to the wind when I'm downrange under fire. "Enjoy your night. Let me know if you need anything," I say.

"You do the same," he croaks. "Though it looks like it may be difficult." His sly gaze flicks to Eva pacing my tiny front porch, fingers laced behind her back.

Shaking my head, I laugh. "Anyone ever tell you, you're a smart old man?"

"All the way home, Leif, my son." With that, he tips his hat over his face and reclines all the way back for an evening nap.

"Eva," I say, cursing under my breath. "While it's always nice to see you" —I roll my eyes so she can see— "We could have discussed Mom's birthday on the phone. You really need to butt out of my life. I have somewhere to be tonight. Plans with my friends, you know?"

Eva huffs, tilts her head to the side and scrunches up her face in that bitchy way she's ace at. "Why did you ignore my phone call?"

Mr. Olsen snorts loudly, a laugh masked by a pretend snore. I grin when Eva peeks over my shoulder. "The heavy metal I was holding over my face prevented me from picking up my cell phone at that particular moment," I fire back, unlocking the door and pushing it open.

Eva flies in first and spins on me. One eyebrow raised she croons, "What, you're so weak you can't hold your gun up now?"

I groan, turning my face to the ceiling. "Bench press, Eva. I was working out when you called. It makes answering the phone hard. What do you have in mind for the party? What do you need me to do? Is your husband gone again?"

Her face changes, and the guilt hits. Eva veers into the kitchen and opens the fridge. "I'll just make you some dinner before you go out, okay?"

Biting my tongue, I set my bag and helmet on the rack by the door and throw the switches to illuminate the living room. "Why did you marry the guy if you were going to be constantly lonely?" And in my fucking business.

"Why would you marry a woman if you were going to be constantly deployed?" she shoots back, turning on the stove. I glance at the ingredients, the ones she bought earlier this week and can't deny I'm excited to eat what she's making. It's one of my favorites.

Leaning on the island bar, I watch her work for a couple

of silent moments. "That's why I haven't committed to anyone, Eva. That logic doesn't work. Flipping the argument doesn't win this time." She sniffles once and tucks her fair blonde hair behind one ear. It's almost the same shade as mine, except hers is a touch darker. I'm in the sun more frequently, and she lives in an office all day long. "Are you happy?" I ask.

She's quiet for a few moments, and an outsider might think it's one of those awkward silences that happen when you're not sure what to say, but when you have siblings like Eva, it's never awkward. There's nothing I can say that would offend her and vice versa. She's calculating how her response is going to be taken, weighing whether it's worth telling the truth. Basically we're having the conversation in her mind before she begins it. "I'm as happy as I can be given the circumstances." She slides a bottle of water to me over the counter. "He is busy with his life. I'm busy with mine. When we're together, it works well and we're happy. Mundane, maybe, but that's what it looks like for most people." She casts a glance letting me know I don't reside in that category.

It sounds fucking awful and I'd tell her so if I felt like arguing. "Here's the thing," I start, clearing my voice. "You here all the time isn't good for business. Even the guys at work think it's weird. I moved here to start a life of my own."

"Shut up. You aren't a child. Why do you care what they think about your family?" Because it's interfering with my life. "We are your family. That means we'll always be a part of your life no matter where you move."

"Can we limit visits to weekends only?" I ask, opening the water and drinking half. "The food and cooking is appreciated. Your ugly mug in my kitchen is fantastic, but Sundays only? That's fair."

Her eyes go wild. After countless hours of training in interrogating suspects, I know what the feral look in her eye means. "We are adults, Eva. You're married. My house," I say, waving an arm around the room. "Your house," I add, pointing at the door. "Please." Manners might get me out of a fight with Celia, but Eva is a fucking shark so I steel my nerves.

She shakes her head and starts muttering under her breath. "You don't even ask about me. How I'm doing. You move right in to how I'm making you feel. It's not always about you, Leif. Despite what the rest of the world leads you to believe."

My cell phone vibrates in my pocket and as subtly as possible, I slide it out and read the text from Sutter. They're heading to Bobby's Bar and want to know when I'll be there. Swallowing hard, I look at my sister, her back facing me. "If you want my friendship and for me to wonder how you're doing you probably need to go away for a while. Absence makes the heart grow fonder and all that. You call me every day. You come over uninvited. There's no guesswork involved."

She spins, the frying pan in her hands. "The IVF didn't take. Again," she says, eyes glassing over. My breath lodges in my throat. "I'm bleeding out $19,500 worth of fertilized eggs that won't attach to my uterus right now." *Oh, fuck.*

tossing it

Where the fuck is Celia? She's good at this. She's the sincere sibling. A lump of dread lodges in my throat, and I work to clear it. "I'm sorry," I reply, voice low. "That must be tough." She can't expect more than that from me. When it comes to emotions, I'm stunted. I block out everything in favor of feeling nothing. I'd blame my job and what I sometimes have to do, but I think I've always been like this. An emotional robot. I round the island and pull my sister into my arms. "I'm sorry, Eva. Maybe next time?"

Her face buried in my chest, she shakes her head. "We're out of fertilized eggs. I don't want to go through all of that again and he told me he doesn't want to use someone else's. I haven't told him it didn't take yet. He had an important business dinner tonight. It would have upset him." Eva is rarely emotional. In fact, this whole process with her infertility is the only time I've seen her upset to this degree. Probably because she always gets what she wants, and for the first time she can't control the outcome. I'm not completely sure she doesn't want a baby so bad because it's harder for her to have one. While we were growing up, she always waxed poetic about never having kids because they're messy and take up too much time. We were all shocked when she announced that not only were she and her husband trying to have a baby, but they were going through fertility treatments to give them the best chance possible. Celia called her a liar and a massive fight broke out. Our parents were happy at the prospect of grandchildren, but even they were wary of her drastically altered plans.

Sighing, I try to be sympathetic because I know how hard she's been trying to have a baby, but in the same breath, personally, I think she's fucking insane for wanting a family. A baby. A child. An actual human being that depends on you in all ways. If you're lucky it's eighteen years, if you're not it's forever and ever. That tether is something I never want. Parenting isn't a no-fail mission, and that's a risk I'm not willing to take.

Ever.

Chapter two

Malena

"I saw Caroline and Tahoe in the parking lot," I tell Shirley after taking a large swallow of my tonic water. The lime is just for looks. I have to sleep with one eye open tonight. The night nurse called in sick and the last thing I need is to have my mind clouded by alcohol. No one has time for that. I have a couple of hours before I need to get back to relieve Mom's daytime caretaker. "That man is really something to look at, isn't he? Caroline was all flushed," I add. Shirley loves to talk men. She likes to talk about them in any form. Even if they belong to someone else. From what I've seen, it's mostly harmless. Everyone knows she's secretly hung up on Caleb, the cook from the diner she is a waitress at. They have torrid sex, see other people, and end up back in bed together.

Shirley shakes her head while gulping down her beer.

tossing it

She wipes her mouth on the sleeve of her fishnet sweater and shakes her head before saying. "His name is Tahoe for fuck's sake. That girl isn't going to know what to do when he kicks that thing into four-wheel drive."

I giggle. "She'll manage I'm sure." It will be a relief if she finally loses her virginity. Maybe the appeal of Caroline May will dull a touch. We all reside inside of Caroline's shadow of innocence. After this long, you can't help but think she's doing something right.

Alternatively, Shirley tells me a story about a fling last night, all the while casting glances at the bartender slinging drinks to customers—his pants baggy and his shirt wet with sweat. Shirley's bleached blonde hair has black roots creeping up a few inches from her scalp, and her makeup looks like she put it on three days ago and forgot it needs to be washed off or redone on a daily basis. I love her, but the woman doesn't love herself. Not enough, anyway. But isn't that the problem every woman faces in different aspects?

"His friends are here," she says, flying from one subject to another as I nod along. "The SEALs."

I'm not sure who she means until I glance in the direction she tilts her empty glass. Bronze Bay has some handsome locals, don't get me wrong, but these small town waters don't produce the type of handsome that the SEALs rolled into town with. They look out of place in surroundings so quaint. Their muscles on display without being ostentatious. It's not like they've cut the sleeves off of T-shirts or something, they have serious bulk and there's no hiding it regardless of what they are wearing. I've seen them sulking around in uniforms, and from a distance in their wetsuits getting off their boats and heading up the docks. Every time it takes me back a bit. It's one thing to hear about the SEALs and what they're doing on the news, it's another thing completely to view them up close, in our local bar, infiltrating our world in all ways. I hone in on one guy in particular, right away, because of the color of his hair.

It's blond. Light blond. Like the surfers in my favorite movies from years ago. He's broad and tall like the rest of his friends, but he's leaner—a self-confident swagger to his walk as he surveys the bar in a wide sweeping glance, not taking in any one thing or person longer than another. He's indifferent, and little does he know, that's one of the main qualities I'm looking for right now.

"The tall one," I whisper under my breath to Shirley, glancing away before his gaze sweeps over us.

She clicks her tongue three times in a rapid succession. "The tall one," she repeats. "If my research is thorough, which when is it not when it comes to hot dudes with muscles who bleed testosterone? His name is Leif," she drawls, and then spells his name to explain the difference between what it sounds like and the letters that form it, and then continues, "He comes into the diner with Tahoe a lot. I haven't heard any gossip about him bed hopping like his friend there on the left. The brown hair and deep dimple," she explains, using her eyes to talk as much as voice. "That's Sutter. He fucks like the Energizer bunny and doesn't spend the night." Shirley laughs when she sees my expression. She shrugs. "What? Not from personal experience, that's what the girls said at the diner. I overheard it," she says, smiling sheepishly. "They really should have kept their voices down if they wanted it to stay a secret." I glance at Sutter and automatically see him naked, and fucking like a jackhammer.

Swallowing hard, I shake my head. "Nothing about the blond one, then? Leif?" I ask, trying out his name. I haven't heard it before, but that doesn't mean much. I have spent most of my years in Bronze Bay where the residents have simple, ordinary names. My name was always the weirdest and I hated it. When I was a baby, my parents moved us to this small town to get out of the city. After my father left, I thought it was because he missed the city and Mom's dementia was just the excuse. It's easy to hate him even more that way. Drop me off here with my city ass name and then disappear. I hate him for too many reasons to count at this point.

"Nothing. He's clean at the moment," Shirley says. "I need to go give Britt this card." She pulls an envelope out of her purse. While this is a bar and we'd all be here anyway tonight, it's also a couple of our friend's engagement party. Britt is one of my good friends, but her fiancé, Whit, is absolutely rotten to the core. I've lost count of how many times he's come on to me. He is a red-headed demon that Britt is too comfortable with to release into the wild. It's a sad state of affairs. With my track record, I'm in no position to tell anyone how to drive their relationship though. I steer clear of anything serious, and it's been a long time since I've seen a man naked, let alone been touched by one. My friends assume

I'm prolific like Shirley, and I don't care to correct them. It makes it easier to explain why I have to skip out on plans. Taking care of my mom is only an acceptable answer for so long before those that care about me try to give me advice. I know she needs more care than I can give her and I feel awful about it.

Shirley and I walk over to where Britt and Whit are talking to Caroline and Tahoe. After a few tense minutes of Whit being an annoying, weaseling asshole we all move our separate ways. I'm lingering in front of the jukebox, my quarters already inserted, when I sense someone waiting behind me. With my last song selected, I move out of the way, toss a friendly smile over my shoulder, and freeze.

"Hasn't been updated in a decade or so, huh?" Leif asks.

I wasn't prepared for conversation. Especially with this man. "Yeah. Probably a few, honestly," I reply, sliding another step away. "It's all yours." I smile wide and check my watch. "There's gotta be something you see that you like," I add as his eyes scan over the choices, and then flit over to meet mine.

He grins. "I'm Leif," he says, extending a hand. A massive, freaking, whopper of a hand. My own gets lost inside his firm shake.

"Malena," I say, my voice wavering. I didn't expect a proper introduction with handshakes and name exchanges. That can't be his normal, can it? "Tahoe's friend?" I add quietly, letting him know I've heard of him.

tossing it

He nods, taking his hand from mine and clasping them behind his back. The picture of a perfect gentleman. His demeanor is unnerving. The swagger he entered the bar with is replaced by polished poise. "Indeed. Are you having a nice time tonight?" he asks. "It's quite a place. This Bobby's Bar," he says, raising both brows as he glances around the small dusty room, lit by old colored lights. The music is loud, but not so loud that I can't hear him, though I do notice when I said my name he leaned toward me to hear me better. "You're the first person who has stopped to chat with me."

Why? What game he's playing at? "I wonder why," I say, flicking my hair over one shoulder. "Get turned down a lot tonight?" I know he arrived to the bar recently, but I don't want him to know I noticed.

"Turned down?" The corner of his eyes slide down, and he frowns in confusion. "I didn't know I was trying to turn anything up." When he's not wearing his smile, I can see how perfect his bone structure is. His cheekbones are high, and his jaw is square and masculine. Blue eyes peek out from underneath thick, blond lashes. The gentleman front slips as he grazes his top teeth over his bottom lip. Leif shows me how shrewd and calculating he is—how utterly mouthwatering he is when he tries.

I tear my gaze from his mouth and pretend to be wildly interested in the jukebox. "I don't want to assume anything, but bless her heart, my friend Shirley knows everything about everyone, and I know about you guys— you SEALs. You don't have to play at the nice guy thing to try to talk to me."

"No? So, if instead of introducing myself I grabbed your perfect ass while you were selecting music you would still be talking to me right now?" Leif bends an arm and posts himself up against the jukebox, his gaze lighting my body on fire.

"No," I reply, letting my shoulders sag. "Probably not." Shirley catches my eye and waves goodbye. I nod back, and she shoots an exaggerated wink.

Leif clears his throat to draw my eyes back to him. "What you're saying then, because you're definitely talking to me right now is, I win," he says, lips pulling up in one corner. "Your ass is perfect, by the way. That was the truth."

I try to catch my breath. Men don't dazzle me, but Leif is paralyzing my thoughts. "Thanks. I think. You're proclaiming your victory in one breath and complimenting my ass in the next. I can't be sure if you want my number or if you're bored," I say, glancing over his shoulder to the hodgepodge of random bar patrons. "You're probably used to places far more stimulating than Bobby's Bar." I meet his eyes and run my fingers through my hair. My song comes on, and I sway my head back and forth while I wait for him to respond.

He groans. "You're right. This place is dead. Want to get out of here?" While he's distracted with thoughts of leaving the bar with me, and what that entails, I study his body. His arms are strong, blue veins cutting ridges across the tops of his hands and forearms. They show a touch more than on a normal person because his skin isn't as dark as a Bronze Bay native. It's more of a creamy beige, the color after you've been outside, but not too long. I bet he burns easily. "This is an awful song, by the way," he returns after several long seconds.

"Why would I leave here with you? You don't like my music choices, and I know nothing about you. What if you're a Ted Bundy copycat?"

His smile is broad. "Are you calling me hot?"

I furrow my brow. "He was a serial killer, Leif. A psycho."

"But he was hot. More attractive than most men. That's why he was such a successful serial killer."

Turning away from him, I start to walk away. "Okay. That's about enough of that. It wasn't nice meeting you, but welcome to Bronze Bay. Officially. If you're thinking about using your looks to kill chicks, stay away from the one in the black fishnet. She'll slit your throat before you get the tip in."

He laughs loudly and grabs my arm. Annoyed, I turn back but don't meet his eyes. "So, you are saying I'm good looking enough to kill chicks."

"Oh my gosh. You're awful!" A smile slips, just because he looks so jovial and pleased with his sadistic jokes. At least, I hope they're jokes.

"Malena," he coos. "You know where I work. You know my friends. You know more about me than I know about you. I'm not killing anyone," he says, looking to the side. "Not tonight at least. I don't think." His face is thoughtful, and a chill creeps down my spine. He does kill.

I widen my eyes. "Comforting. Really. This

conversation is really something. I'll give you that much. Can't say I've ever had a pick-up line quite like this."

"It's not a pick-up line," Leif says. "You can see the dust motes in the air in here. I'm asking if you want to get out of here. We could walk down to the beach and talk about serial killers and hot men. I'm not coming on to you. My friends are busy," he explains, eyeing his friends trying to pick up a few Bronze Bay ladies. "And I don't want to go back home yet in case my sister hasn't left." Leif looks like he wants to explain, but decides against it.

I look at my watch once more. I have an hour. I can give him an hour. "Only because the air quality really is something I worry about," I reply, smirking. "And only if you dance with me to my song choice."

He leans off the jukebox, arms held wide. "I am your man for that job, Malena of Bronze Bay." His shoulders rise up and down as he bends his knees and juts his hips. One of his friends catcalls, witnessing his atrocious attempt at what I assume is a form of dancing.

Leif bites his bottom lip and doesn't take his gaze off mine. His blue eyes are challenging, searching, blazing with anything except indifference. "You going to join me?" he asks.

"It was one of my most unforgivable mistakes asking you to dance with me. I rescind my invitation."

He shakes his head. "I called your ass perfect." His sway becomes more severe as the beat drops, and I laugh out loud. People are noticing the show he's putting on. "Show me you can move it."

"Air quality, remember?" I pick up my watered down drink and take a sip. "Beach?"

Leif narrows his eyes and doesn't stop dancing. "It would be a crime if you don't dance with me," he says, noticing the attention he's getting. "Any other ladies want to dance with me? Malena here isn't up for the challenge." His voice is booming with command and I know they'll come.

My face heats as two skanky river rats wind their way into our vicinity and start working their bodies against Leif. One in front of him and one behind him. He's thoroughly engrossed in watching me as he dances with the girls—trying to decipher my reaction. His friends are now shouting his name, and women are shouting out joyfully. The first time he looks down to the girl in front of him is my chance to escape, putting my drink down on the nearest table, I back into the hoard of people surrounding us.

I rush down the dark hallway with the peeling wallpaper and old posters advertising live mic nights and hit the back door at a jog. He was right about one thing. The fresh air really is a relief. I have to be back home in forty-five minutes and while I dread returning, especially even a minute early, there's no way I'm staying here to talk to my friends after the Leif show. How embarrassing? It reminds me why men are more trouble than they're worth. Rounding the dumpsters, I head to the side lot and find my parked car.

"I thought we were heading to the beach," Leif says, appearing on the passenger side of my car. He's grinning like a complete lunatic, utterly pleased with himself. If I wasn't so annoyed, I'd probably smile back. At the moment my resting bitch face is at full tilt.

"Bringing your dance partners to the beach," I ask.

"You invited me to dance and then turned me down," he replies. "Rude."

I bring a hand to my chest. "I'm rude? You're crazy. I don't have room for any more crazy in my life."

"I don't want to be in your life, Malena. I want to go to the beach with you, right now." He says the words right now like they're the words he wants me to focus on. "Be my beach friend," he adds.

"I'm going against every womanly instinct by agreeing to this. You're lucky I have some time before I have to be home."

His forehead wrinkles. "Before you *have* to be home? Do you have a boyfriend? Husband?"

Releasing my door handle, I turn toward the edge of the lot where it dips down to a path which leads to the beach. When he's next to me, I answer. "Would my husband or boyfriend be okay with me walking down to the beach with my new beach friend?" I let my gaze flick from the top of his head down to his toes very methodically.

He kicks up his flip-flops and catches them when we hit the sand section of the path. I scoop up mine in one hand. "I suppose he wouldn't, would he? So why do you have to go home?" Leif clears his throat and looks at my profile. "You have a kid?"

He's perfectly uncomfortable now, and I relish the

feeling he gave me back in the bar. "Do I look like a mama?" I ask, smiling at the dusty pink and dark blue swirls of the sky butting up against a glass calm ocean.

His eyes slant down in the corner, deep in thought, trying to figure out how best to answer such a pivotal, possibly offensive, question. We stop before we hit the packed, wet sand and stay perfectly still as we take in the beautiful night. Leif takes in a deep breath and finally replies, "Honestly, your ass says no, but your age, location, and desire to be at home, say yes."

"Age and location, huh?" A few seagulls call out overhead and break up the sound of waves lapping against the shore.

"Forgive me if this is a stereotype, but I have discovered that many of the women who look about your age," he finally glances over to meet my gaze. "Have kids and husbands. There's nothing wrong with that, mind you, but it's not that way where I'm from. The big city and everything. City people are busy doing everything except settling down."

I don't say anything. I keep my face neutral and pretend to be offended. The longer I stay silent, the more he moves—his body rocking back and forth, from foot to foot. "You are a serial killer, aren't you?" I say. "Making sure I don't have a family that will look for me. Rest assured, I'm more like the city people you speak of. I don't have any kids or a husband. Not even a boyfriend. Or prospects."

He blows out a long breath. "You had me worried."

"Don't like kids?" I smile.

He shakes his head. "Or families," he jokes. "For the record, I feel like I need to say it right now, I'm not going to kill you."

"My mom has dementia," I blurt. He looks surprised. "Her nurse leaves in about thirty minutes and someone has to be there all the time. She forgets where she's at and will try to leave. It's a pretty shitty situation."

He nods. "I see. I'm sorry. No one else to help out then? Sisters or brothers?"

Sighing, I turn my eyes back to the ocean. "Unfortunately not. Just me, and the person she's turned into. I shouldn't be telling you this. You don't care. I don't talk about her often. It's a depressing subject and I don't want anyone to feel sorry for me. So don't."

He clears his throat. "Family is important. You shouldn't worry about what people think. It's not depressing, it's life. I'd never feel sorry for you."

I quirk one brow and sit down in the soft, dry sand. Looking up at him, I'm greeted with a mammoth figure. "What if I told you to feel sorry for me?" I smirk, trying to sway the mood of the conversation to something lighter.

He sits down next to me, his long legs stretched out way past mine, and puts an arm around my shoulder. "You're the most pathetic excuse for a woman I've ever met. I am more than sorry for you, I feel bad for you, and I'm going to be your beach friend anyways." He sighs. "Better?"

I nod. "So much better."

"Good."

tossing it

The silence beats on, and I know I have to go soon, and for the first time in a long time, I'm happy right where I am. Random questions are always the safest. You can discover things about another person without getting too personal. "What would you do if you won the lottery?" I ask.

"We don't have enough time for that question tonight," he replies. "What would you have done if I had pulled you to my chest and danced with you inside the bar?"

I swallow hard. "I would have danced with you."

"Noted. What would you do if I asked you out to lunch tomorrow?" Leif asks. I started the harmless game, but he's giving it a life of its own, taking it to dangerous places.

"I'd say no."

"Why?" He looks at me, and I feel his gaze boring into the side of my head.

"I work tomorrow," I reply, turning to take the full-on seduction of his eyes. My breaths quicken and my pulse skyrockets—I can feel it slamming against my neck. "So I can't go to lunch with you tomorrow. I would go to lunch with you on another day."

He leans back on his elbows. "I'll take that."

"You'll take what? I'm the one accepting a lunch date with a serial killer."

He pulls me back so I'm on my elbows next to him, my body buzzes where my arm skin meets his. "A hot serial killer," he admonishes.

"How could I forget," I add, my tone sarcastic. "You are a horrible dancer, though. It makes me trust you a little more."

"I don't trust you at all," he returns.

I laugh. "You shouldn't." Running my hand through my hair, I catch him watching my face. "What would you do if I asked you to come home with me? Hypothetically, of course."

Leif tilts his head to the side, and his brows tilt inwards. "I'd tell you yes, and probably make it halfway to your house before I would turn around and decide it was a bad idea."

"Huh," I say, nodding thoughtfully. "Interesting. Why a bad idea?"

"I don't even know your last name, Malena. What kind of man do you think I am?" Leif stands, and clasps his hands behind his back, looking like that picture of a gentleman he was when he introduced himself.

He's grinning as he extends one hand down to help me stand. I take it and make an effort to stand closer to him when I rise. "Winterset," I say, pulling my bottom lip in with my top teeth. "My last name is Winterset."

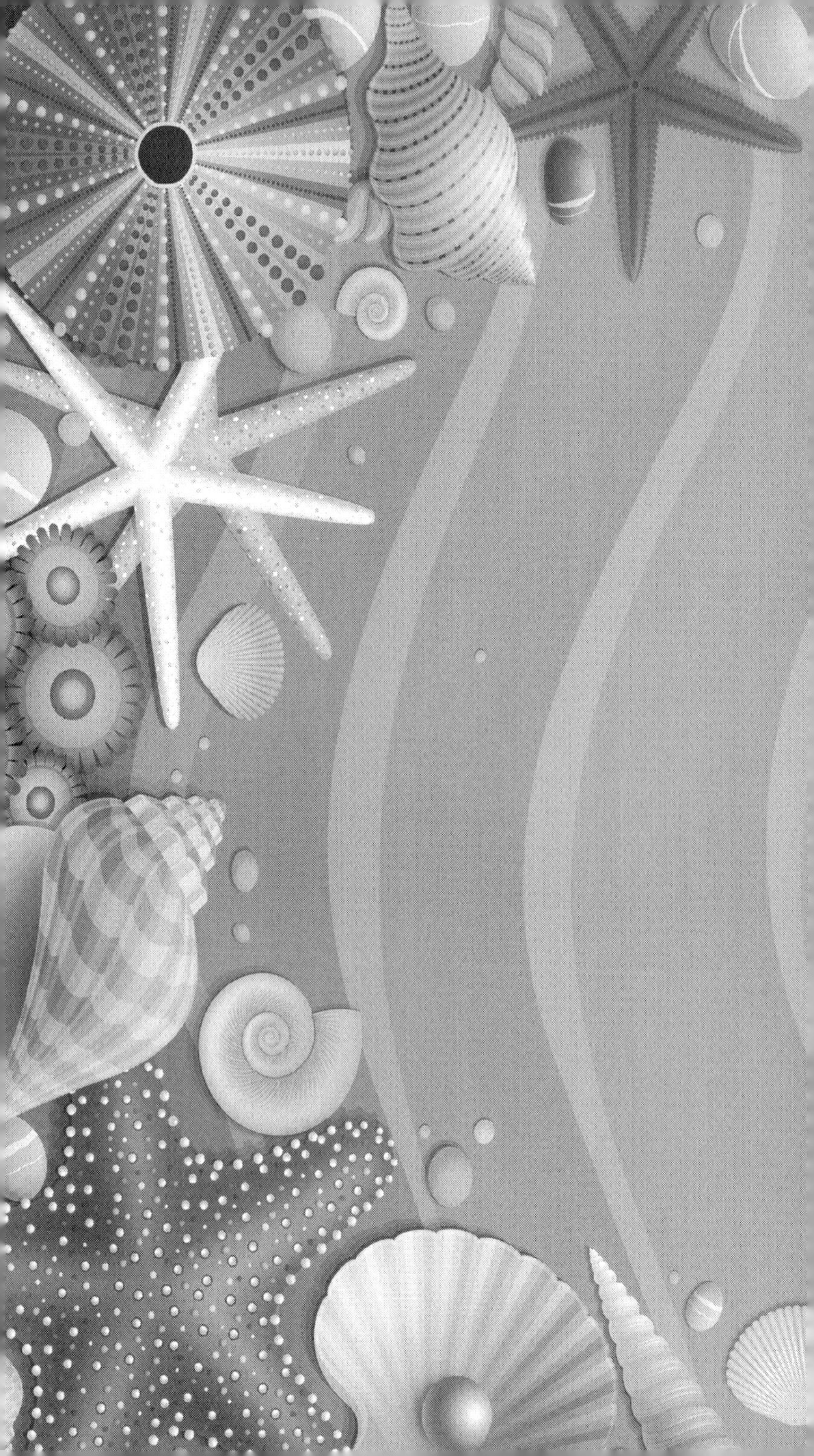

Chapter three

Leif

When I told Malena I would have turned around instead of following her to her house, I wasn't being completely honest. I would have loved nothing more than to see that woman naked and writhing underneath me, but I have unfinished business at the office. I have to keep my priorities straight, even if sex is on the menu and I haven't had a cheeseburger that juicy in a long ass time. Even now, while I'm sitting at work reading through the reports, trying to pick apart what went wrong, where the weak points reside, and how I can catch the bastard next time; half of my brain is still back at the beach with that woman.

I shake my head. "Task at hand. Task at hand," I mutter, no one to hear me in the dark, empty building. He's on the east coast, in my territory. Or that's what Intel is pegging, and I want him for myself. I start making mental bets with myself. If I get the motherfucker this time, then I get Malena. Something to work toward. A goal. A prize no one will know about except me. I hate that my next thought is whether my sisters would approve of her. Probably not. It would be too easy if they did. Focus is what I need if I'm going to be successful with the mission this time around. So much focus there won't be room for anything or anyone else.

I stay at my desk longer than I planned and it's well past midnight when I creep across the porches to reach my house. I grin when the faint hint of cigarette smoke hits the wind right as I pass my neighbor's residence. Upon entering my house, the acrid smell is erased by the delicious meals Eva cooked earlier. Stacked in my fridge and labeled, are my dinners for the week. There's a note on the counter in Eva's scrawl saying I'm in charge of securing a location for Mom's birthday party and she'll call me tomorrow. "Great," I say, sighing. Popping the top off a beer with my forearm, I meander toward the front door and out to the dock. Leaning over, I brace myself with one arm and listen to the noises of the ocean. It's calming. After hours of wracking my brain, it's imperative I empty it.

Sleep doesn't come easy for me. It never has. On my light complexion, the heavy, deep bags under my eyes are a signature trait. It has less to do with me being tired, because there have been times I'm nothing except exhausted, it's because my mind won't stop. Alcohol helps a bit. Sex, too. But nothing is a consistent trigger for a restful sleep. The Team doctors poke us and prod us. They wire us up, study our blood, our body composition, our minds, organs, and sleep patterns. Most of us have problems sleeping to some degree. We can't take any sort of sleeping pills because that's not a healthy dependency when we're awoken in the middle of the night to head on a spur of the moment mission. We need clear, fogless minds and accurate trigger fingers. I drain the rest of my beer and toss it in the mini trash can Eva put out here for exactly this reason. She was tired of seeing empties lined up on the wooden railing.

Showering is the first step to sleep, even if I've already showered multiple times during the day after workouts or diving, it gives me the best chance of decent shut-eye. Unwinding happens slowly. I think of Malena instead of missions and bad guys. I think of her deep brown eyes and the way her eyes crinkled at the corner when she smiled wide. Just once, though. She doesn't smile that big for no good reason. There was definitely something about her that I connected with on a base level. Maybe it was her mother, her family, affecting her life to such a degree that it dictates her time without permission. I know how that feels.

As I stumble through my bedtime routine, I let my mind wander to past relationships. While fleeting, they all did have something in common. Nothing. I didn't have anything in common with those women. Sometimes it's the opposites-attract type of chemistry, and now I have to believe maybe that's why I haven't been successful in finding someone to stick around. I need someone who has monsters that play well with my own. The same breed.

tossing it

Ironically, thinking about this kind of coincidence thwarts my mind from spinning too precariously and when my head hits the pillow, I fall blissfully asleep, my dreams lighter than they've ever been.

I wasn't planning on calling Malena Winterset the morning after officially meeting her. That's not my style, especially after how much I've been thinking about her, but I have to. She's the only person who plans parties in Bronze Bay. Her contact list will be exactly what I need when it comes to selecting a location for my mom's birthday. I dial the number displayed on my laptop screen, beneath a dated, fuzzy photo of Malena. She looks like a kid.

She picks up on the third ring, breathing heavily. "Hello, Malena here, can I help you?"

I swallow hard. Cool. Calm. Collected. My heart hammers away after she's spoken one word of her standard greeting. "Word on the street is you're the woman I need to talk to. I need to plan a party," I say.

She breathes heavy a couple more times before saying, "Yes. That's me. What can I do for you?"

She has no clue who I am. "Are you busy right now?" It sounds like she's wrestling an anaconda by the way her pants ricochet through the receiver. "I can call back." *And maybe you'll recognize my voice*, my wounded pride sneers.

"Uh, no. Sorry. Hold on for one second, please."

"Sure," I return.

I hear her in the background talking to someone, her voice soothing. The kind of tone that would calm a young child. I'd tune it out if I could, because it's too personal, but I press the phone to my ear even farther to hear her clearer. My hearing isn't what it used to be after years of blasts, gunfire, and explosions. Mostly I don't notice it, but when I do, it's frustrating. Malena says, "Sit right here. I'm not going anywhere, okay? Not yet." It's all I can make out in between a mumbling, one-sided conversation.

There is a scratchy noise on her end of the receiver. "I'm sorry. This is so unprofessional of me. What can I help you with, sir?"

Sir. I'm a sir. Ouch. I decide against telling her who I am and give her the details. "I need a location on the water to host a birthday party. I'm sure we'll need food and tables and stuff too, but right now I just would like to see options for locations." I give her the date of the party and she asks a few other pertinent questions, and then after taking down my phone number and email address we hang up. She'll have to reach out again. I make a promise to myself that I won't contact her again until she gets back to me about locations for the party and not a moment sooner. Even if I have a full afternoon with fuck all planned, and a raging hard-on when I think about the shape of her ass.

tossing it

I dial up Sutter and ask if he wants to meet me at the beach. He's always down for beers and the beach on our days off. After he agrees to meet me there in an hour, I offer to pick up beer and supplies if he brings the company. Not the specific company I want, but that's the only way he'll agree to show up. Hanging up, I pocket both of my cell phones and grab a cooler from the bottom shelf in my pantry. I toss in a bag of almonds, because even if it's a day off of work and the gym, we aren't eating shit. Staying in high performance form requires sacrifice on our off days, too. Beer doesn't count. That's like water.

Mr. Olsen isn't around when the wave of humidity overtakes me as I step outside. His door is closed and his chair is back up close to his door, where he drags it every night before he goes in for the night. I make a mental note to pick up a bag of dried figs while I'm at the store. He loves them more than anything. He told me they're one of the only things he loves that he can still eat without vomiting. Getting old and sick looks like my worst nightmare. As my friendship with my sickly neighbor grew, I became acutely aware of how I don't want to end up. If I don't go out with a blaze of gunfire raining above my head, I don't want to die lonely, withering away each day with nothing more than a sunset to look forward to every evening.

My moped winces as I sit down and turn the ignition. There's a compartment in the back for my cooler and a clamp that items can be strapped to. When I moved here, I sold everything I'd worked for my entire life— a fancy sports car, a bachelor pad decorated to the nines, and most of its contents. As a single man without any dependents, my disposable income is something most will only ever dream of. Every five years or so they offer hefty reenlistment bonuses. Those go into an account that sit and make me richer with interest. I'm fortunate in that money is something I'll never have to worry about.

I can live in a tiny apartment and drive a scooter fitting a college kid just as easily as living in a penthouse with a garage kept C6. It makes little difference to me as long as I have my career—my reason for living and breathing. The tiny engine that sounds like a go-kart splutters as I turn into the dusty parking lot of the General Store. I park right by the front door and slide my helmet onto the seat. This is the kind of store that has everything. The Bronze Bay General Store is a drugstore, department store, grocery store, and a gas station all wrapped up in a white-washed façade.

Waving to the cashier, I veer left to the refrigerated section of the store. Beer and sandwiches first. There are little black baskets on the corner of an aisle and I pick one up just as an employee arrives with a stack of them so high they're covering her face. "Let me help you with those," I say, taking the stack from the bottom, placing mine in the top.

"Thank you," she says.

As quickly as lightning striking a brand-new television in the state of Florida, my dick hardens. *Her voice.* Setting the baskets down, I turn my face to her. "Malena?"

Her eyebrows rise in confusion. "You," she says, swallowing hard. "What are you doing here?"

Smiling, I stand, and subtly jiggle my leg to readjust. "Buying groceries," I say, eyeing her apron. "I'd ask what you're doing here, but something tells me you're working."

Malena shakes her head. "Yes. Working."

"You didn't tell me you worked here," I say, trying to recall seeing her here before. This is one of the few places I frequent on a regular basis. The General Store and the diner.

Her face turns down as shame washes over her features. "Yeah, I pick up shifts from time to time to make things easier at home." Her answer makes me uncomfortable even though she's merely speaking the truth.

Party planning in a small town must not be lucrative. I instantly want to help her in whatever way I can. I'll make it my mission. Her big brown eyes fringed with thick lashes slide up to meet mine. Her face is beautiful. She's wearing less makeup today than she was last night. Surprisingly, she's more appealing this way. "I, ah," I stutter, hiking my thumb over my shoulder. "Beer and sandwiches," I manage, like an idiotic Neanderthal.

She blushes. "I'm sure you know where to find those," she replies without missing a beat. "But let me know if you need help finding anything else," she supplies, a sunny smile taking the place of the deep frown. She turns to leave, her tight ass encased in a pair of black pants. Closing my eyes, I silently let a string of curse words flit through my mind.

My face heats. "Malena," I call.

She stops in her tracks and turns her face to the side. "Yeah?"

"When are we getting lunch?" So much for waiting for her to get back to me about the locations. So much for a lot of things. Apparently, her face and ass dictate I make rash decisions, something I am not used to doing. "You were busy today. What about tomorrow? It's Sunday. Are you off?"

Malena opens her mouth to shoot me down. I can tell by the set in her shoulders. I've approached her in a place she isn't comfortable in. "The diner?" I supply, when her reply isn't immediate. "Or we can grab Chinese at the spot in the next town over? It's worth the drive. I've been there a handful of times since I moved here."

She shakes her head, her long brown ponytail brushing the collar of her shirt. "I can't tomorrow. I have some work to do from home and I need to be there for my mom."

Rash decisions, right. "I'll bring over lunch. Can I? For your mom, too?"

That gets her attention. She turns all the way around to face me, peering over my shoulder at the girl at the register. I'm sure she's glaring at her coworker. "Come help me find the beer while you think about it," I say, nodding my head to the side. "I need your help." I say it

tossing it

loud enough to be heard by all. Smirking, she nods.

"Was that a yes, I can bring over lunch?"

Malena is much shorter than I am, so I have to look down at her and lean away a bit to see her face as she says, "I'm still thinking about it. People don't come to my house," she explains, meeting my eyes. "Not that I don't want you to, you understand?"

"You're not comfortable having me there?" I ask.

"A little of that," she says. "Leave me your number and I'll get back to you after my shift is over."

She slides her cell phone out of the apron pocket and looks confused as she enters in my phone number. "I haven't switched to a Florida area code yet," I respond. "The last piece of California that I am hanging on to is my number."

My other cell chimes in my pocket. I'm sure it's Sutter wondering where I am. He never distinguishes between which phone he's calling. He doesn't care. Pulling it out, I glance at a text message from my friend. It's a photo of three blonde chicks in barely-there bikinis. According to the words below the photo, he's waiting for me.

Even though I shouldn't care, I try to click off the message quickly before Malena sees. Her face tells me I wasn't successful. She sighs as I pick up a case of beer and two sandwiches from the premade section. "Need any more help, *sir*?"

I don't need help from her, but I do need a few other things. I shake my head. "I'll see you tomorrow at noon."

"I'll text you," she fires back, mouth hanging open.

"It's probably a no."

Sighing, I narrow my eyes at her. "You can text me what you want for lunch. I'll see you tomorrow."

Malena smirks. "You're so rude." I have her. I have her. When my head is clear, I can spit the game she wants to hear. It's when I'm all hard dicked for her that I'm fucking shit up. She folds her arms across her chest, a glint of challenge in her eye.

I grab the end of the ponytail laying down one shoulder. "And you're fucking beautiful," I reply.

She looks away, then remembers where we are and takes a step away from me. "See you tomorrow Ms. Winterset," I tell her, reminding her of the end of last night's conversation.

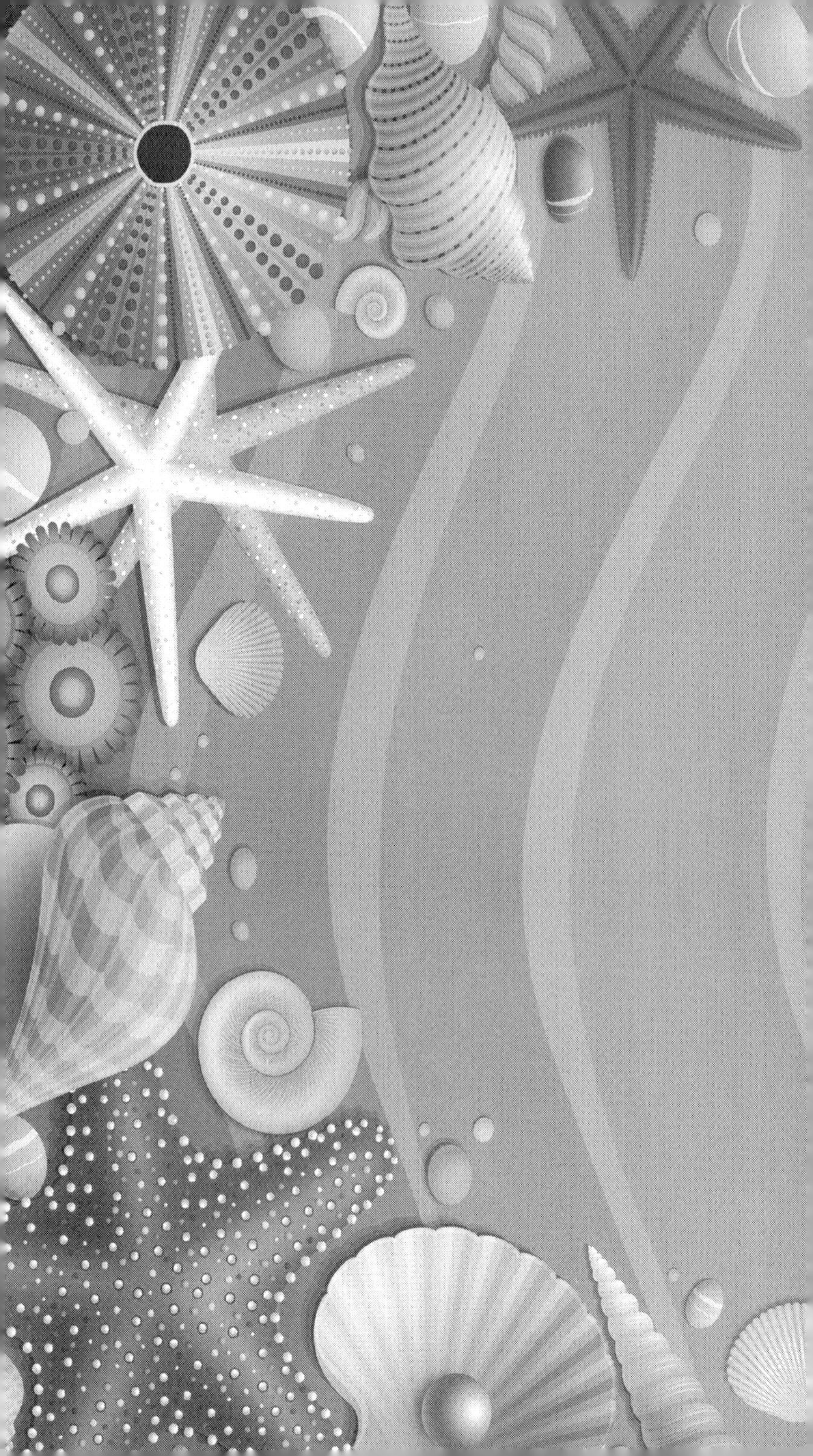

Chapter Four

Malena

My shift crawls as I stock shelves in the canned goods aisle, the dreaded task no one wants that I always get because I'm not a full-time employee. The other women have worked here for decades. Those old bats probably worked here while they attended Bronze Bay High School and decided they liked it so much they never wanted anything more. Could I do this forever? I'd like to think no, but I could if I had to. My dream to be a full-time event planner isn't something that seems out of reach, but it's hard to do anything while my mom needs my help. The guilt rears anytime I align my goals aside her needs, and I squash my desires to instead meet her needs.

With my familiar guilt, I'm reminded of the handsome shadow wafting around in my world. Leif is pursuing me and he's making it blatantly evident. It's something

tossing it

to ponder during the mundane hours of minimum wage tasks and menial customer conversation. Why is he trying so hard? Why me? Wouldn't a hookup squelch the inevitable, and save us both time? Leif must think I want to be courted, wooed, and primed for bedroom action like the typical woman my age. I don't want what the typical woman my age wants, though. Rather, I can't have it because of my living situation so I try to avoid it if I can help it.

When I asked him at the beach what he would say if I asked him to come home with me, I thought I was making my intentions clear, that I don't have patience for the subtleties of casual dating, nor the time to date. Shirley gave me the full lowdown on Leif Andersson when I called her late last night. She's seen his sisters around town and knows he lives down by the water next door to Mr. Olsen. I know where that's at because the sunsets along that road are the best. We'd ride our bikes out there on weekend nights as children just to see the watercolor splashes in the sky. There are fiery oranges and reds that overtake the bright blue. Right before the sun dips behind the ocean, the horizon looks like the world has tipped upside down. I'd stand on my head and get my hair all sandy watching that moment, trying to dissect it—trying to make sense of it.

My brown card slides into the slot, and I bring down the handle on the machine to punch my hours for the day. Stepping away from the time clock so the woman behind me can clock out, I take off my apron and straighten my hair in an antique mirror that has hung here so long, the glass is aged, all speckled black in places around the frame. Leaning in, I wipe under my tired eyes. "You doing anything fun?" Marian asks from behind me, catching my eyes in the mirror.

"Nah. Heading home," I reply. "What about you?"

She sighs. "Youth is wasted on the young and you don't even use it." Marian reaches behind her ample body and unties her own apron. "Live your life."

Not too much though. Just enough to give them something fun to gossip about. If you live too much, they'll cast you to the sharks. "I may head to the beach. Itching to see the sunset. Been in this fluorescent light all day. Makes me a little crazy."

Marian looks as if I've offended her by stating facts. The lighting is indeed fluorescent and fake. "Good. Get on out of here. Tell your mama, I said—" Marian halts her sentence, cheeks flushed when she realizes her blunder. "Bye now, Malena." Marian tugs at the bottom of her shirt, and sniffles several times.

"It's not your job to remember every person's ailments. She's doing okay. I'll mention you said hi," I say, trying to comfort my mother's old friend even if she doesn't deserve it. "She still has flashes." The moments of clarity are few and far between, but when they happen, it's like having snippets of my mom back instead of the slack-jawed, wide-eyed zombie that has taken her place.

Marian rolls her eyes. "This is Bronze Bay. We take care of our own. We keep up. I'm sorry, sweetie, I should have remembered. Have a good one." She wrestles her oversized purse out of a locker and exits through the back

tossing it

door. It's easy to forget when she's never mentioned.

"You too," I say, speaking to empty air. The beach was a lie to cover for my absence of a life, but seeing a sunset would brighten my mood, and keep me from texting Leif. There's no way he's still at the beach. I bet he's at his house, watching the sunset from the dock in front of his house. That's what I'd be doing if I were him. After Mom goes to bed tonight, I have to research a few locations for availability for the upcoming party I got a call about this morning. I'm thrilled to have an event planning task, no matter how small it is.

Tucking my bag under my arm, I exit into the swampy heat and start up my car, the air conditioning blasts at the same time since I rarely turn it off. The drive home is quick, and I'll pass the beach on my way. The paved roads are bad, potholes littering both sides for as long as the road stretches. The dirt roads are usually lined with sea shells and they make a satisfying crunch as you drive or bike over them—or cut your feet if your flip-flops slip off. The public beach comes into view and the small parking lot is surprisingly jam-packed. Then I see the moped. The one Shirley described as belonging to Leif and I know why it's so busy. I'm focused on the beach and trying to pick him out in the raucous crowd and turn my eyes from the road for too long and I hit the long ass pothole we've named *gravedigger*. The frame of my car scrapes and the engine whines as I gas it to make it through the deep hole.

"Fuck," I yell, as I finally get through it and begin to listen to my vehicle for signs of distress. "That's a trip to the mechanic," I whine under my breath, and then lose it at the same time. Dylan. The man I married on a whim because we were so madly in love. The man who left me two years into the union because I couldn't give him what he wanted. A baby. It was a blessing in disguise, I realize now. If the time comes where I get to marry again, I want a man who wants to love me in any form no matter how deranged and barren my body may be.

Dylan was my high school sweetheart. There were no false pretenses with him. His dad owned the local mechanic shop and Dylan was primed to take it over when he graduated high school. That was comforting. A piece of stability in our little world. He was well liked, we thought we were in love, and marriage and family was what we thought we wanted. He wanted the stereotypical Bronze Bay life. I was barely out of high school and trying to have his baby. My periods were never the same time every month and they told me it was my fault I wasn't able to have his baby. They used terminology I didn't understand, and never thought about since because it wasn't something I really wanted. It was an act I thought I had to do to mesh with my chosen life.

Returning to reality, I pull the car to the side of the road, the beach still in view. The clock in my car tells me I have twenty minutes before I need to be home to relieve Mom's day nurse. I watch the people dancing to music I can't hear, clanking beer bottles with huge, carefree laughs. Leif is there, off to the side, sitting down, facing the ocean. It looks like a few bikini-clad women are gathered around him, but thank God, his hands seem to be to himself. Sighing, I give in to my desires. Pulling out my cell phone, I text the number he gave me earlier.

Lunch tomorrow at my house. Bring fried chicken wings and all the patience you can muster. Also, condoms. I hit send, grinning.

Leif stands, and my heart races hoping he'll look beyond the parking lot and come my way. To talk to me and to get far away from those women. He slides his hand into the side pocket of his board shorts and pulls out his phone. The smile on his face, when he sees my text, is evident from here.

"You really are into me," I say, raising my brows. Looking at my phone, I wait for his response.

You really want to date me? comes his reply.

Laughing, I text back, **Didn't you see the last thing on my list? That's not really dating.**

Now, we're on familiar territory. A place I can thrive in. His face looks jubilant, as he paces away from the crowd, toward the parking lot. The pull is almost magnetic as he gets closer to me. *Come here. I want you next to me. You want me too.* Then reality hits.

Why are you being so nice to me? What's the catch? I tap out and send.

You're hot and I want to get to know you better. Why does there have to be a catch?

Because you're a man, I think. **I guess. Not into a one-night stand, then?**

He stares at his phone for several beats before replying. **Trick question?**

No. I don't have time for much, and dating is

definitely time-consuming. A quickie here or there, though? Totally doable. Pun intended. He did call me fucking beautiful. That's an easy ask. He'll be pleased with my body and won't have to seek what's inside my mind. The scary stuff.

Leif runs his hand through his hair and looks to the side, the hand holding his phone down by his side. He's upset by my candid response and I'm shocked for the second time at the realization of Leif wanting something more than I'm offering. Could I date him? Do I have the time? The patience? The room for heartbreak if it evolves? Everyone in town knows why I don't have serious relationships, but there's a chance Leif has no clue about my past. This could be my fresh start. The life I would have had if I dated a Bronze Bay native. It's easy to think I'm not a good match for a man like Leif. He's so beautiful and I'm dull in comparison. What could I possibly bring to a relationship with an outsider? The thought of not being good enough is terrifying.

Let's see how lunch goes and then we can discuss quickies and dating, I amend. He's going to run when he sees what I have to deal with. No one wants to take part in that burden unless they're being paid. My own father abandoned me with the task of caring for a person who is as good as a stranger on most days. My cell phone buzzes and it's a message from my girlfriend Caroline, answering a question I'd asked earlier in the day regarding Leif. She confirmed Shirley's information. He is a good guy. Without baggage, and he's not known for tearing around town.

tossing it

An embedded niggling feeling whispers that he sounds too good to be true. Maybe I was on the right track with the serial killer persona.

Thanks, Caroline. You're a peach. Don't say anything to him please, I write back. As soon as I send that text, another from Leif's number bubbles up.

To you, it says. It confuses me until I look out my car window and see him raising a beer toward me, a grin plastered on his face. He found me.

So much for having the upper hand. **I hit a pothole**, I tap back.

If by pothole, you mean you slammed into my beautiful, chiseled body and had to stop and ogle, then I agree.

I gasp at his forward text but laugh. My gaze dips down to his rock-hard body and my own body heats—a tingling of need ignites between my legs.

His head is still bowed over his phone, so I don't text back yet. Another text from him chimes, **So, this one is for you. And to the only relationship in the history of time that began with chicken wings.**

I swallow down my pride and go with it. Because it's easier than fighting against the riptide current of my sensibilities.

To chicken, I text to him, raising my phone so he can view it.

He chugs his beer as the sun sets behind him. It's the magnificent shade of red that I love, punctuated by the most sculpted, chiseled, man I've ever seen in my life. A man that at this moment in time, only has eyes for me.

My chest tightens with something akin to excitement, but it's unlike anything I've ever felt. This could be the start of something amazing. I let the swell of excitement take over before real life crushes it to bits.

Lunch tomorrow can't come soon enough.

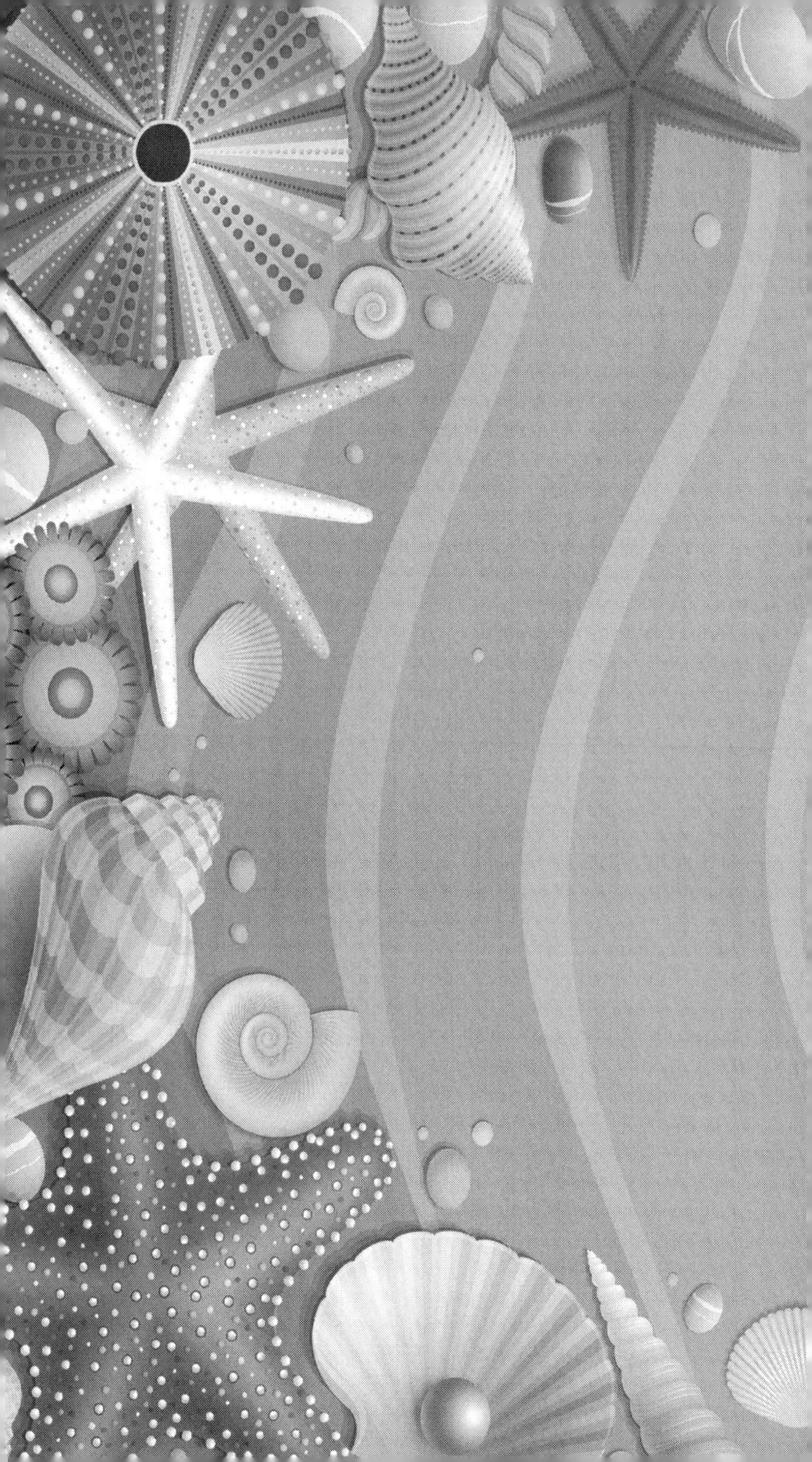

Chapter Five

Leif

I bought every flavor of chicken wings the diner made. On the off chance she was fucking with me, I also bought salads, burgers, and a fish and chips basket. Malena is sitting across from me at her glass kitchen table, her mother seated to her left rambling on about the bird she saw in the backyard this morning. We both respond to her at the same time and grin at each other when it happens.

"You really brought way too much food. What were you thinking? That you needed to feed an army?" Malena puffs out her cheeks and pulls a face. "Pass me the goblet of chicken wings fine, sir." As I slide the platter, she removes a hair tie from her wrist and pulls her hair back against the nape of her neck. "Gets a little messy." She shrugs as she digs into a wing, tilting her head to the side to get a better angle. When she pulls away, she has a smear of orange sauce on each corner of her mouth. She leaves it there.

tossing it

My eyes light up when I realize she actually loves wings. They are my favorite cheat meal. Even though today isn't that day for me, I know I'll eat every single one she doesn't to prove we have something in common. It's an irrational need for Malena to understand I'm worth more than a one-night stand. It's a fair assessment if she's judging me against most of my friends, but it's also a little irritating. I can't control how I'm perceived regardless of my efforts to do things the right, normal way. I didn't bring condoms like she asked and that was to also drive that point home. When she opened the door wearing a pair of tiny board shorts and a bikini top, I realized I fucked up big time on the condom front. Instead of none, I'll need seventeen boxes. For one day.

Ms. Winterset picks at the array of food in front of her and Malena asks if she needs anything several times. It's odd, as I know it's her mother, but she is definitely more her patient. Malena is her caretaker. She reaches over to tuck a strand of hair behind her ear, so it doesn't get into her mouth when she takes her next bite.

"Mom, what do you think of Leif?" Malena coos, a sarcastic edge to her voice. She glances at me, "She always tells the truth. Even if she shouldn't. It's very entertaining."

"Don't ask her that," I hiss. "I'm not ready for the truth."

Malena quirks a knowing brow. "I'm ready for it though. Consider me a truth-seeking missile."

"Leif, you say?" Ms. Winterset interrupts, her tone high and unsure. "This is Dylan. Right, son?" She turns to me. "You got a fancy new hair-do though."

Grinning, I reply. "Yes, ma'am. Very fancy." *Tell me more about Dylan and what he has to do with Malena, please.* "When was the last time we saw each other?" I hedge, flicking my gaze to the side to see Malena's reaction.

Malena places a hand on top of her mother's, ignoring me completely. "Mom, this isn't Dylan. He's not around anymore, remember? This is Leif. He wants to take me out," she explains. Ms. Winterset has clear dark eyes, I'd think her a shrewd woman, the kind that knows a lot of things, but never gives their hand away. That is if I didn't know better. Her face is an older version of Malena's, but her skin is pale in opposition to her daughter's.

Lines between Ms. Winterset's eyes appear and her eyes turn down in the corner as she surveys Malena. "What happened to Dylan? Are you okay?" Motherly concern for her daughter's welfare creeps in and that must feel nice, that she still has traces of herself even if they're misguided.

"I'm fine, Mom. It didn't work out. Are you full?" Malena asks, nodding to her mother's plate. "I can get you something else, or are you ready to lie down for a bit?"

Ms. Winterset looks at me, an all-consuming emptiness now evident. "I'm a bit tired. It was nice seeing you, Dylan. Tell your daddy I said hello."

I swallow hard. All I can manage is a nod. This is a lot to take in—to deal with when I'm not really sure what I want. The wooden chair legs scrape the floor as they both stand and then make their way down a hallway to the bedrooms. I'm thinking about how quickly I can run, and my chances of avoiding Malena for the rest of my life when she saunters back in, a weary expression on her face.

"You can go if you want. Thank you for lunch," she says, forcing a smile and adjusting the string around her neck, then adds, "I'm sorry about that. I want to say it's not usually that bad, but that wouldn't be the truth."

This is it. The moment I can politely excuse myself from getting entangled in her life. I can walk out of the door with a clear conscious and a new gratitude for my annoying, completely normal sisters and family. Malena sits back down in her spot and sets a baby monitor on the table. "In case she tries to run," she explains. "Not hungry anymore?"

No, not at all. I stand and pace toward the front door, but then spin. The moment has passed and my mind has been swayed. It's because her hips are perfect, and her eyes scream, save me, save me, please save me. She's invoked my weakness unknowingly. "Who is Dylan?" I fire out.

She smirks. "I thought you were leaving." She chews a bite of a buffalo wing. "Just an ex. No one important."

I take a step toward the dining area and run a hand through my hair. "How long ago was Dylan?"

Malena sighs. "Why are you interested in my relationship history?"

"Answer my question," I reply. "You can ask me whatever you want in return. I need to know certain things." Sliding my hands into my board shorts, I try to keep my nerves at bay. "Because if I'm going to date you, I need to know who to watch out for." I take another three steps toward her. There's a string on her hip peeking out from her board shorts. If I pulled it, her bottoms would loosen. Training my eyes on her face is hard when I'm so desperate for her body.

Pushing away from the table, she stands and turns to face me. "You're worried about my exes?" Malena eyes my arms, my neck, and then lets her gaze travel down the length of my body. "They aren't anything to worry about. Not compared to you. I dated Dylan in high school." Her gaze shifts to the left and then meets mine again.

My heart hammers. She's so close I could reach out and touch the bare skin on her stomach, arms, and the sliver right above the waist of her shorts. "Who else here? In Bronze Bay?" I ask, my voice catching on the last word.

She steps forward. "A few one-night stands here and there. I don't do relationships. Feelings are messy when it doesn't work out in a small town. It's best to leave them out altogether. I don't want anyone to have to deal with my problems. Er, my responsibilities. So, tell me, what about you? Any exes you hold a burning torch for?"

"I don't hold torches," I say, lifting one brow. "I also don't want a one-night stand with you."

"Why? Am I not good enough for you?" she asks.

I laugh once, loudly.

She holds one finger over her lips to silence me. "She's going to sleep."

"You're too good for me. I plan on being in Bronze Bay for a long time and I don't want to leave a bad taste in anyone's mouth. Sometimes it's for the best to do things the way you're supposed to do them. The right way."

"Who is giving these rules to go by here? Who exactly told you how it's supposed to be?" Malena sasses, her brown eyes challenging me, but her smirk telling me she's enjoying the banter.

"Rules. Ah, me? I'm doling those out," I reply, removing my hands from my pockets and clasping them behind my back. "If you're amenable, of course."

"Such a gentleman," she says, stepping closer. "Tell me about the rules, Leif."

I swallow down any remaining hesitation about diving into something I'm unfamiliar with and go for it. "We have rules in life, right? We have laws and guidelines, traffic rules, and common courtesy—all to keep us a highly functioning society," I say.

She nods but looks somewhat confused, her lips pressed into a firm line. She makes a noise to signal for me to go on. "If we give whatever is between us rules, it would make sense that it would be highly functioning as well."

"But I don't get a say in said rules?" she asks, turning back to glance at the baby monitor on the table. "That doesn't seem fair," she finishes.

"They're up for debate. It can be a team effort. I'll tell you the ones that I've been thinking about and you can tell me if you agree with them."

"You've been thinking about relationship rules? That is so weird! How would you know if I'd even agree?"

I shrug, a gesture that catches her eye. "I didn't, but I'm persuasive when I want something."

Malena rolls her eyes and steps back into a stance that tells me she's waiting for my almighty knowledge. "Go on. Hit me with it. What do you got?"

I'm able to formulate multiple plans in a short amount of time because of my chosen career path. It's one of the skills that translates perfectly outside of work. I'm an expert decision maker. Malena makes me feel like I'm a little out of my league, but I'm going for it. "One," I say. "We must use two forms of birth control." A slight pink rises to her cheeks at the unstated mention of sex.

She nods once, blinking rapidly. "Good one. I agree. Next."

"You can never leave stuff at my place," I say. My sisters. My family. I don't want questions, or have to give answers laced with lies.

She narrows her eyes. "And you can't leave stuff at my house. In the spirit of keeping things even."

"Deal," I reply. "Number three." I shift to the side and have to remind myself to keep my hands to myself. "You can't meet my family."

Malena scoffs. "So, it's not like a real, real relationship then?"

I shake my head. "That one was for you. I figured you don't want strings attached, but there has to be some commitment if we aren't going to see other people at the same time, which we're not. Meeting my family would be too…much." Will she accept this reasoning?

"Your sisters?" she jumps. Of course she's heard about the dynamic duo. Of course. "Fine. I agree with that." Malena looks a little less enchanted with my rules and with me at the mention of number three. But I made a vow to myself that I wouldn't get any woman entangled with my parents or sisters until I was sure it was going somewhere. God knows how long that will take to figure out. "Even if it does feel a little like we are doing the one-night stand thing," she adds.

"I would have fucked you on the beach the night I met you if I wanted a one-night stand, Malena. This is just a way to keep things less complicated. You said it yourself, relationships are complicated in a small town. Isn't simplicity what you want?" *Say no. Tell me you want me and only me.* The realization that I'm desperately seeking her approval makes my head swim and my stomach flip. I don't need her approval. I don't need her. *I want her*.

She folds her arms across her chest as a trail of goosebumps wash over her exposed skin. "If you say so, Leif. I never would have fucked you on the beach. Just so we're clear about that. Go on. What's the next rule? I'm intrigued."

"But you would have taken me home and fucked me here?" I ask, stepping forward to close the distance between our bodies because I can't stand it. I need to taste her breaths. "Like you asked. Remember?" Reaching out, a tentative move, I let a couple fingers glide down her side ending at those fucking exposed bikini bottom strings. "Right?" My gaze rises from her tight body up to her face. "Malena," I add. Her eyes look sleepy, and her resolve is faltering.

"Yes," she answers.

"Why?"

The chemistry between us crackles. There's a current of desire laced with need exiting my body and entering hers. "There's something about you," she says, voice low. "I know it will be...good between us."

"Good?" I pick up on her word usage. "It will just be good?" There are a million words I could use to describe what being with Malena would feel like. Good isn't one of them.

"You know what I mean," she says, looking down at my hand, the one stroking her soft skin. My hardon is raging out of control as I let my other hand wander to the other side of her waist. My fingers can almost touch on her back when I hold the smallest part of her stomach.

Shaking my head. "I don't know what you mean. Explain," I order, raising a brow in challenge. Malena looks at me, eyes wide, lips parted, and I know something resembling truth is coming, and I crave it.

Licking her perfect fucking lips, she says, "There's something about you that makes me...want you. Do you feel that way about me?" I want her because she's a walking billboard of everything I'm subconsciously drawn to. I have a type. Most men do, it is almost as if I didn't know what I was looking for until I saw her. Malena doesn't fit into my usual hook-up box. Her brown hair and realness isn't my typical attraction du jour. The bottle blondes from my past don't hold a candle to Malena's beauty. The attraction to her was immediate and all-consuming.

I meet her eyes instead of watching her skin react to my touch. "It's why I'm here right now," I reply honestly, a time I should have lied. "There's something about you that I can't turn away from. I want you to be mine." An understatement, I hope she realizes as her own gaze darts down to the front of my shorts and all that she's creating.

A flush rises from her chest to spread across her high cheekbones. "Any more rules?" Her voice cracks, her breaths heavier than they were moments before.

Swallowing hard, I run my hands up her delicate arms. "Just one more rule. The most important one," I reply. I pause for a beat or two then say, "You can't fall in love with me, Malena Winterset."

She jumps a little when I say the word *love*, and rears out of my grasp. I've shocked her. I meant to, because she needs to know it's integral to whatever might happen between us. "Okay," she agrees. "You definitely don't have to worry about that." Except the tone of her voice tells me I do have to worry about that. There's a softness about her demeanor that signals weakness.

"We're in agreeance?" I confirm, closing the distance between us once more, leaning my head down. She smells like coconut and clean hair. My mouth waters and my balls ache. "To explain further, I'm not the type of man you fall in love with. I'm the kind of man you use for a bit and then toss." I shake my head. "I'm sure my life will be short, and I don't want to leave any threads behind when I go in a blaze of glory. Do you understand?" While my statement makes it seem as if I'm being altruistic, I'm not. Life is easier when you live with your guard up. My career has also taught me that some guards should never be lowered.

"Yes," she says, interrupting my thoughts. "We're in agreeance." Licking her lips, her brown eyes widen, her frame leaning in closer to my chest.

"Now that the details are out of the way, I'm going to kiss you." Her smile is wide and white as she sets her hands on top of mine. "If you're up for it," I add.

"Let's go to my room," she replies, tugging one of my hands. My stomach flips as her eyes finish the sentence for me. "If you're up for it?" Malena uses my words, grabbing the monitor from the table.

Guiding me to the opposite side of the house, she opens the door to a wing of the house that looks like it was added after the fact. "This is my space," she says, spinning on her toe to face me as I take in my surroundings. "I had it modified when I realized I'd probably be spending the rest of my life here," she says, glancing at the device in her right hand. She sets it down on a bookshelf to her right. "When my dad left, I knew it was up to me to take care of things. He left a good amount of money in our checking account. I used some of it to make this section of the house my own and left most of it untouched to pay for Mom's care. The day and night nurses and stuff. The treatments and medicines are expensive," she rattles on, her demeanor changing completely. Shaking her head, she whispers, "Shut up, Malena." Looking at me she grins. "I'm sorry. You don't want to know that. It's one of my flaws. I over explain things. Instead of a 'this is my room,' I give you my life run down."

It's warmer in here, and I see why she's wearing her bathing suit. The windows are cracked and the ceiling fan is wobbling out a staccato beat, pushing around the heat. There are books, and antique toys sitting on shelves and tables. "As much as I want to kiss you, learning about you comes in a close second. You can over explain anytime you want. This is really nice," I exclaim, walking in a few more steps.

"You're just saying that," she says, eyes focused on the light hardwood beneath her bare feet. "I live with my mom. That's not sexy."

I laugh and reach behind my head to shrug out of my T-shirt. It slides off, and I toss it on the giant, pale purple bedspread. "And you have toys in your room. Lucky for you, sex appeal isn't something you have to worry about, Malena." Cocking my head to the side, I let my gaze wander over her body very obviously up and down. "I'd want you if you lived in a convent." Clearing my throat, I walk to the window. "Was this a garage?" One of the walls is exposed red brick. It lends a loft-like feel that isn't typical for single-family homes.

"Yeah," she says, dragging a finger along the rough wall. "I liked the brick and didn't want to cover it up. Makes it feel a little bit like a city apartment or something," she explains. "Something of my own."

I raise one brow. "You like the city?"

Clearing her throat, she shakes her head. "I'm indifferent," she says. The questions are there. Behind her chocolate colored eyes. "Why do you think you aren't going to live a long life?" Her question is aimed like a dagger.

"Still thinking about that, huh?" Facing the wide window, I readjust my dick and try to will my libido to slow down. This room smells like her and it's been a long time since I've been in a woman's bedroom. The only time I'm ever in one, it isn't to talk. "My career is dangerous. It's not a foregone conclusion that I will die young, but it's also more probable given statistics that I'm in more risky situations on a daily basis."

She nods, lips pressed into a thin line. Stop thinking, Malena. Stop thinking and kiss me. Give me what I need.

"When you say you're the kind of guy you toss? What exactly does that mean?"

Sighing, I approach her. The buzz of chemistry strengthening the closer I get to her body. "There are keepers and tossers in life. Good guys and bad guys. I've spent too much time with bad guys, you understand? I'm not in the business of letting people down. I have a one-track mind that doesn't leave much space for anything other than what I'm focused on in the moment. It's why relationships in my past have failed. I don't know how to compartmentalize the different areas of my life. I'm okay with that, you have to understand it, though. We can have fun. Just you and me. For as long as it works out."

Her eyes flare. "It's doomed before it begins. Don't get me wrong, I'm not the type of girl to ask for more, but I haven't been in anything committed for a while and this isn't the typical way of things." She waves a hand between us. Pausing, in thought, she adds, "You know what? Never mind. Never mind. Kiss me," she orders. "If you still want to."

Narrowing my eyes, I wish I could read her mind. "Do I want to?" I grin.

She smiles back, her cheeks bubbling out on the sides. It's adorable and hot at the same time. Leaning down, I set my hands on the top of her shoulders and brush my lips against the corner of her mouth. Malena lets out an audible sigh, and I pull her in closer to feel her warm skin against mine. The heat is immediate—the scent of her skin hitting me like a flood. Tilting my head down farther to make up for our height difference, I brush my nose and mouth along the side of her face, grazing her ear. "I want to," I tell her, growling the words one at a time.

"That feels so good," Malena sighs. "Kiss me now." Her face turns, seeking my lips, the kiss that I so desperately want to give her.

I hear soft footsteps. "Does Dylan know about this?" Ms. Winterset screeches from the doorway, an accusing finger aimed at me. Malena pushes away, her palms holding me at arm's length, except her fingers are tangled in my ab muscles and that makes my dick harden even further. The situation looks bad, rather, what Ms. Winterset assumes seems worse than it actually is.

Dropping her hands, Malena says, "Mom, I told you Dylan and I have been over for years. Remember? This is Leif. He brought over lunch. He wants to take me out on a date?"

Her mom purses her lips. "Looks like he's doing far more than taking you out on a date. What did I tell you about giving away free milk? No one is gonna buy the cow that way, sweetie. This is so…confusing. I'm confused." That makes two of us, wait, no three of us. My dick is pretty damn stumped right now, too.

So much for taking a nice long nap. Irritation laces through my veins like fire. Using the patience I reserve for my own family, and my annoying sisters, I say, "I was just leaving, Ms. Winterset. I was merely giving her a quick kiss goodbye. Surely you don't think I'd do anything untoward with your daughter, with the door open." I make a mental note for next time to shut and lock the motherfucking door. My phone buzzes in my pocket. I put it on vibrate when I got here, and this is the second time I've felt it. I take it out just enough to see a text from Eva.

"I have work to do anyway," Malena says, convincing her mother of my departure. "Maybe you can help me, Mom? I need to check some availability of the beach pavilions down by Sandy Tides beach," Malena explains, trying to calm her mother by distraction. That's a tactic I use with Eva, so I applaud her efforts. "You can help me choose which photos are best to send to the client?"

Ms. Winterset seems pleased to be asked to help, her posture changing, easing. "Does Dylan know about him?"

To me, Malena holds up one finger and says, "Wait here, one second, please."

I nod, stifling my irritation.

"Be right back," she whispers to me. "Come on Mom. I'll get you on the computer. You can scroll through some pictures. Doesn't that sound like fun? Maybe you'll get tired and we can try for a nap again."

"I'm not tired, I'm mad! I raised you to be better than this, Malena Louise!"

Sighing, I sit on the edge of the bed and run a hand through my hair. Reaching behind me, I find my shirt and slide it back on. Their conversation fades off as I check my messages. According to my texts, Eva is at my house right now. The next message is a photo her disgruntled face with the caption. **Because you refuse to give me a house key.**

I tap back. **I will be home soon. Check on Mr. Olsen or something. HE will love your company.**

She texts back. **Where are you at?!**

Malena walks in, eyeing the phone in my hands. "Sorry about that." She shrugs. "Seems she's not going to let me live that mistake down today. Probably not tomorrow either." Her eyes are sad, a touch haunted.

"It must be hard," I say, sighing to show my frustrations for her. "To have to relive things you don't want to. To have to maintain the patience of a saint." Of a God. Of a Deity. More patience than I'll ever own throughout the duration of my life.

"That obvious, huh?" she asks, sitting next to me. "Dylan was around the longest and I guess that's why she remembers him the most or repeatedly remembers him I should say." I set a hand on her leg. "You put your shirt back on," she says, frowning. "I liked it when it was off."

Tilting my head back, I laugh. "I liked it off, too. But I have to get going. My sister is waiting for me at home. She's liable to break a window trying to get into my house. Then she'll go through everything I own in an effort to discover new things about me that she thinks I'm keeping from her."

Malena winces. "Eeek. Sounds like a personal problem to me. Not my circus," she replies, shaking her head. "Rule number three. Not my monkey, right?"

"You'll thank me later for rule number three," I reply. "They're a lot to handle. My family."

"No complications," Malena says, setting her hand on top of mine and squeezing. "This has to go down in history as the worst first date known to man. I bet even the cavemen would cringe at this awkward attempt to get to know one another." She flops back on her bed and stares at the ceiling. "You can call me, you know if you still want to call me after this disaster, and I'll try to work on a time to meet up with you again. Probably sometime in the next century at the rate in which my schedule fills up with...life."

Trying my best to keep my gaze directed above her neck, a hard feat, I keep my voice low. "I have to ask because it seems like a logical solution, and logistical planning is one of my things, have you thought about finding a place that could better care for her? Full time?"

Her face belies little emotion. I can tell this is a subject that's been broached and considered many times before. "Care for her better than her own daughter? Is that possible? Even if those places didn't scare me, I don't have the money for something like that long term." Malena sits up. "Spilling too many details again. Sorry. Have you seen what happens to the elderly in those group homes? Horrible, awful things. I wouldn't be with her. Imagine what could be accomplished to an old woman who doesn't remember anything! They could neglect her or be cruel to her one day, and she'd forget about it the next." Malena swallows hard, and her eyes shine with threatening tears. I regret my choice in question.

"Hey, you're doing the best you can. I'm sorry for bringing that up."

She shrugs, tells me about a facility she's toured a couple of times. She says she knows eventually her mother will end up there, and she likes to keep track and make sure it's kept up well when she pops in. The way she talks about it tells a story all of its own. The hesitance wars with what she knows is the right thing. I make a mental note to do research about the facility later. My sister Celia is a nurse and might be able to help me. She'll have information about Ms. Winterset's diagnosis at the very least. I'm clueless.

I follow Malena out and into a den where Ms. Winterset is scrolling through photos on an old desktop computer. After the welfare check is complete, Malena walks me to the front door. After a longing look at the table covered with lunch, she turns her attention back to me. I halt whatever she's about to say by speaking.

"I may not be a good man, Malena, but I think I can be good for you. Thank you for letting me in today."

She folds her arms across her chest. "I don't see how you could possibly mean that, but I hope you do. Today was a bright spot for me." Malena's lips are taunting me, but the chance to own her lips is gone. Not today. I can't kiss her now. Timing is everything, and this would mar anything I'm trying to prove to her. Take the high road, Leif, I remind myself.

"Thanks for lunch. I'll probably go eat the rest of the wings right now."

"I'll call you," I say.

She leans against the doorframe, a smirk in place. "You're that crazy, aren't you? I thought your rules were a little nuts, but you're actually going to call me after what you've seen today."

Pressing my lips into a firm line, I keep my face stoic. "Only because I want to see more of you," I tease, flicking my gaze over her body.

She nods. "That's believable," she deadpans, puffing out her chest a bit. "Until we meet or chat again then."

I smile.

She smiles, then closes the door on my face.

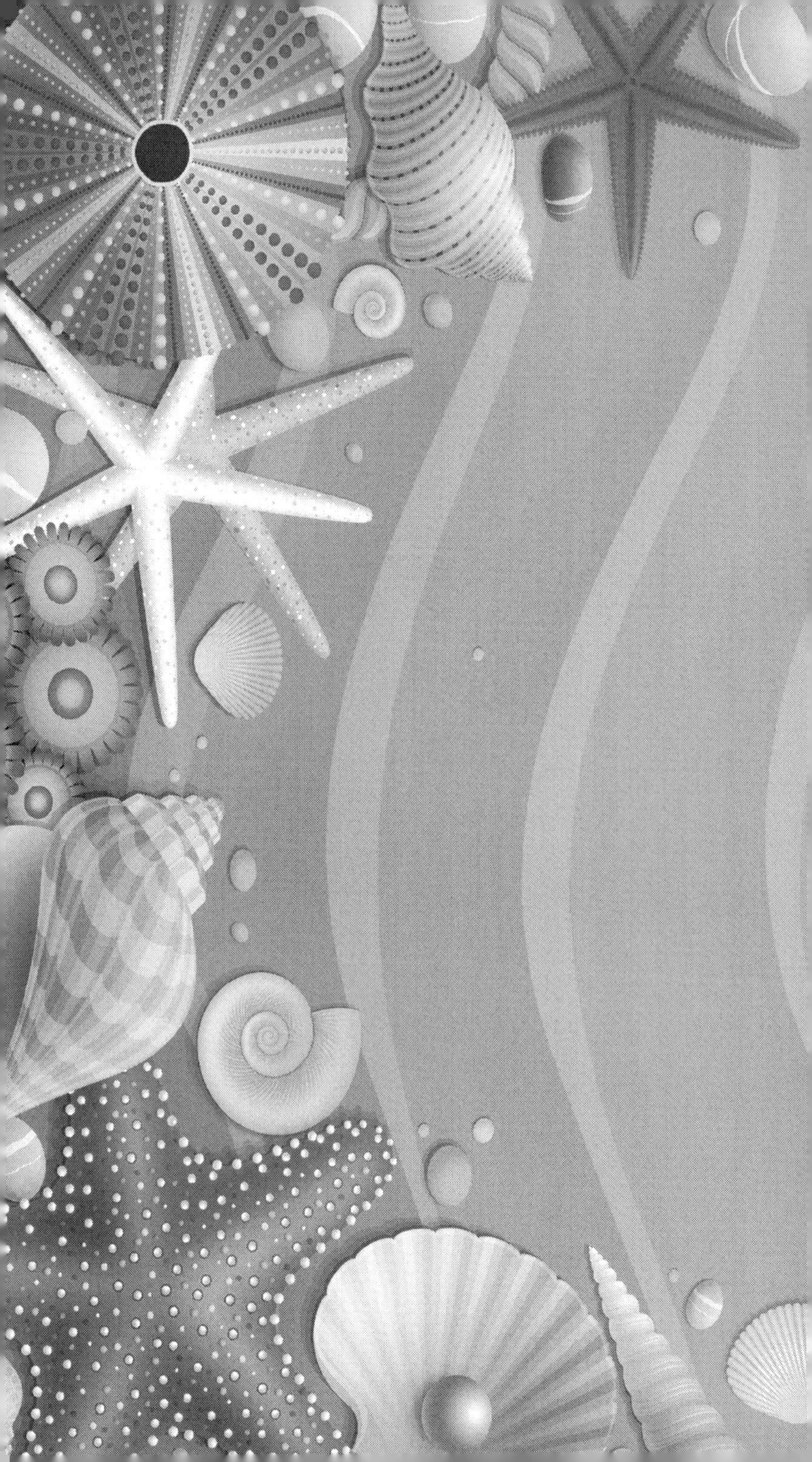

Chapter Six

Malena

"I told them not to worry about Mom's birthday, that I would plan it all myself," Leif splutters on the other end of the phone. "It's not my fault you're the only person who plans parties in this small ass town."

I smile, thinking about the phone call with his sister that turned into an inquisition. The second I called Leif to give him information on beach venues for his mother's birthday party, I recognized his voice straight away. After chastising him for not telling me it was him the first time he called, and then giving him the information, we ended up talking long into the night. About everything—including my father, what it was like to grow up in a small town, and my hopes for the future. We chatted about almost as much as I talked to Eva about.

"You told them about me. That was your first mistake," I finally counter, joking but not letting him know that. "The rules remember?"

tossing it

"I wasn't breaking any," he says, breathing heavily. "I accidentally mentioned you when she asked about the venue."

"And? There has to be more to it than that. She wanted to know my life's history, Leif. She asked me if my period was regular," I reply. I'm pretty sure she was joking, but I answered honestly because she caught me off guard. "Come on now. What did you really tell her?"

The breathing on the other end of the line intensifies, an animal caught in a perfectly laid trap. "They know what's inside my mind. Eva knows me as well as I know myself. I didn't have to tell her anything else. I merely said your name and she attacked."

I laugh. "Come on, Leif. I'm not giving up. Tell me," I order, checking my watch. I'm on a break at the General Store, sitting in the dimly lit backroom, echoing my voice. The other workers take breaks with each other. I'm the odd man out and have to eat my packed lunch in a dungeon hole without another person in sight. I like the peace. I like it even more now that I have Leif to talk to. "Why did she want to know how many exes I had? Questions aimed in the dating department."

He groans. "I might have mentioned that we were… friends. Eva took it from there and it's snowballed into her planning our wedding and naming the nonexistent children. I'm sorry. I shouldn't have said anything. Eva is relentless in her pursuit to match me up with someone. And to have kids of her own. It rubs off on everyone around her."

This got a lot more serious in the span of thirty

seconds. He's basically admitting to having feelings for me. To his family. Sisters. People who mean something to him. He's also simultaneously telling me this isn't going past the dating phase.

"You can breathe easy, Leif. I don't care about talking to Eva. She was nice enough. I honestly thought you'd be upset because we were breaking some dumb rule. Sure, she was asking more questions than I have to answer on my yearly physical form, but it's because she cares about you." A novel idea to me, a woman without siblings. My cousin lives a few towns over. I don't see her near enough, but she's always been the closest thing I'll ever have to a sister. She's busy with her life and I'm busy with mine, but I know she'll make time for me if I need her.

"No. You don't know Eva. She doesn't care about me, she wants to own me."

Tilting my head back, I let a giggle slip. Shaking my head, I reply, "You're being such a dude. It was a little weird. I'm over it already. You scared me when you called today. By the sound of your voice, I would have guessed someone died." I swallow hard and try to mask my unease by taking a bite of my sandwich. "Which would be an occurrence in your daily life, wouldn't it?" I ask when my mouth is empty. It's a hard thing to wrap my brain around. The whole SEAL career and all that it entails. He's given me details here and there when I ask pointed questions about Hell Week and the breakdown of where all the different Teams are around the country. He promptly shuts down the conversation when I ask specific questions about missions and things I've seen on the news. Top secret Leif gives nothing away.

"Not daily," he fires back. "More than it should. It happens more than I want it to. Though things are slower than they were at the start of the war. It's dying down. No pun in intended," he replies, clearing his throat.

I take another bite and chew slowly, digesting this information. "Is dying down a good thing?" I edge. "Safer for you? Safer for our world?"

The scratch of his five o'clock shadow rubs against the phone. "Yeah. Yeah," he says. "It would make me sort of twisted if I admitted I enjoy war, right?"

"Yes," I say.

"I definitely don't enjoy it then."

I slurp the rest of my drink. "But you do enjoy it."

"I never said that."

"You do," I reply.

"I'm happy here. In Bronze Bay. Not deployed."

"Hmm," I grumble into the phone. "Yeah?"

"With you."

My face flushes and my stomach flips the contents like a roller coaster. The tone of his voice pierces my thick skin—silently filling me with something I never dreamed possible. Hope. I ball up my napkin until it can't get any smaller. Leif stays silent, waiting for a response. "I have to get back to work," I whisper.

"Can you come over tonight?" Leif asks. "We could watch the sunset, drink beers. Or wine, if you think that's a more acceptable date."

I laugh, and my stomach sinks. "I can't. The night

nurse isn't around and I can't ask the daytime one, she's been there all day while I'm here."

After a beat or two, Leif asks me how much I pay the nurses, and I tell him. He asks me a few other questions about my finances. I have no reason to lie to him or feel ashamed. His sister knows when I'm having my monthly, surely my income and bills aren't that taboo to talk about. Leif has told me he's really good with numbers and he wants to help me. For whatever reason, maybe because help isn't something that's offered to me very often, I accept willingly.

"Last question," he asks, voice hesitant. "I had Celia look into a few facilities in our area. Don't get upset. I just asked her very casually. She's a nurse and knows a lot of people."

I make a noise of acceptance, mostly because I'm not sure what to say and I'm a little upset. We never established boundaries, but this kind of seems like he's stepped over some.

"If she can pull some strings and get your mom the help she needs, would you accept it?"

A lump lodges in my throat. This is what I've always wanted for her. A place she would be safe at all hours of the day regardless of my location. Would I be able to live with the guilt of passing her to someone else? "Can we talk about this later? I'll think about it," I tell him, sniffling.

"Did I make you upset?"

I shake my head. "No. It's just I'm happy you're trying to help me and sad because I didn't think it would happen this fast. It's a lot. I've been on my own, save for my friends and the nurses I pay, for a long time. Giving up control will be complicated."

"We can talk about it later, okay? Something to think about is all."

"Sure," I tell him. "I have to go back to work. The birds are staring daggers at me," I say, narrowing my eyes at my coworkers trying to listen to my conversation. "Call me later?"

"Of course," Leif says. "Malena."

"Yeah?"

"You're an amazing person. In case no one has told you that today." He clicks off the line, and my heart rate ratchets up even though he's not in front of me. Shaking my head, I pocket my cell, slam my lunch box in my locker and exit the break room without so much as looking at the rest of the General Store employees.

I rub her clammy forehead. She woke up flailing and crying again. Because she forgot he left us. I calmed her as best as I could, but I'll be on high alert for another hour or so. That's about how long it takes for Mom to fade back into REM sleep where she has to be for me to be confident she won't wake up and try to leave the house. After leaving her room, I double check the locks on every exit in the house. I had trigger alarms installed on every single door and window after the first time she went for a walk at two in the morning. I hoped the alarms would take the place of the night nurse and save me some money, but it wasn't enough and I had to keep working. It will never be enough.

Rubbing my tired eyes, I pull a glass out of the cabinet and hold it under the faucet to fill it. Standing over the sink, I drink the contents, tipping my head back. Deep breaths, Malena. Deep breaths. Leif is right. A facility would be able to better handle her at this point. She's not only a prisoner of her own mind, she's a prisoner in this house. I grab my novel off the kitchen table, and head back to my side of the house, taking the monitor with me. I grab a stress ball off a shelf and begin crushing it in my palm. This is the point when I usually start to feel sorry for myself. The point when I let the guilt ease, and let myself actually feel mad about my predicament, my lack of life because of the responsibilities I bear.

A rock hits my window instead. Glancing at the gauzy curtain, I look back at my book. Another tiny rock hits. Then another three in a fast succession. Padding over, I pull aside the curtains and see Leif leaning against a palm tree, in my front yard, a bicycle next to him. Shaking my head, I deactivate the alarms using my cell phone and open the window as high as it will go.

"You scared me," I hiss out. "What are you doing here in the middle of the night?"

"I wanted to see you," Leif replies, the tension in his shoulders and neck evident from my perch several yards away. His white shirt has a sweat stain. "I couldn't wait until our next date," he explains when I don't reply. "Can

I come in?" The air is thick, the humidity clinging to anything that will hold it.

I'm acutely aware of my tousled hair, crappy old T-shirt hitting mid-thigh, and what it means when a man comes over in the middle of the night unannounced. "Is this a booty call, Leif?" He approaches and my heart thumps a little more wildly with each of his thunderous steps in my direction.

He smirks. "No way." Under his breath, he says, "I wish." But I know without a doubt I wasn't meant to hear it, so I take the goosebumps and the panty buzz and step back so a burly man can remove my screen and crawl through my window.

"I can't believe you rode all the way here." I pull my fingers through my hair, glancing in the large mirror above my dresser trying to calm the tangle. I let my gaze flick to Leif in the mirror—he's staring at me, a fierce smolder about to set my skin on fire. In favor of seeing that in person, I meet his eyes, smiling. "It's late for a workout, isn't it? Didn't know bike rides were your thing either."

"I wasn't working out. I just…couldn't stop thinking about you," he says. "You're so beautiful." His eyes dip down to my shirt and bare thighs. "I'm out of my league here and while I'm sure me showing up in the middle of the night to talk to you isn't the best idea, you should know I almost didn't wake you up. I was standing out there just thinking. Looking like a burglar or something worse. Figured I better just do what I came to do." *What did you come to do?*

"If it makes you feel better, I wasn't sleeping. You didn't wake me up." For once, I keep a lid on the details. Ruining this mood would be criminal.

"Good," he replies, breathing heavy. "I need to try something."

"Try something?"

He steps toward me, putting one hand on my hip, raising my shirt on one side by gliding his hand up to my waist. When my black lace panties show, he lets the shirt fall back down. "Like I thought," he growls, swallowing hard. Leif leans his forehead down on mine. "Malena, I can't stop thinking about kissing you. I can't stop," he repeats. "If I kiss you, maybe I can get my head on straight. I'm not a man that makes excuses, but I need to try. You're driving me fucking crazy. Talking to you. Getting to know you. Giving a shit. It's all messing with me. A kiss. All I need is a kiss."

Running my hands under his T-shirt, he shudders as my fingers make contact with his bare skin. "I'm not sure if that's a compliment or not," I reply after he hisses out a pleased breath.

Nodding emphatically, he says, "It is."

"Sounds like we have an experiment on our hands," I reply, removing my hands from his rippling abs to glide my palms on top of his biceps and forearms, watching as my touch prickles his skin. "Just a kiss? Nothing more?"

Biting his lip, he nods, leans down and pushes my lips apart with his tongue. His hands circle my lower back as the kiss deepens—my lips on his, and our bodies pressed together, no space for the Lord in this embrace. It's gritty with need and electrified with pent-up desire. His teeth bump against mine, as he tilts his head the opposite direction to possess my mouth from a different angle. Backing up, he follows me until my legs hit my bed.

Leif breaks from the kiss only long enough to remove his shirt, as I scoot back toward the pillows. "Consider the experiment a failure," he breathes, eyes wild, gaze flicking from my mouth to my eyes. "I'll never get enough of your lips."

I grin in reply and he's on me in the next second. His kiss truly is an out of body experience. My skin is on fire from feeling his large hands on my hips, tingles of need flush every part of my skin that touches his. This isn't because I haven't been with a man in a long time, it's because it's him. Wrapping my legs around his waist, I clasp my hands around his neck, lacing my fingers in his hair. Our height difference isn't as obvious when we're lying down, limbs entwined, heart to heart. Leif drags his lips across my neck, leaving a trail of fire as he goes. His kiss finds my ear and I whisper his name. A tiny plea for everything he's not giving me. Everything he can't give. His lips find mine again and I let my eyes close to feel every sensation crawling through my body.

His muscles are tightly coiled, strong. Leif's body is saying everything his words never have. He wants me. Us. This. Just as much as I do. When he pulls away from the kiss, I meet his eyes. The light blue is exquisite this close—a liquid ocean full of torment and satisfaction. He pushes breaths through his full lips as he pants, the only exertion being him holding himself back. A flood of wetness soaks my panties, a mere look turning me to culpable putty in his hands. I'd give up anything to have him. This look. I feel it everywhere.

"Malena," he says, licking his lips. "I can't stop. I don't want to stop."

"Then don't. Kiss me."

Wetting his lips, he looks at me reverently laying beneath his strong frame. "I want to do a fuck ton more than kiss you," he says, leaning back, his legs on either side of my own. My shirt rode up, and there's an ample amount of under boob exposed. "A kiss didn't fix anything." Leif shakes his head. "A kiss sealed my fucking fate." Sighing, he bends his head and drags his lips up my stomach to my breasts, teasing my shirt up with his tongue, until his mouth seals over my nipple.

He slides his mouth over to the other side and repeats the gesture, his lips and tongue worshipping my skin—slowly, methodically. I'm lost in the moment, his touch, the way he's looking at me, testing my reactions like he's trying to play an instrument. My breaths come quicker, and my stomach flips when he finally brings his kiss back to my mouth. A soft rain begins falling outside my window, the wind blowing it around signaling a night storm.

"You kiss like you've had a lot of practice," I say, my words brushing across his wet lips.

He shakes his head slowly, dragging his tongue along my bottom lip as he does. "You make me feel like this is my first time."

His words hit me everywhere this time, including

my heart. "You're so smooth." I guide his head back to mine and steal the knowing smirk off his face with another kiss. He groans into my mouth as he presses his erection between my legs. The hard bulge is exactly where I want it minus our pesky clothing. His face tells me he's thinking the same thing as he glances between our bodies, his bottom lip clutched between his teeth.

The moment turns to dust as the first roll of thunder breaks around us. We both jump. Leif puts a hand on his chest. "I'm not used to that yet. This shit comes out of the middle of nowhere."

"I know. It's not something you get used to either. Sort of comes out of the middle of nowhere most of the time," I say, my heart rate hammering more from his touch than from the scare.

Kneeling, I hug him around his neck. His hands hold me, but his attention is focused at my open window. That thunder must have really shocked him. "Did you hear that?"

"Yeah, obviously," I reply.

He shakes his head. "No, not the thunder or the rain. It sounded like a crash," he says. "In the distance." Nope. I didn't hear anything. His cat-like, SEAL reflexes must be on alert. When he pulls away from me and stands from the bed his eyes are narrowed out the window, his gait sure, steady, it looks like he's entered another mode—another skin.

"My bike is gone," he whispers.

I jump out of bed and grab my phone and then the horrified sickening feeling rages in my stomach. "I didn't turn the alarm back on," I whisper.

"What?" Leif says, turning to look at me over his shoulder.

I run to the living room and sure enough, the front door is wide open, the rain blowing in anytime a gust of wind strikes. "My mom. She's gone. She left," I scream out, but Leif is already out the front door at a pace that seems inhuman. "I didn't turn the alarms back on," I say to myself. How could I forget? Why would I turn them off and forget? What is wrong with me? Staring at the cell phone screen and the red disarmed buttons, I close my eyes and take a silent, horrified breath. "I did this. It's my fault. It's always my fault."

I step into the rain and am soaked in seconds, my hair plastered across my forehead. With bare feet, I make my way down the driveway to the main road and look both left and right. When do I call the police? Now? The road is silent, we only have a few houses on our street, but there are a ton of trails cutting through the thick brush-like woods that surround our house. It's from one of these trails that Leif appears several feet from where I stand, a rain-soaked hero, my mother, sobbing silently, in his arms.

"Get the car, Malena," he calls out the order. "Her wrist is broken. She took a fall on the bike." Her pink nightgown is covered in dark muddy spots highlighted by a lone, blinking street light. Turning on my heel, I start my car and run back to the house to throw on actual clothing and grab Leif's shirt off the edge of the bed, a sight I'll probably never see again.

He's buckling her into the backseat when I peer out the window on my way to Mom's room to get her clean clothes. When I get to the front door to exit, Leif is standing there, running his hands through his soaked hair. "I'm sorry I didn't hear her sooner," he mutters, shaking his head, unable to meet my eyes. "I'm losing it."

"No, I'm sorry," I say, tears threatening. "I'm always going to be the one who needs you more than you need me. That's not fair to you."

Leif puts his hands on either side of my face. "Malena, stop it. You can't help what happened. This isn't your fault," he says, anger lacing his words. This time, I do cry. Hard and furious. He folds me into his cold, wet arms. "This is going to keep happening," Leif adds. I hear it. The words he left unsaid. *If you don't do something about it.*

This is my lifeline. My phone a friend. My Hail Mary. If I don't recognize it, I'd be a daft, dumb woman, and I'm not that. "Please help me, Leif. Call Celia? I need more help. She needs more," I whisper through sobs. "She deserves more."

He nods against my head and promises to get everything sorted as quickly as humanly possible. I believe him. He shrugs on the shirt I offer and shivers against the cold rain. I get in the driver's side and he shuts the door behind me. Rolling down the window, I'm going to thank him again, but he leans in and kisses me instead.

"Drive safe. Call me when you get there," he says, then

turns his eyes to my mom. "Feel better Ms. Winterset." Leif meets my gaze, the rain soaking through his shirt. "Call me," he says, nodding his head. "I'm going to fix everything. Don't worry about a thing." He kisses me again. Slower this time, a hesitance to let me go, lips lingering, fingers caressing my face.

It was a kiss of a man who cares about a woman.

Leif just entered my bloodstream. With a kiss, he arrived and will never leave. His mouth left a stain on my soul. Bringing my fingers up to my own lips as I drive toward the emergency room, I let the shock of my realization seep in. I'm falling for Leif Andersson, better yet, I've already fallen for him.

All at once.

Because of a connection so strong I never knew it could exist. Is it breaking a rule if I don't tell him?

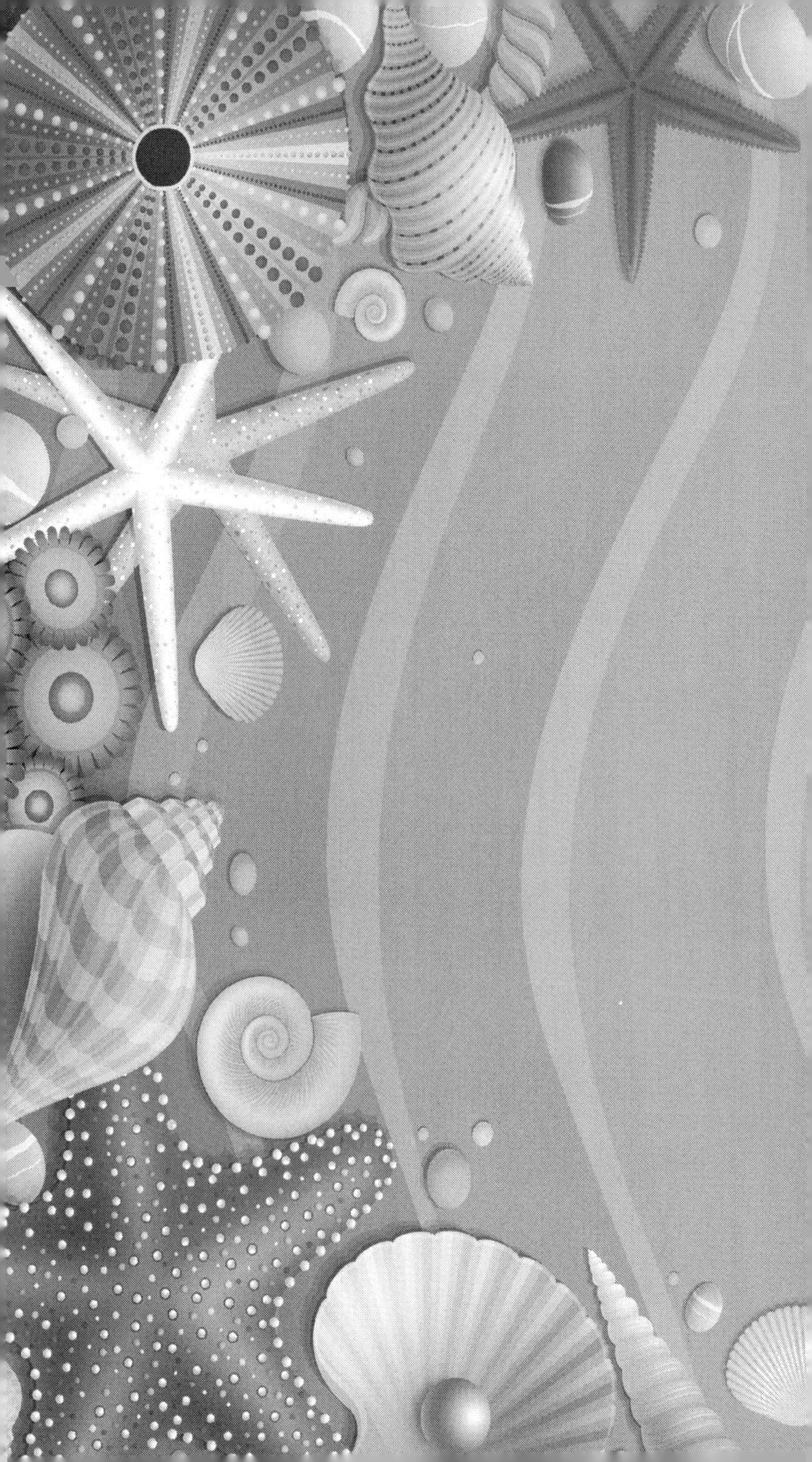

Chapter Seven

Leif

Eva and Celia are sitting across from me at the diner, the concerned looks on their faces making my stomach flip. They're in parenting mode even though they aren't my parents. Silently, I wonder if this is what every youngest sibling has to go through. This time it's my fault. I asked them to meet me here in an effort to put it all on the table. Well, most of it anyway.

"She doesn't seem stable. Are you sure you want to get mixed up in this?" Eva asks, glancing at Celia, then me. She sips her coffee slowly, giving me a chance to pick the correct words.

How do I tell her it's too late? That I broke my own damn rule without my own consent. Talking to Malena all week, learning things about her, character traits I didn't know I wanted, culminated in a desire so strong I ended up at her house in the middle of the damn night. I chug down half of my water bottle.

tossing it

Celia inserts, "We're good people, Eva. I'll help Malena regardless of Leif getting mixed up with her problems. It's the right thing to do."

Eva sends a pointed look to our sister. "We both know that's not the question," Eva barks, looks at me, and continues, "Why are you helping her this much. You told me you're her friend. This is more than friend, just as I suspected. Her home life is a wreck. A father that abandoned her, a mother who is certifiable."

"Hey," I cut in. "Don't talk like that."

Celia says, "I agree, Eva. Don't be a bitch. Just because our family is ideal doesn't mean that's the norm."

"Ideal?" I ask, eyes wide. "This isn't ideal, or normal. An ideal family would help without question. Without judging." I shake my head, settling back into the booth. I remind myself to keep my voice down. Caroline, one of Malena's best friends, works here and she's glanced over here a few times since this insane conversation began. "Celia," I say, looking at the more rational sister—the one who has already helped me without asking too many questions about my emotions. "You got Ms. Winterset into Garden Breeze. That's the best one in the surrounding areas, right? When can she check in?"

Celia nods. "How is she going to afford it, Leif? Eva told me about their phone conversation and it doesn't sound like she has a lot of…resources to make a switch this permanent."

Closing my eyes, I swallow down the lie that was on the tip of my tongue. "Don't worry about that part. It's taken care of and Malena won't have to worry about it." Celia presses her lips together and I thank God, she doesn't say what she really wants to. She tells me about the facility and the doctors she's familiar with. The care will be top notch. It's heavily guarded, but still has access to the beach and a year-round garden that has both flowers and vegetables. A hobby Malena told me Ms. Winterset had a passion for before dementia set it.

Throughout this conversation, I feel Eva's gaze boring holes into my soul. "You're in love with the woman. How the fuck is that possible?"

Deny. Deny. "I'm helping a friend, Eva. Stop trying to read more into it."

Celia clears her throat. "You never helped any of the other women more than to see them out of your bed and out the front door. You have to see why we're at least a little bit curious. The interest for anything other than your career hasn't been there before. It's sort of exciting."

"Only my sisters would think my interest in a woman is exciting. We're adults."

Eva bangs a hand on the table. "He admitted interest."

Celia scoffs. "Of course, he's interested. He's paying for his girlfriend's mother to enter the best facility in the area. Answer us one question and we'll leave you alone. We need to get back to work."

Sighing, I run both of my hands down my face. "What?"

Eva butts in. "Let me pick the question."

Celia shakes her head, narrowing her eyes at me. "No, if we only get one I want to make it count. You're too hot-headed."

tossing it

Sighing, Eva says, "True."

I throw my hand up to get the attention of our waitress. It's Shirley, Malena's other friend. This place doesn't leave any room for secrets, that's for sure. I told my sisters this when we sat down for lunch, I'm hoping they fucking watch their mouths.

Shirley saunters over, a glint of mischief in her eye. "Since I'm not following any of your rules, will you please give me the formal introduction to your lovely sisters?" Shirley coos, setting the check down in the center of the table, gaze locked on mine. Fuck. Why wouldn't I assume Malena talks to her friends about us? Why wouldn't she, especially since she knows I am talking to my sisters?

Clearing my throat over my sisters' sighs, and shifting frames in the seats in front of me, I feel like I'm on trial. "Shirley, this is Eva and Celia. My lovely, benevolent sisters."

Eva shakes her hand first, giving her a polite smile. Celia follows with a grin a little more believable. They exchange pleasantries for a minute or two, chatting about Bronze Bay, the beaches, and the like.

Then, like a shark scenting blood, Eva turns her fire back on me. "Rules? Do tell us about these rules, dear brother." She looks at Shirley and she grins widely. My armpits start sweating, and a sheen breaks across my forehead. Reaching into my pocket, I grab cash, throw it on the table and stand to leave.

"None of your damn business," I deadpan. "I have to get back to work."

Celia scoots out and follows me to the door. "Does she know? Have you told her?" she asks, her words against my retreating back.

When we get out into the parking lot, I spin. "What are you talking about? I'm exhausted from talking to you guys. It's never easy. You know that? Does who know what?" I get to my moped and lean against the seat, so we're eye level.

Celia looks crestfallen, and I feel a touch of guilt for being so rash, but I can only take so much from them. "Listen, I got her into Garden Breeze when they were pulling from the insanely long wait list. You owe me. Remember that."

Hanging my head, I sigh. "I'm sorry. Eva just pisses me off with her questions. Why does it matter? Can't I want to do something for someone of the opposite sex without her jumping the gun?"

"Does Malena know that you...care about her?"

Oh. "I'm helping her. That has to be some indication."

Celia shakes her head. "You are so bad at this. She probably thinks you feel bad for her or something. You're not a bad guy, Leif." Celia lays a hand on my arm. "You are worthy of someone's love. The first step is admitting to yourself that you care for Malena. That's what all of this is. You realize that right?" She waves her arm between us. "You wanting the best for a person *she* cares about. Paying for it. Giving a damn about things other than yourself is a prime indicator. You don't have to admit it to us, but you need to admit it to yourself. Life is too short."

tossing it

I nod. Mostly to halt the conversation, but I hear truth in her words and while it does scare me, I'm already there. The time to flip a bitch passed, and now I'm stuck with feelings and unsure what the fuck to do with them.

Eva and Shirley are visible through the diner windows and through Shirley's exaggerated gestures I can only assume my evil sister is getting a rundown on my dating rules. Fuck. Closing my eyes, I mount my moped. "Thank you, Celia. For everything. It means a lot to me."

"Because it means a lot to Malena," Celia adds. "Drive safe, scooter McGee." She ruffles my hair before I smash the helmet down on top of it. Celia walks away, back to the diner to get caught up no doubt, and I make my way back to work.

The sea salt air clears my mind and I try to simplify my world to the lowest common denominator. I can have my work and Malena. I can stay in Bronze Bay. That doesn't require any huge sacrifices on either of our parts. I care about Malena and her life, but I know for a fact my sister is right. I wouldn't do this for anyone in my past. Malena needs me and I want to be needed by her. Because I care about her heart.

What's going to happen when I sleep with her? The rules will be fucked, that's what, and there will be nothing to guard me…or her. After I show my ID to the gate guard, I find my spot while contemplating my future.

"Hey man," I tell Sutter as I walk into the office and toss down my gym bag. "Anything going on?"

"Nah. Skydiving on Friday. I can't fucking wait. It's been so long. I need to keep up on my quals for when

I get back to a west coast team," he mutters while scrolling through updates on our top-secret network. To get the clearance for our system is time-consuming and painstaking. Setting it up was the longest part of the process when we moved to Bronze Bay. It gives us all of the information we need in real time and keeps our emails safe. Sutter can't wait to leave here.

Settling into a chair, I open my laptop and check out the website for Garden Breeze and find the phone number. Dialing it, I walk into the empty conference room and make arrangements for Ms. Winterset's stay and give them the indefinite payment information. I also tell them not to make my information public. I'm sure Malena will assume, but I don't want my generosity to be in her face. Then she'll read into it, and we'll both have to confront what such an act actually means. The girl on the phone is helpful and promises me Ms. Winterset is expected this afternoon when she's discharged from the hospital.

Malena is going to need me to help her. Be there for her. My heart races when I think about seeing her again and it's asinine to even me. It was just last night that the whole broken wrist debacle took place. More, it's when I knew that no matter what happened, I wasn't going to be able to turn my back on her in any way shape or form.

As I hang up the call with Garden Breeze, I get a text from Malena telling me she called out of work today because she was at the hospital all night long—is still there. It's a long paragraph thanking me for pulling strings to get her into the facility and how she's going to repay me. Malena feels guilty, I can tell through word choice, but mostly she sounds tired—ready to do the inevitable.

I text back. **Don't mention it. It was nothing getting her in. She needs to be there, she'll be happy. Celia says it's the best place around. Try not to worry. You'll have to get as many of her medical records to them when you get a chance. Tell me if you need anything else. I'm sorry about last night**. While I wouldn't have fucked her—I didn't have a condom on me, I would have made her toes curl multiple times if we weren't interrupted. I have to keep reminding myself there will be plenty of time.

Her reply is swift. **Last night was simultaneously the best and worst night of my life. But don't quote me on that because I'm running on about thirty minutes of sleep. I'm going to get Mom settled in at Garden Breeze and then I'm going to sleep for a decade.** My mood deflates as my hope to see her tonight is crushed like a tiny bug. *Think about her. Not yourself.* This is an enormous step she's making. It will leave her alone in her house. That's going to be a vast change from what she's used to.

I keep it easy, happy, my thumbs flying to tap out the message. **If you need company. Let me know. I'm only a bike ride away. Though, I'll probably take my moped now that I'm not stalking you.** I expect a serial killer joke to follow.

She doesn't respond as quickly, though. **I want to see your house.**

I swallow hard. **Yes. Come over.**

I might have to leave a toothbrush there.

I grin. "**Not allowed** ☺ In reality, Malena could leave a limb at my house if it meant she was there, in my space—my bed.

Can't come then. Sorry.

You can use mine, I counter.

That's abhorrent, Leif. I can't be your friend anymore.

Fine. Bring a toothbrush as long as you take it with you when you go. I didn't know we were 'friends.'

Such a swift kick in the ass. You charmer, you. What would you call me if not a friend?

My heart rate ratchets up to adrenaline junkie mode. It doesn't make sense, but I'll over analyze it later. I slink back into my office chair. Sutter says something to me, but I'm too lost in my thoughts to respond to him. Grinning at my phone, I text, **Mine. I'd call you mine.** My dick rises to the occasion, making me uncomfortably aware that while she may be mine, I have yet to stake my claim in a consummate way.

While I'd typically reject such a strongly worded statement, I'm so tired that it actually pleases me to read it. Being yours has a nice ring to it.

Good. I'll make it official when you come over.

That might be worth the exhaustion, her text comes, and then another, **I have to go. Sorry. A van arrived to take Mom and I'm going to go home to pack some things**.

It's going to be a good thing, I remind her. **Don't be scared. Call me if you need anything. Or just swing by.**

She doesn't reply, but I remind her where my condo is and offer to swing by tonight if she asks me to.

Sutter, who was reading over my shoulder this entire time I was wrapped up in Malena cackles like a drunken clown. "Dude, you are so fucking chained. When did this happen? You've kept a good ass secret man. Not like Tahoe. What is in this fucking water? Turning men into pets left and right," he whoops out, bent over laughing.

I click the side button to darken my cell phone's screen. "Fuck off, Sutter." "No fuck you, man. Do you guys have balls left? These chicks aren't anything special. I've dicked plenty of them and walked away unscathed. What is it about them that makes them so desirable? The southern drawl? The coconut laced hair shampoo? The tans? These small town ladies are the Kryptonite of this whole fucking SEAL Team." Sutter shakes his head. "I need to get back to San Diego where the women are women and the men stay men. I'm surrounded by pussies and I can't fuck any of them."

"Calm your tits, dude. Maybe if you had a woman to go home to at night, you wouldn't be such an asshole all the time."

"What is it about her then? Explain," Sutter says, sitting in an office chair, and scooting toward me until we're knee to knee. "Make me understand."

Swallowing hard, I blow out a breath. "You're serious? I just came from lunch with my sisters. I don't think I'm ready for this kind of conversation. I haven't even had sex with her so I don't want to call it before the ref does, man." It's a slight lie because I already know sex with Malena will be amazing because the chemistry is off the motherfucking charts. "There's nothing to understand, really. Why do you care? You're a bachelor for life. Don't worry about what I'm doing."

Sutter shakes his head. "No. Not for life. But it's not going to be some small town chick to keep me. These women have never seen outside this place." He's generalizing, but he knows it. I don't need to remind him.

Narrowing my eyes, I ask, "How is that a bad thing?"

Sutter appears to actually consider my question instead of slinging an insult.

I go on, "Listen, they sent me here for a break. It's why most of us are here. I don't know about you, but since the war began, I haven't even paused to consider what might be good for me. What I wanted outside of the Teams, what would fulfill and make me happy. Have you?"

Sutter looks at me with wide eyes, shaking his head. "You've turned into a pussy before you tapped it. I didn't know it was possible. I'm witnessing the death of your manhood right now."

I roll my eyes. "Fuck you, Sutter. I thought you wanted to be serious for half a second. I want to help Malena and…I like her," I say, turning away from him to read emails on our server.

"It's the hero complex," Sutter says. "Once she's saved, you'll get bored and join the fuck team again. That's what it is. I've diagnosed you. Go forth and swoop in with your red cape and awesome biceps. Fuck a few times, then return to me wiser and stronger."

"You're wrong," I say, praying to God he's not right. He makes sense in the fucked up way only Sutter can make sense.

"I'm not wrong. I'll be here waiting."

For the first time, I don't want to be on whatever team Sutter is on. I don't think I was ever the angry, single asshole that he is, but I might have been. I pull up the itinerary for skydiving on Friday and save the few emails that contain details about the whereabouts of *my* bad guy.

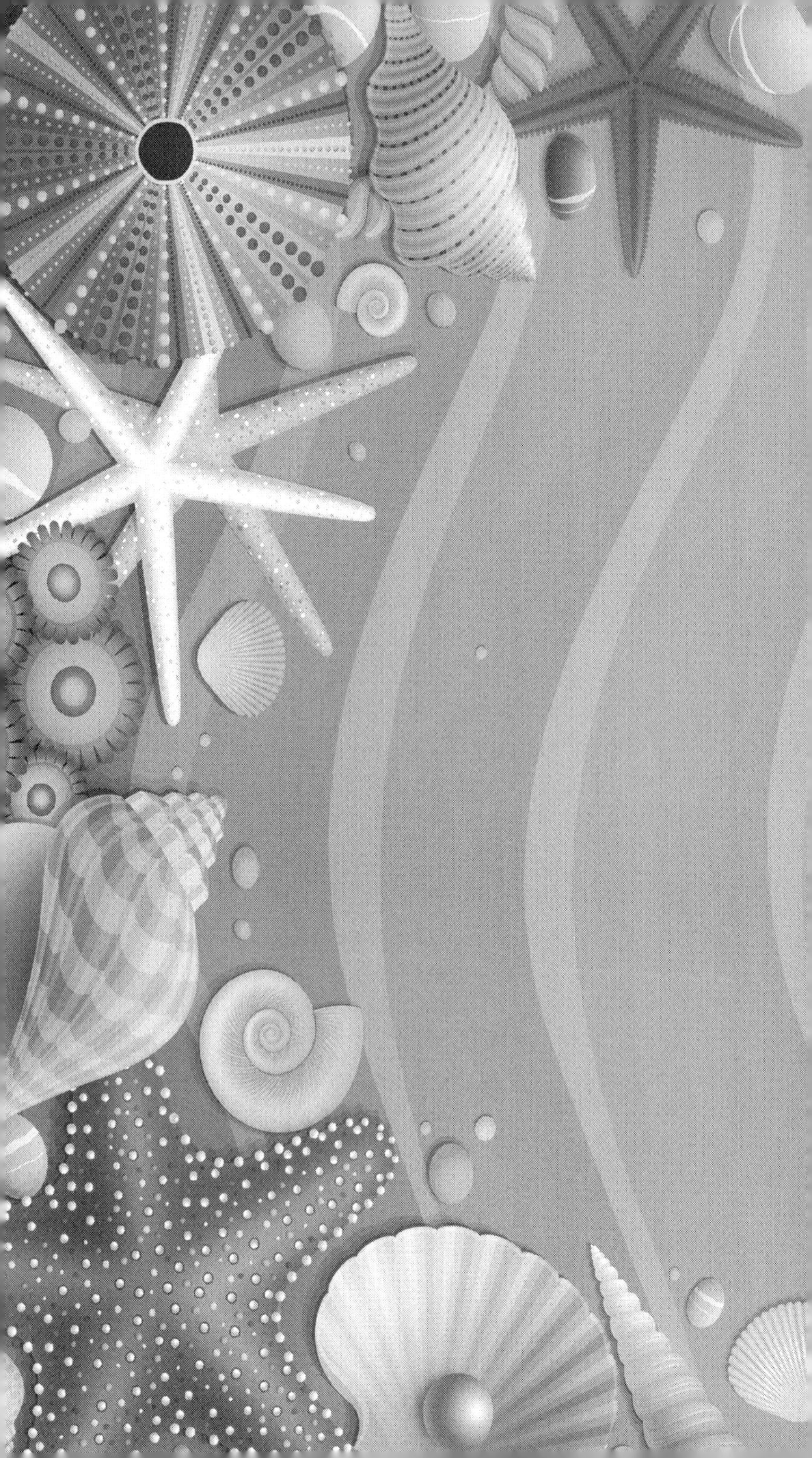

Chapter Eight

Malena

"She's so confused. Are you sure she's going to be okay?" I ask, eyes rimmed red from crying and lack of sleep. Everyone at Garden Breeze has been overtly cheerful and helpful. So much so that I wonder if it's all an act, like the second I leave they'll start being mean to my mom or something. I'm so jaded by life. Nothing has ever been this easy—seamless, during my existence.

The doctor puts her hand on my shoulder, a white-toothed grin wide and ready. "I promise to call you to give you an update. This is what I specialize in. Your mother is in the best hands possible for her condition. I'm surprised you managed her by yourself for this long." The doctor's smile fades and the ball of daughter-guilt hardens in my stomach. "Her dementia is further along than we are used to seeing in a newly admitted patient. We are well equipped to handle anything that may come along during her stabilization in a new residence."

tossing it

I nod, a continuous motion, as the doctor goes on. She uses all the words I already knew but always feared. I don't have to fear them anymore. These people are here to help her...and me. "And I can call to check in on her anytime?" Glancing in Mom's beautiful suite, I see that she's calmed down, and is now sitting in a chair gazing out the window, looking at the expansive garden, a slight smile on her face. There are several bouquets of fresh flowers arranged in vases around the room. When I remarked on them, a nurse told me no expense was spared to make sure Mom's integration was smooth and pleasant. Leif did this. All of this. The ball of guilt morphs into something more pleasant, yet horrifying. I'll never be able to repay him for this. Not ever. Not in this lifetime. Not with money, not with all that I have to offer.

The wrist break wasn't severe and didn't need surgery which was surprising when you consider the angle at which it was bent after the fall off the bicycle. I cringe at the day-old memory.

"I'm going to slip out while she's calm," I say, heart pounding in trepidation. I'm given paperwork and with one longing glance at the woman I love, I leave. I'm leaving here. Without my mom. The person who cared for me for as long as she was capable. The only person who has ever been there for me in all capacities.

Dragging both of her large, empty, rolling suitcases behind me, I exit into the hot air. I feel both tortured and free at the exact same time. There has to be some lesson in this. Some releasing of control, and winning some battles, yet losing others, but right now I'm so tired

I can't think straight. The lines in the road blur as I hit the Bronze Bay city limits and familiar territory, my eyes blinking slowly on their own. I barely make it home and into my bed before crashing. I wake up to my cell phone, which is on my bedroom floor, buzzing loudly.

My limbs are stiff and sore from sleeping so long. "How long did I sleep?" I mutter, grabbing the back of my neck as I amble into my bathroom, and stuff my toothbrush into my mouth. I squint my eyes at the analog clock on the wall. "Fifteen hours." My voice is hoarse as I reach down for my phone and start figuring out my life. I've missed several text messages from Shirley, one from Caroline, a call from Garden Breeze, and sixteen calls from Leif. I listen to the voicemail from Garden Breeze first. I quickly call them back. They were merely calling to give me an update that Mom had a great night, slept through and everything. She is playing a game of cards with one of the other residents and seems very happy. It gives me a pang. She's not playing cards with me. That's when I realize how empty my house is going to be. I thank them for the update and hang up with tears falling down my face.

Loud pounding on the front door breaks me from my thoughts. I rinse the remaining toothpaste from my mouth, throw my hair in a ponytail and answer the door. I open the door to a worried Leif.

"Where is your phone?" he snaps, looking me up and down, like he's assessing for damage. Just my heart, I think. "Are you okay?"

"If you count sleeping for fifteen hours okay, I guess

tossing it

so. I passed out. The emotional exhaustion kicked me in my rear," I admit. Leif looks amazing, a tight shirt stretches across his wide chest, and the scent of his body wash hits the air like his battle song. Give me war, Leif. Give it to me. "In desperate need of a shower," I add, thinking about the last time I bathed. "Like, big time."

Leif's worry transforms into relief, as he pushes inside. "I'll wait for you to shower," he says.

"No, you don't have to! Don't you have work? You've done enough for me lately. Don't be late on my account," I breathe out. "It's all so much, Leif. I don't have the money to repay you and I don't think a lifetime of sexual favors would even put a dent in the Garden Breeze bill." My stomach churns, and I lay a hand on it. "It's really too much."

Leif sits on the sofa, elbows on his knees, and head clutched in his hands. "Malena let's not talk about it, okay? It's nothing. What makes you think I want sexual favors?"

"It's nothing?" I retort, the pitch of my voice increasing as I continue, "How can you say that what you did is nothing?"

"Sexual favors?" he mutters again, ignoring my question, yet demanding a response.

I swallow hard. "That was a joke mostly because it's the only way I can repay you for your kindness. That's all. You're either the most generous man alive if you consider this nothing, or you're downplaying it because you don't want things to get weird."

He doesn't look up. "Go shower. I'll make some

breakfast. You must be hungry." At the reminder of food, my stomach grumbles. "Saying it's nothing doesn't mean it's not important. It just means it doesn't affect me. The money is a non-issue. Do you understand?" His gaze finally rises to meet mine. "I don't want anything as repayment. Not money, and definitely not sexual favors. Just so we're clear. I wasn't aware you were into prostitution though."

Oh. He'd told me living the single life did very good things for his bank account. Bonuses and home sales, and paychecks that couldn't be spent while overseas added up over the years. I guess I never connected those dots. I wince. "I understand, but I still think it matters. It means something to me." I cross one foot over the other. "I'd be your prostitute," I try to joke, but only a small corner of his mouth pulls up. "Only yours." The other side pulls up and he shakes his head.

Leif runs a hand over the scruff on his jaw. "It means something to me too. That's why I did it," he says, standing and brushing past me to enter the kitchen. I hear banging as he tries to find a pan, and I don't make a move to help him. I watch him, this big, beautiful man who has shown me his heart.

"This is the nicest thing anyone has ever done for me before," I deadpan.

Leif stops, a frying pan in his hand and turns back to look at me. He opens his mouth to say something, then closes it again. The tears rise in my eyes, and I don't want to cry again, lest it come across as ungrateful, so I hold up one finger and excuse myself to the shower. I let the hot water wash off the past two days. My mom is fine. My life can change. There is a man who cares for me cooking for me in my kitchen right now. There has to be something to be said about this. The General Store job was only so I could pay for Mom's occasional night nurse, a person I no longer need. I can be a full-time party planner now. Just last week I turned down a job because I couldn't fit it into my insane schedule. Maybe I will still keep my gig at the store to try to pay back Leif, little by little. That would be the right thing to do, but I don't want him to be upset if I try to offer him money.

For the first time in a long time, I have time. Time for myself. At the cost of my family, though. Once I'm scrubbed clean, I throw on a tank top and shorts and steel myself for Leif and the wall of sexual desire that hits anytime I'm in his vicinity. The wall that did in fact leave room for my mom to escape our house in the middle of the night.

There are two plates on the table when I come out. Eggs, toast, blueberries, and avocado, all separated in perfect fourths on the plates. He's opened the curtains to let light in and the space already has a fresh energy running through it. He interrupts my thoughts, "Here's the thing, Malena. You can't thank me constantly for everything. You're welcome and all, because that's the polite thing to say, but I need you to drop it from here on out. You asked me for help and I helped." He heaves his shoulders up and down. "Consider it the universe repaying you for all the slack you had to pick up when your dad left, but let's build something from the ground up, not on Garden Breeze, money, or broken wrists. Is that a possibility?" he asks, leaning on a dining chair, clear blue eyes earnest, relieved he's finally spoken the peace he's been forming since my shower began.

"I won't forget it, but I won't talk about it if that's what you want. It changes a lot for me and it's going to take a lot of getting used to. I want to build something with you, Leif. More than I've ever wanted anything else. You're the first thing I've ever let myself desire to this…degree." I sit down, keeping my gaze distracted with the breakfast plate. "My life has taught me to keep my expectations low. Self-preservation and all that." He must understand that. Leif has told me of the sacrifices he's had to make over the years. Creature comforts are zilch when you're overseas living in a dirty hut for months at a time.

Leif sits down next to me, picking up his fork. "I'm here. I want to be here," Leif says, pausing waiting for me to meet his bewitching eyes. When I do, he goes on, "Set your expectations higher. I have."

Grinning, I stop any sort of word vomit from arriving by shoving toast in my face. It makes him laugh. If I'm selecting expectations for myself, then I want Leif. All to myself forever. I want to keep his kindness in my pocket as a defense mechanism against the cruel world. I want him to only ever want me in return. His emotion-filled gazes. His touches filled with fire. All of him. He seems to know what I'm thinking, which I hope isn't true or I'd crumble under the weight of my own desires. Leif licks his lips and tips up his chin as he surveys me, watching him. "What should we do today?" he asks.

"We?" I blurt out, my mouth full of food. "You have work."

"There wasn't anything going on in the office today. They don't need me. We're skydiving tomorrow, so I wanted to make sure your first day…alone, well, wasn't really alone. What do you want to do today? I figured we could do something now and then visit your mom later on this afternoon. That's when there's free time and when most guests visit." He backtracks. Almost as if he doesn't want me to know how much he knows. "I think that's what they said when I called. You can call to check and be sure."

I choke on the bread sticking to the roof of my mouth. Banging a fist on my chest, I make an exaggerated unpleasant noise. "Are you even real?" I ask. "I slept for fifteen hours and time warped. Maybe I'm still sleeping." Pinching myself on the arm, I sit back in my chair. "Definitely awake. You're definitely real." I shake my head.

"Touch me. Find out for sure," he growls, chewing slowly, eyes on mine. Oh, the ways in which I want to touch him.

We both eat, looking at each other, back and forth, like a game of wits. "Please tell me I'm not some charity case. This bubble is going to pop when you realize you can't fix me." I'm half joking, but Leif's smile falls from his face completely.

Swallowing food, he pauses, then says, "Who said I wanted to fix you?"

"That's what people like you do."

Leif scoffs. "People like me?"

"The perfect ones," I say.

He shakes his head. "I'm so far from perfect, the word isn't even in my vocabulary. I don't think you need to fix anything about yourself, Malena." Leif puffs out his chest and stretches a bit. "It seems you're not used to others helping you."

The father sized lump in my heart pounds a bit, a jagged reminder. "You're right," I say, casting my gaze downward.

"And all my family does is help. Even when I don't want it, but that's the price I pay. When I'm far from home, they send care packages filled with my favorite things—trying to make my life easier—more comfortable." He pauses, and I try to put myself in his shoes, shoes that seem gilded in comparison to the tattered ones I've been forced to wear. "They moved to be closer to me when I decided to make Bronze Bay my permanent residence. Mom has always wanted to retire in Florida so it wasn't a crazy stretch, but that's just another example of how we help each other."

"I'm not your family though," I say, narrowing my eyes. "Why me?"

He seems taken aback by that question. He takes a bite of toast and chews, nodding his head, looking at me up and down. "I've spent some time thinking about this," Leif says, tilting his head to the side. "It's a combination of things. You're beautiful, and I want you. You're caring and compassionate, and I want you. You tell me things most people wouldn't dream of saying out loud, and I want you. The thought of your lips on anyone else drives me mad with jealousy, and I want you. You look like that," he says, jutting his chin in my haggard, wet direction. "You taste like heaven. You seem to enjoy spending time with me. One last thing," he says, taking my hand in his.

He nods his head as he says, "I know for a fact I'll never *not* want you."

My heart stops as my hand automatically clasps around his. "You can't know that for sure. People change. Grow. Move on. Move out."

Leif repeats, "I'll never not want you." His confidence is unwavering.

I can't accept that answer. It turns everything I've believed about humans on its head. It's backward. Nonsensical. Coughing, I take a sip of water. "Want me in what kind of way?"

"Every kind of way," he fires back. "Why don't you go change your shirt and we can get out of here."

I'm still reeling from his confession, my mind spinning and my stomach flipping. "What? My shirt?"

"If you want to wear that any other time, I'm cool with it, but I can see your nipples and it's distracting me from any sort of gentlemanly plans I had for today."

Waiting for my response, he pops a few blueberries in his mouth. "I don't want gentlemanly Leif," I say. "Actually, after all of the nice things you just said, I'm kind of thinking I want the opposite of nice to balance it out."

"That so?" Leif replies. He wipes his mouth with a napkin and slides his chair back, his knees wide. "Opposite of nice?" He fishes. "I just finished telling you how good you are. Why don't we see how bad you can be?" He holds his big, muscular arms out to the side—an invitation. "Do your worst, Malena Winterset," he says, raising one brow. "I know your last name this time and in case you had any doubts…I *do* want *you*."

He is a picture of pure masculine perfection. Leif says he's not perfect, isn't intimate with the word, but in this moment I see no faults in any way, and I recognize that for what it truly means. It's terrifying, but not so much that I'm not willing to give in to my feelings. "I want you too," I return, standing from my chair and approaching him. "You know my last name, you've proven you're not a serial killer…I think, and you're so charming I can't even see straight." His gaze is on my chest and the offending shirt, so I wiggle it down to expose more cleavage. He licks his lips. I sit down on top of him, straddling his narrow waist. A sigh of relief and built up desire vibrates his throat as I nuzzle my face into his neck and inhale his clean scent. My head feels fuzzy, and my face heats with nervous energy. Without thinking about how I feel, I grasp his cheeks in my hands and bring my lips to his. Leif wraps his arms around my lower back and pulls me tighter against his body. It's hardened with muscles and coiled from the act of holding himself back—letting me guide this kiss. He tastes like blueberries, and I know that I'll never be able to smell or taste blueberries again without thinking about Leif and this exact moment. The moment of clarity and understanding—the moment of truth.

Working my lips against his sends waves of pleasure throughout my body. I remember Shirley telling me once that you can make out with a man and not get turned on. That's how she controls the mood and the pace when she's with a man. I don't have that option. Being this close to Leif, our tongues entwined, our bodies rubbing against each other renders me useless but for what he's making me feel, how I'm touching him. Sliding my fingers into his hair, I pull him closer—until the kiss is almost painful.

There are no sounds but for our jagged exhales, and wet lips taking each other hostage. I grind myself on top of him, feeling his erection pulse beneath me. He breaks our mouths to run his lips and tongue across my jaw and down my throat. Gently, he bites the skin on my neck and groans—a sound that ricochets directly between my legs. I throw my head back to give him better access and to better control my breathing which is completely out of my control.

"My room?" I say, my words aimed at the ceiling.

"Not yet. Right here for now," Leif growls, lifting my shirt over my head and tossing it aside. He leans his forehead on my bare chest while cradling my back. His warm breaths puff against my skin creating a wild sensation of being warm and cool at the same time. "You're so beautiful," he says, palming my back, dragging his fingers over every inch of exposed skin. "I want you so badly."

Chuckling, I say, "You've mentioned that." There's usually that few seconds of bashful insecurity when you expose yourself to a new person, but strangely that doesn't come. Being with Leif like this seems right—like this is how it's supposed to be, what I've waited for. "I want to see all of you," he whispers as he rains kisses on my breasts, the hollow of my throat, and my collarbone. He stands easily, my weight not an inconvenience in the least. Turning, he sets me down on the island in the center of my kitchen and pushes me back gently. He's removed my shorts and panties in the next instant, his gaze raking over me voraciously—like I'm the grand prize in his favorite game show.

He bends my knees up and I have a brief flash of the last time I was getting my yearly exam, and laugh. "What's funny?" Leif asks, his big hands on my knees spreading my legs apart, hands gliding down my thighs. "This moment is anything but funny for me."

To lie, or to tell the truth and ruin this? Lie. Definitely lie. "Kiss me," I order instead.

He hikes himself up, settles his clothed body on top of mine, between my legs, and presses his lips to mine. "This has to be the hottest thing I've ever seen in a kitchen," Leif says, a sly grin on his face. Wrapping my arms around his neck, I silence him with my tongue against his. My mind is void of anything else except for him, and I've never, in my entire life, felt such relief and freedom. Everything else can slip through my fingers, but he's here. Firmly planted in my reality, and I have to blink a few times to make sure this is real.

He pulls away and pushes up on his arms to look down at me. His lips are glistening and red from our punishing kisses. "I've seen hotter things in my kitchen," I admit, smiling, to break the sexual tension.

"Yeah?" Leif asks, quirking one beautifully edible brow. "Who?"

"Not a who. A what," I reply, biting my bottom lip in a smile. "Pots and pans. Boiling water, hot oil sizzling and popping. You know? Normal kitchen stuff."

"I'll sizzle your ass. And pop it," he replies, laughing a short burst, his eyes crinkling in the corner. Leif uses one arm to roll me to my side a bit, and then swats my ass playfully. I grab him around his neck and let my legs lock around his waist.

Scooting back, he pulls us off the island and moves to the other room to lay me down on the couch. Goosebumps rise on my skin as the air conditioning hits every exposed, vulnerable piece of skin. Leif kneels in front of me and puts my legs on his shoulders. "I need to taste you everywhere," he says, swallowing hard, meeting my eyes. It's a question.

"Yes," I say, a zing of anticipation striking, my heart rate picking up. "Only if you're good at it," I tease.

"It's been a while," he replies. "I think I can manage an orgasm or two. Just a guess." My core clenches as his lips glide down my inner thigh and land exactly where I want them. The cold bereft feeling is replaced by heat, his kisses, and a slick wetness as his tongue folds up and down in a steady rhythm. I sigh and grab his hair as he attacks the task at hand like he was born to only do one thing. The pleasure that was already there from merely kissing him skyrockets into something so pure, full, and mind-bending that I can't describe what he's making me feel. Never have I felt so out of control. Leif makes a ravenous noise and closes his eyes like he's feasting on his last meal. It's unthinkable indulgence, a man wild with lust, offering everything he has. His hands wrap around my thighs and he uses them to pull me onto his tongue, inserting it as far inside me as he can, all the while his finger is circling my clit in a steadily increasing manner. I come undone, my legs tightening and the fiery orgasm hitting me, the pulsing waves felt from the tips of my toes to the top of my head.

He digs his face into me harder as I come, not wanting to miss a second of my pleasure. My mind is still fuzzy when he finishes, kissing my core once, long and hard. I clench again in response. Lifting my head to look at him is almost too much work. "Oh my gosh," I say, in between ragged breaths. "That was the hottest thing that's ever happened in the living room," I say. "No jokes there."

"Good," Leif replies, licking his lips. "Felt okay?" he asks, eyes wide.

"You were lying. It has been a long time since you've done that," I ask incredulously. When he doesn't reply, I say, "I've never had an orgasm that strong…ever. The only thing that could have made it better would be if you were inside me while it happened."

His eyes go feral, and he swallows hard. "Do you want that?"

tossing it

"What do you think? Honesty is the best policy, and I'm not lying," I say, teasing my legs open, so he can see the slick mess he just created. "I've probably never wanted a dick more." Biting my bottom lip, I let my naughty words soak in. He wanted to see how bad I can be. There aren't walls between us. I think maybe there never was. From the moment I met him, I laid it all on the table. I didn't give him excuses or lies about my real world. Exposed in every way, he took it all and continued to pursue me.

Sliding my hand between my legs, I wait for his gaze to follow my fingers, and then rub the wetness once, dragging a trail up my stomach and up to my breasts. He leans over and takes a nipple into his mouth. He's unbuttoning his pants with one hand. "I really did want to be gentlemanly, Malena," he rasps at my chest. "You deserve so much more."

He says things like this, things that don't make any sense. He is the walking definition of a perfect catch. "Leif, this is the best thing you can possibly do for me today. I need this more than I need a day date. Be with me," I say, pulling his face up to mine. When his blue eyes are locked with mine, I grab his bottom lip with my teeth. I shake my head no and release his lip. "This is what I want from you right now. Can you help me? You don't say no when I ask for help, right?"

He grins, and it makes me hyper-aware of where his hands are, where his steely shaft is. "Do you want to go to your bedroom now?" he asks. "Least I can do is make our first time a little more memorable...or comfortable."

"You don't get it," I say. "You are memorable. Everything about you is memorable. I'll never forget one kiss."

Leif stands and removes his shirt and shorts in a speed that doesn't seem human. Then he leans over to pick me up and sets me on my feet in front of him. I can't help but admire his Adonis-like physique. He's so tall. The opposite of me in almost every way physically. His skin a pale shade compared to my own. His blond hair. Mine dark. We stand there in front of each other for several seconds, just looking at each other. The chemistry flying off the charts, my hands itching to reach out and take his girth in my hand. Leif breaks the fiery silence first.

"While that may be so, I still want to fuck you in your bed. That's what I've been thinking about since the moment I saw it." He shakes his head. "You have me. You have me so completely." Taking in the weight of his words, I try to formulate the right thing to say, but I can't.

I nod instead. "Let's go."

He wastes no time scooping me into his strong arms. I wrap my legs around his waist and kiss his neck, trailing my tongue up to his ear. When we've made it to my bedroom, Leif only has one thing on his mind. "How do you want it?" he asks. "I'm tall. You're small. Tell me how you want it before I take you any which way I can."

I kiss his lips once. "I want to taste your lips while you're inside me."

He nods, eyes falling closed. "That's a really good plan," he says, sucking in a jagged breath. "Let's execute it right now."

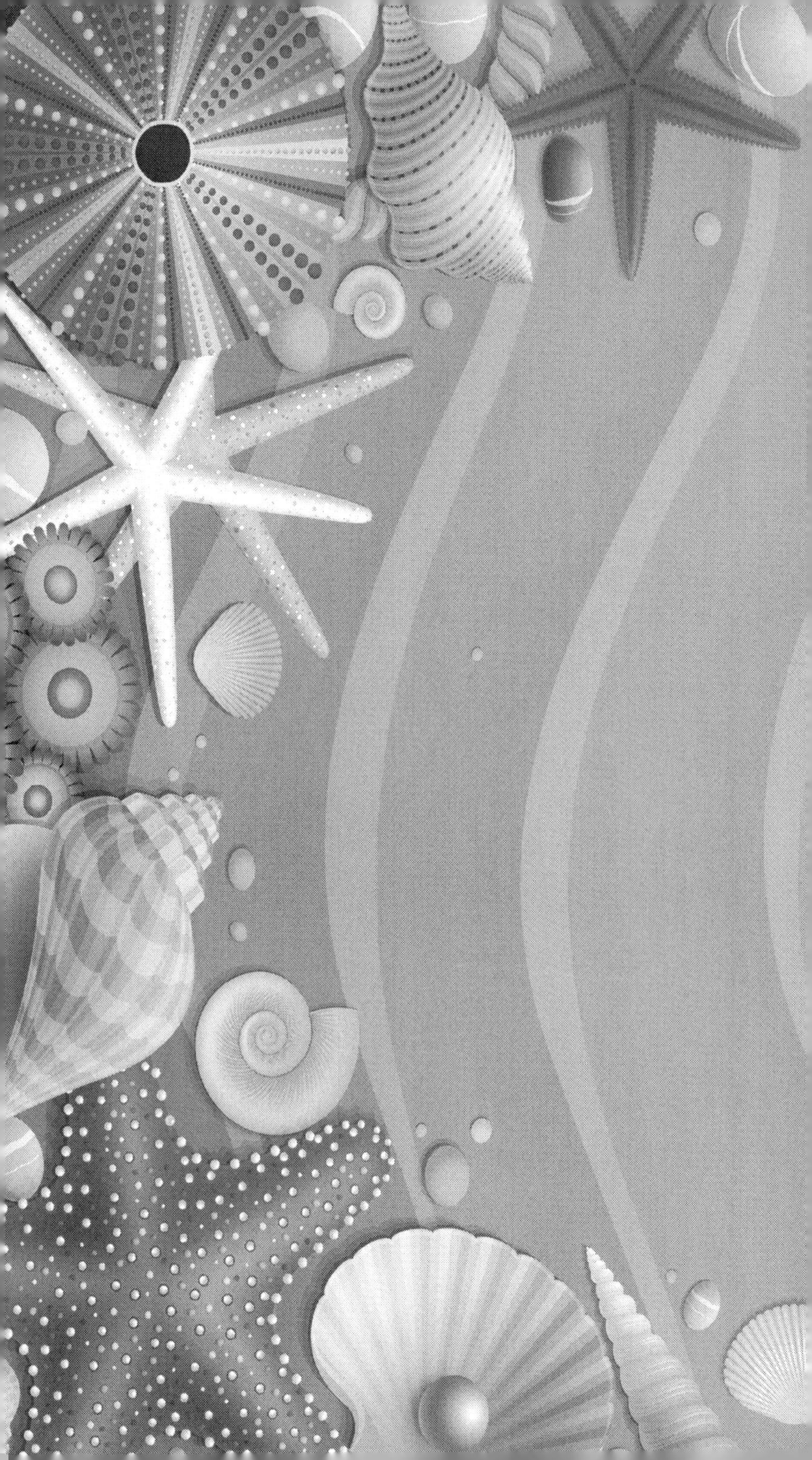

Chapter Nine

Leif

It's surpassed a want and entered the realm of need. I need to possess Malena in every possible way right now. If I were to list in order the things I need for survival, fucking her would be first on the list, above oxygen. I can hold my breath for a few minutes. I'll be good.

Setting her down on the edge of the bed, I let her wet pussy slide down my abs as I lower her ass. She sighs a sexy fucking noise that sends a jolt to my cock. When I came over here, I was worried about her. Malena wasn't answering my calls and no one could get ahold of her, not even Garden Breeze. My intentions were to make sure she was okay and be on my way. I wanted to give her more time to process everything that happened over the past few days.

As I gaze down at her naked body, I realize just how awry my plan has gone. Her skin, every inch, is flawless. Malena's body is this pint-sized playground that has been taunting my dreams. It's been months, hell, maybe even a year since I've been with a woman. One that I'm this attracted to? That's *never* happened.

"I want this to be the hottest thing that's ever happened in your bedroom, but you're so fucking hot it may be short-lived," I admit, licking my lips.

"So that means you don't want me to suck your dick first?"

I shake my head no, even if my cock is nodding in opposition. "You're on birth control?" I grind out, my erection in my hand, ready. This is probably the only intelligent thing I've asked today and I'm surprised I'm functioning enough to bring it up. Whether her answer matters at this point is another matter entirely. I don't have a condom on me. I don't own any. Not because I didn't think it was going to happen, but because I didn't think it was going to happen yet.

Malena sits straight up. "I…uh…yeah, I'm on birth control," she stammers. "You don't have to worry about that." She swallows hard and meets my gaze. "I promise," Malena adds, a deceptive gleam to her eye. She goes on to tell me she hasn't slept with anyone in a long time, giving me way more information than I want or need about birth control to regulate irregular cycles, in the fashion I've come to expect from her.

"Malena," I say. "Enough. My dick's getting soft talking about STDs." I've already told her I get tested at work constantly for everything under the sun. That came up in conversation last week.

She giggles and that has a reverse effect. "I want you.

I don't want a family," I say, shaking my head. "I trust you if you say you're on birth control, and I hate to be the horny bastard to break my own rules about two forms of baby blockers. I don't have a condom. You okay with that?"

"You're breaking your own rules? I'm okay with that," Malena coos, raising a brow and leaning back on the bed. "You lose some street cred, but I can live with it," she adds.

I grin. "I can earn it back," I reply, touching her lower stomach and trailing my fingers between her legs. Malena closes her eyes and murmurs a contented sigh. "Open your eyes," I command.

She does as I ask. "Can we get back to the plan," she says, her words a breathless plea. "Kissing and filling."

Swallowing down hesitation, I kiss her hard—opening her mouth with my tongue. Positioning myself between her legs, I tease her entrance with the head of my dick and relish the slick, warm sensation. There's no other feeling that compares to this, the moment in which you enter a woman. This fucking feeling of nirvana is why nations have fallen, and good men have done bad things. I press into her slowly, letting her adjust as I kiss her. "How's that?" I ask.

She nods her approval while wrapping her legs around my waist, and bringing my lips back to hers. When I'm buried inside her, stretching her fully, I let my head fall into the nape of her neck, breaking our mouths. "You feel so good," I whisper, as I begin thrusting, driving my cock into her tight body. Malena matches my thrusts,

tossing it

taking everything I'm giving in stride.

"Fuck me harder," she says, grazing my ear with her teeth. It's in that moment that I know I won't last long. Not when she's saying all the right things, and looking the way she does, like she was made for me and me alone.

Cupping her face with one hand, I look down at her while I pick up the pace, thrusting into her as hard as I can. The loving sweet pace, all but forgotten in favor of straight up fucking. Our sexual chemistry has exploded, our desire winning over practicality. I'm filling her, she's clinging to me, moaning, chanting my name. I'm focused on not coming, trying to block out the desperate tenor of her voice. She announces she's almost there as she clings to my shoulders, positioning herself so her clit is rubbing against the base of my shaft each time I enter her deeply. Keeping my mind on my pace, not on her pussy gripping my cock like a vise, I watch her come undone beneath me. Her cheeks are flushed and her eyes closed. Malena in this state is something to behold. I've never watched a woman as closely as I watch her while she comes, never cared other than it would be my turn next, and it does something to me. Something I'm not ready to admit. A deeper acknowledgment that someone else is more important. Another person is above me in the hierarchy of my own life, and I have no fucking clue how or why it happened.

It happens fast, and I'm lost in watching her and analyzing every nuance that makes Malena so entrancing when I come hard. Deep and rough inside her small body. It's not a, hey, I jacked off for fun because I was bored type of load. It is waves of hot bursts so intense, my face screws up as I ride the pleasure. I collapse on top of her, holding the majority of my weight off her with my elbows. I breathe into her neck, sucking in Malena tinged oxygen over and over. I feel her chest rising and falling under me and we stay like that for a long time, me still inside her, the whole experience of claiming her more than I can fully process in one sitting. I broke so many of my own rules. Not the ones I gave Malena, rules I've held myself to for as long as I've been dating.

I roll off her minutes later and stare at the ceiling. Clearing my throat, I wait for her to say something. Anything. Did that feel as fucking life changing for her as it did for me? Her ceiling fan is wobbling at a slow speed and I can hear gulls cry outside in the distance. Seconds tick on. Malena catches her breath and I start to wonder how big of a mistake I just made. She must be upset.

"You okay?" I ask.

"Still trying to figure out why that was so amazing," she replies, rolling toward me on her side, moving one hand on my chest over my heart. It's warm. "That was the best sex I've ever had."

"Me too," I reply, holding her hand. Before it gets awkward, I have to address the elephant in the room. "I, uh, didn't mean to…without a condom on, that is," I ramble, my face heating. "We can grab the morning-after pill when we leave here. To be safe," I add. Real fucking gentlemanly, man. Fuck. "If you want."

She smiles—it reaches her eyes. "You really don't

want kids? That wasn't a line?"

Her question takes me aback. This isn't a topic of conversation I've ever broached with a woman before. How to prevent kids? Yes. Always. Having kids? "No. It's never been something I felt the desire to do. They seem like more work than I have time for, you know?" I want to ask if she wants kids, but most women do, and I really want to stay in this lust fog a little while longer.

Malena nods, eyes steely with resolve. "I don't need the morning-after pill. I'll never need it. No matter how much come you can funnel inside me." Malena giggles. "I can't have kids. They've run a bunch of tests to make sure and things don't work." Her gaze darts to her hand on my chest. "I don't tell people usually. I'm sorry. It's not something I think about very often, but when you mentioned birth control and come, and morning-after pills, I figured I might as well tell you. I hope you don't think I'm being too forward." Too forward? She's my motherfucking dream girl. Add one more thing to the list of things of why she's my one and only match.

Rolling toward her so we're face to face, I say, "Never apologize for something you can't change, Malena, or for being honest. I appreciate your honesty and if we're being frank, that fact only makes me want you more." I cup her face and press my lips against hers in a passionate kiss. "It's like you were made for me," I say, brushing my lips against hers.

"I was thinking something of the same when you said you didn't want kids. I'm glad this conversation is out of the way."

"Why," I ask. "I can put all of my come inside you whenever I want?" I smirk, my hand wandering between her wet thighs—the evidence of my mistake.

She nods, eyes closed. "That, and so you don't have to worry about your rule."

"Fair point," I reply. "Want to fuck one more time? I've been wanting to get inside you since that first night on the beach." *My whole life.* "Once isn't near enough." *I'll never have enough of you.*

Malena slings a leg over my waist and my dick hardens again. "I was thinking a couple more times, actually. If you can hang," she says, taking me into her hand and guiding me inside her slick folds. I jut my hips up and watch my cock disappear into her body. Then she starts riding me, hands splayed on my abs, facial features in a state of rapture as she works her hips.

With my hands free, I palm her breasts and caress her waist and hips. I let her set the pace and just enjoy the view. She isn't alone. Nor is she sad. Perhaps I am being a gentleman after all.

"Did you see her in the garden?" Malena asks, shaking her head. "I haven't seen her that happy in years. I would have put in a garden at my house, you know? If I didn't worry about her wandering away anytime she went out there." She casts her gaze skyward at the sunset beyond the dock at my house. The visit at Garden Breeze was short and sweet, long enough to confirm that not only is Ms. Winterset settling in, she's happy there. One of the nurses told Malena that typically this kind of move is harder on the family members than it is on the patient. "I should have done this sooner. God, it's been years that she's been miserable at home." Malena shakes her head, damning herself to an eternity in hell.

"You couldn't possibly know she'd be this happy elsewhere. She was really enjoying herself at Garden Breeze, though. There's no reason to worry about her. That's for sure." Ms. Winterset didn't recognize Malena today. A fact that almost made it easier when it was time to leave. I tried to let her visit without my presence, hanging in the lobby area, dodging the women trying to flirt with me at the front desk. Malena left her mother a stationary set and a handwritten note. Ms. Winterset likes to write letters when she has flashes of clarity, and Malena hoped the letter would ease her mother in case she remembered that she'd been dropped off at Garden Breeze and left by herself in a strange new world. I walk up behind her and set my beer down on the railing.

"Do you like to garden?" I broach, wrapping an arm around her shoulders.

She reaches around my waist with an arm. "I don't know. I should try, right? It's something she has always loved and it's the only thing she remembers that she still loves." I hear the resentment in her voice. "Might be therapeutic for me. It's always hot and sunny here. I could garden year-round. There would always be something in season."

"Or you can throw yourself into planning my mom's birthday at the beach instead?" I try to change the subject to something on more neutral territory. "It will be a pretty awesome surprise."

Malena grins. "I've already got everything handled," she replies, eyes lighting. "You know I'm going to have to be there to make sure everything goes smoothly, right?"

"Yes," I reply.

"That means your sisters. Your family. They'll all be there. At the same place I'll be."

I quirk a brow. "That doesn't mean I have to introduce you to them."

Malena swats me on the arm playfully. "You're awful."

"You're beautiful."

She blushes. "I'm hungry."

A car door closes in the parking lot adjacent to my building. *Right on time*, I think. "I'll introduce you to them now," I say, sighing. Eva didn't call, but call it brotherly intuition—I knew she would be coming over tonight. I have no doubt in my mind that Celia told her we dropped Ms. Winterset off at Garden Breeze yesterday. Malena tightens under my hands, the nerves reacting immediately.

"What do you mean?" Malena says, scrambling out of my grasp. "She's here? Now?"

I sigh again. "I don't want them to be. Not because you're here. Because she never calls before she comes over," I bark loudly, so Eva can hear as she approaches.

Malena spins toward the sound of footsteps on the pathway to my front door.

"You never answer my calls, Leif. Don't be a dick," Eva croons, gaze lighting on Malena even though she's talking to me. "Looks like I came over at a perfect time," she adds. "I've been dying to meet her in the flesh." Eva walks toward us, a proud stride, and much to my surprise, a pleasant smile on her face. My stomach flips at the realization of what's about to happen. Worlds colliding.

Malena shrinks into me, but I push her forward, to sense the evil I have to deal with on a regular basis. *We all have our demons, Malena*, I think. "Malena this is my older sister, Eva. She's married and has her own house, but likes to harass her brother at his place instead of living her own life. Is Celia on her way?" I ask, tilting my head. "I can only surmise you've telepathically told her to get her ass over here as quickly as possible because I'm in a weak spot."

Eva cackles, her blonde hair sliding over her shoulder as she tips her head back. Taking out her phone, she sends a text. Of course. Malena extends her hand, baffled or taken aback by sibling rivalry. "It's nice to meet you in person, Eva," she says. "Your brother led me to believe I might never get to meet you. Which would be a shame as I don't think anyone can put him in his place so… gracefully."

Eva ignores Malena's offered hand in favor of bringing her in for a hug, trapping Malena's hands by her sides. "You don't know how relieved I am to see you do actually exist in his world. I thought he was gay," Eva says, pulling away to look Malena over more thoroughly, like a judge in a baking competition or something. "Not that there would be anything wrong with him being gay, but I really wanted another woman around. Why would you think you'd never meet me?" Eva narrows her eyes at me.

I make an irritated groan behind them. "I'm right here," I say. "You knew she existed. Don't play dumb. You've been hassling me about her. Hell, you've been hassling her too!"

"I thought maybe he was delusional, that's all. He's never really cared about anyone other than himself before. I knew you existed, I just wasn't sure you were actually spending time with my brother," Eva explains, making me seem like even more of a vapid monster. "I didn't hassle Malena. I merely wanted to be friends with her. Why wasn't he going to introduce you to me?" Eva asks Malena.

I push open the door and hold my arm out so they'll both enter. Mr. Olsen laughs as he ambles outside to take up residence in his chair. "You kids doing okay out here?"

I respond to Mr. Olsen as Eva and Malena offer warm smiles and ask him if he needs anything. He looks a little tired today—worn down. I help him sit down even though he tries to push me away, I can tell he appreciates the attention.

"I'm going to cook dinner," Eva proclaims.

Malena walks up next to me and pats Mr. Olsen on the arm. "Do you want to have dinner with us?" Malena asks.

"Yes," Eva adds. "You'll have dinner with us." They're already a united front, and I have to admit. I kind of like it. There isn't any hostility between my sister and Malena.

Mr. Olsen lays back and waves a thin veiny arm. "No, No. I'm not going to interrupt your dinner. But you can bring me a plate if you want to. I'm going to take a little nap."

The women enter the house and busy themselves in the kitchen. I watch as Malena and Eva chat. It's easy, effortless banter, like they've been friends for life. Eva asks about Ms. Winterset and how Mom's party planning is progressing. Malena asks about how I was as a child. They relish in the story about how I almost drowned at the beach.

"That's not a funny story. I almost died," I chime in.

Eva rolls her eyes as she washes her hands. "It's funny because you're a SEAL now. Water is your thing. You're like one with it. Right?"

"I guess so," I say. "It's still not funny."

Malena smiles but keeps her eyes down to the knife and cutting board.

"You have something to add? Something funny? Me almost dying is funny?"

"You act like that's the closest to death that you've been. When in actuality it's probably child's play. Literally," Malena explains, meeting my eyes.

"Fair," I say.

Celia walks in the front door. "He's snoring like a

giant," Celia says, hiking her thumb to my front deck. "Smells good. What's for dinner?"

She's wearing her scrubs and her hair is in a messy bun. I see her check out Malena to gauge the amount of shade happening. Malena swallows hard and pauses chopping. "Hey Celia," she says, as my sister rounds the corner into the kitchen. Malena's eyes glass over. I'm not sure if it's because of onions or because she's about to break down.

"Thank you so much" —Malena breathes— "for my mother." They talk for a few minutes. It's mostly Malena telling her how grateful she is for finding the spot for her mother and Celia reassuring her that she doesn't owe her anything. It's a little painful to watch. Malena is so unused to others helping her that it's hard for her to accept a kind gesture for what it is. A kind gesture.

Celia shakes her hand. "Don't even mention it. I was happy to help you out. You've made my brother a more bearable person in recent days." Celia washes her hands. "What can I help with? I should text Momma and Daddy and see if they can come over."

"There's enough. I'm cooking for an army," Eva says. "Text them now."

Malena's gaze darts up to meet mine—panic written on her features. "Come here," I say, tilting my chin to Malena. "I have to show you something. They can handle the cooking for a second," I say.

"Yes. We got this. Go ahead," Celia says. "Go listen to Mr. Olsen snore. I've never heard anything like it in my life." Thank God Celia is gracious and can tell that

tossing it

Malena needs a moment to process all that's happened in the past hour.

Malena wipes her hands on the dish rag. "Okay," she replies drying her hands on her shorts. She walks around the island and stands in front of me. I don't care about being subtle, so I lean over to kiss her lips once, full and deep. I can tell she thinks about pulling away, but the attraction is too strong so she doesn't. Eva clears her throat. Celia laughs. And I just took my weakness from their hands and owned it for myself.

When I break the kiss, Malena brings her fingers up to her lips and looks to my sisters. They're busy, but both are wearing devious smirks. "It's done. Don't question anything else. Got it?" I ask.

Eva sighs, and Celia chimes, "Is this like the time you took that girl to prom and you made a big deal of making Mom buy that corsage that matched her dress? Like you were so serious about the dance and the girl. But then you left her at the dance to party with your buddies and drink beer in the woods? Then the cops made you jog in front of their cop car all the way back home?" A story they will never let me live down. I hate them. But I also love them because while I like to think Malena knows me, at least she's getting another side of me. No secrets, my sisters will make sure of that.

I sigh. "You guys really are unbearable. No, it's not like that at all. My date was in on it the whole time. She knew I wasn't actually going to the dance." Partly true. I took photos with her so she had something to show her parents and then I bolted. It was a mutually beneficial arrangement.

Celia shrugs. "Just making sure." She winks at Malena. "He's a real catch. Promise."

"Seems that way, doesn't it?" Malena replies, shaking her head. Eva makes an annoyed noise while looking at Celia's phone. "Mom and Dad already have plans for dinner they can't make it tonight. Though I'm sure she's utterly devastated she can't talk Dad into coming here instead."

"I am a good catch," I say, snaking an arm around Malena's waist. I pull Malena down the hall to my bedroom. She pauses, trying to look at the random awards I have lining my hallway, but I have her hand in mine. By my age, most have hallways lined with photos of their children. Memories from happy vacations. Wedding days. None of those things belong to me. My career accomplishments adorn the walls in my house. They are things I'm proud of, but I can't be sure they mean the same thing to me as family photos mean to others. That's the best thing about not knowing. You can't miss what you've never had.

"These are really awesome, Leif," Malena whispers, as she reads the small inscription on a plaque. She goes on her tiptoes to read the one on the wall next to my bedroom door. She laughs at the funny poem my teammates wrote for me when I left the command.

"Were you not impressed with me before?" I tease. "My sisters will make sure you're never impressed with me in any way. I can tell them to go away. I do it all the time. Just let me know. I'm never expecting them.

tossing it

This is kind of an introduction by fire, but it's also a very accurate portrayal of me. Of what I came from. Of why I am the way I am."

We enter my bedroom and she looks around. "Are they the real reason why you don't want children?" she asks, meeting my gaze once her appraisal is over. "Because they are…so much," she whispers.

I tilt my head back and forth. "You could be on to something. I never really thought of it that way. Could be," I admit. Malena nods, walking toward my four-poster bed that's far too large for this space, her delicate fingers dragging against the dark wood. "It's just we went from never meeting family to having a full-on reunion. You were quite the bachelor it seems."

Shaking my head, I approach her wrapping my hands around her rib cage. She's so small, so perfectly made to fit into my hands. "Not a bachelor in the sense you're thinking. I've never met someone worth breaking rules for. There's a difference. I didn't give the women from my past time because they weren't worthy of it."

"I'm worth it?"

I grin. "More than worth it. Anytime I'm not with you, I'm wishing I was." That's never happened before. I have never dreamed I'd want to be anywhere as much as I want to be next to Malena. Inside her.

"Don't send them home. I want to hear more stories about you."

"They won't cloud your good judgment?" I ask. "Send you running to the hills?"

She shakes her head. "They only add to your appeal."

Her eyes dart to the side and she gets a far-off look in her eye. "A shame I don't have any siblings to appeal on my behalf, huh?"

"Nah, they'd probably be hot older sisters and I'd go after them instead."

Malena laughs, a soft smile pulling up one corner of her mouth. "That's not funny."

One finger under her chin, I tilt her face up. The setting sun blazes through the house and into my bedroom through the open door like a fiery reminder of what this woman is doing to my life. Setting everything on fire. Bringing me to life by singeing me from the inside out. Leaning into me, she kisses me, allowing her tongue to twine against mine. A battle. A duel. My wits. Her kiss. Malena is in my space, a place no other woman has been. I want to scream it from the rooftops and also bury it like a skeleton. When you become attached to things, they become weaknesses—a guise of security.

I've seen it before, with friends, with enemies. A lump forms in my throat, as I pull her closer, wrapping her in my arms. She's safe. The kiss finishes slowly, our chests pressed together.

As she catches her breath, her forehead against mine, I suck in air.

I breathe in love. I exhale pain.

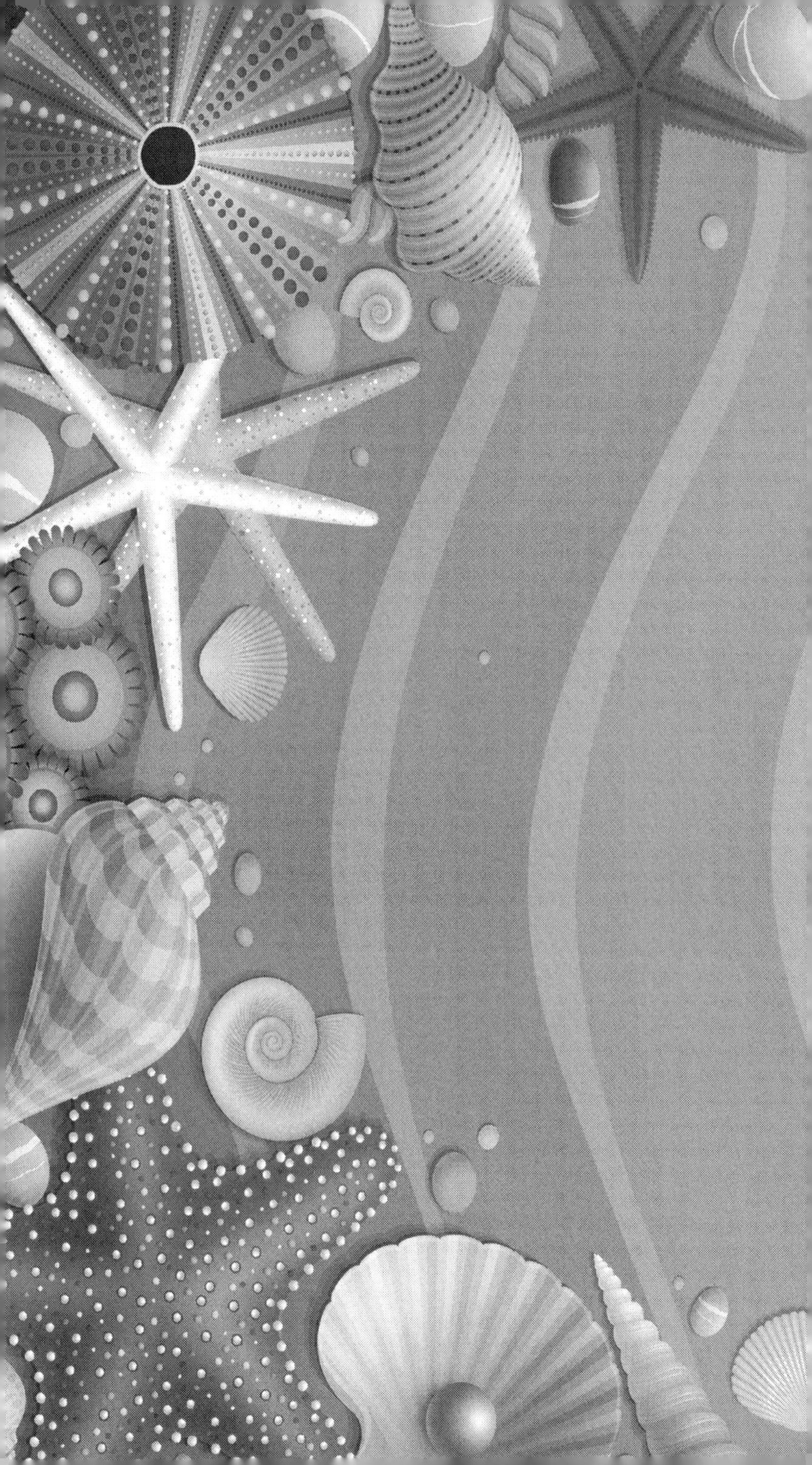

Chapter ten

Malena

"How painful was that? Scale of one to ten?" Leif asks, shutting and locking his front door. "Mr. Olsen is in bed. I put the leftovers in his fridge. I'll stop by in the morning before I head to the airport for jumping to make sure he knows they're there." He eyes me up and down almost as if he's appraising for damage.

Eva and Celia were delightful during dinner. I think they had a coming to God moment while Leif and I spoke alone in the bedroom. After we returned to the kitchen, they seemed to be on their best behavior. Leif didn't question their change in demeanor, and I was relieved because it made things easier on me. For all intents and purposes, it was a nice family meal. Something I've not had in years. It made me miss my mom.

Sighing, I dry the last dish and put it away in the correct cabinet, and then turn to meet his steely, blue gaze. "Zero. It was actually pretty awesome. They aren't nearly as bad as you say," I reply, smiling. "They love you."

"To death," he adds. "Listen, I know we didn't plan for tonight to go down like that, but I want you to know I'm glad you met them. I want you to see all of me."

I swallow down the fear of the unknown. "Leif, I see you whether you realize it or not, you showed your heart to me far before your sisters told me you're a weak swimmer."

He palms his chest. "I am a fucking amazing swimmer," he returns. "And there's nothing wrong with my swimmers." His face pinks. "That just came out. Sorry. That's insensitive." I flop down on his sofa. "There isn't anything wrong with your swimmers. That's okay to say. Remember, I've dealt with infertility for most of my adult life. I have a spine—can handle any joke," I explain. "Though, I'm glad your parents didn't come over tonight. I want to fix myself up before I meet them. Be a presentable human," I say, picking up the edge of my shirt and setting it back down. "I look like a slob. If your sisters say anything about me, anything at all, you are bound to tell me."

He grins. "There's no way you want to know what they're going to say."

"Why?" I swallow down all of my insecurities. They go down like razor blades. I know I'm not good enough for Leif. His sisters will have noticed that right away. They've already had to bail me out of a situation and their brother is footing the bill. I'm a charity case. Now it's my job to prove to them I'm more than that. That I am a deserving person even if I don't feel like one. That I'm worthy of a man like Leif Andersson.

"Because they are inappropriate, Malena. No other reason than they'll probably discuss our sex and foreplay routine as casual conversation. Their filters are broken. I'd never subject you to that kind of talk. They won't have anything negative to say about you. You guys got along perfectly. You can't really be worried about what they think about you. Are you? They loved you."

I shrug. He closes the space between us. "Don't. Don't do that," Leif says.

"You say you're not, but in my eyes, you're pretty damn close to perfect. You have an amazing career, a caring family, a sense of honor and humor," I say, licking my lips. "Leif," I add, "You are generous and kind." I wave an arm at his body. "You're fucking sculpted like a marble statue. Museum quality. Except better, because you're not missing a head or a hand or a finger." Leif presses his lips into a firm line, trying his best not to laugh at my comparison.

"And I, well, I struggle with almost everything. It doesn't take a rocket scientist to see we aren't a balanced pair. What if I always need you more? More of your time. More of your attention. More of everything? Because that's probably how it's going to be. You still have to give as much to your job as you were before we met." Using my other arm, I wave to the hallway of awards, signs he's amazing in his career as well. "What if you don't have time or energy for me?"

"Are we arguing? Is this our first argument?" he asks,

tilting his head, smiling.

I shake my head. "Don't smile at me that way. I'm serious. This is hard for me to accept."

Leif sighs, and sits down next to me, laying his hand on my bare leg. "Am I greedy if I say I want you to want more of me? That's not a negative. Not at all," Leif says.

I try to concentrate on his words, but he's touching me, and any time he touches me, I turn into a rabid sex creature with only one thing on my mind.

"I am busy. My commitments are heavy, but that doesn't mean I can't rearrange things to fit you in my life. Especially because that's what I want. When I want something, I make it happen. In case you forgot," he says. "Chicken wings."

I rub my forehead. "The past few days have been a lot. You've been amazing. I guess I'm waiting for the other shoe to drop because good things don't happen to me very often."

"When is the last time someone did something nice for you?"

My friends will do small gestures here and there. It's not like my life is completely devoid of kindness, but Leif has gone above and beyond. I try to explain to him the difference between a friend favor and a family favor, which is what he's done for me. He tells me he understands, but he's rubbing my leg up and down.

I watch his hand intently, and abruptly stand and step away from him. "It's probably time I get home. You have to be up early and I have to quit the store tomorrow, or at least give my two weeks' notice I guess."

Leif stands. "I have a crazy idea."

"Oh, no."

"Spend the night with me?"

I swallow hard. "Is it the sex? You want me for sex. That's it." I try to keep a straight face. "You've had a taste and now that's all that it's going to be about between us."

"I won't fuck you tonight even if you beg me," he replies, shaking his head. When he bites his lip, my panties soak all the way through. We didn't get enough of each other earlier. It's a fact we're both aware of. The glances are steamy, our bodies find a way to touch each other without our permission. All of the signs of dangerous chemistry ignite the oxygen surrounding us. "We can stay up late and talk. Like a chick sleepover. I know how those work. My sisters were good for some things."

That gets me. I laugh, holding my stomach as I bend over in hysterics. When he doesn't laugh, I meet his gaze, mystified. "You're serious? You want to have an actual sleepover? Like, fuzzy slippers and popcorn?"

Leif lays a hand on his chest. "I am serious. Will you have a sleepover with me?"

I tap my chin, considering. "There will be rules."

He raises one brow. "Yes. I like where your head is at."

"Rule one." I clear my throat, making it more official. "Naked sleepover. No one wears clothes."

Leif's eyes go dark—feral. He nods once. My legs turn to jelly in response.

"Rule two. No sex. Or foreplay of any kind. It has to

be a true chick sleepover."

Another manly lip bite. My stomach quivers. I'm sealing my own fate with these rules. I want to prove I'm able to set some framework of rules like he tried to do. "Kissing is okay. Just kissing," I amend, watching his freaking delicious lips as he licks them. "Rule three," I say, my voice trembling. His eyes on mine, he tips his chin up. "You can't fall in love with me tonight."

Leif blinks once, swallows hard, blinks again. "That won't happen," he says, voice a husky whisper. "Anything else?"

There are a multitude of things I'm thinking of right now—equations I'm trying to work out in my head because sometimes things in life make perfect sense. Sometimes they don't. Sometimes there's a fuzzy haze you can't quite see through, or figure out why it exists. I recognize the haze is there with Leif, but I'm past the point of caring. I'm in deep and utterly addicted to everything that makes him quality, top shelf, goods. "Yeah, sleepovers start with skinny dipping," I say, dropping my gaze to his hands as they unbutton his pants. When his erection springs free, I lose my breath.

Leif shakes a finger in front of my face. "Ah, ah, ah, that's not for you. Not during our sleepover." I take my shirt and bra off and slide my shorts and panties down my legs. He watches, an appraising smirk rising to his lips when I'm completely bare. Bending over, right in front of him, I pick up my clothing from the floor. His dick brushes my ass as I stand. Leif groans. "Though right now I wish it was for you."

Tossing my clothing on the sofa, I spin to face him. "Me too. Looking at it hard makes me wet," I reply.

He runs both hands through his hair and down his face. "Torture. That's what this is going to be. The best kind of torture." He steps closer and pulls my naked body against his. Leaning down he puts his lips next to my ear. "I make you wet?"

My heart races, and I can hear the blood whooshing in my ears. "Yes," I pant.

He drags his tongue along my ear, and his cock jerks against my stomach. "Let's see how wet I can make you." Leif traces his hands down my sides, creating a wave of desire so strong my legs give out. He catches me and lifts me into his arms until my legs are locked around him, and then he walks out the back door of his condo. Laughing, I bury my face in his neck and close my eyes. I know we're alone out here. It's secluded but for his neighbors and there's tall sawgrass on either side of the path leading around the houses and down to the beach. The waves rush the shore in hisses and bubbles and Leif picks up his pace, running for the water at a speed that scares me.

"You're going to be so wet after I get finished with you," he says, breathing raggedly into my ear. "Dripping," he adds.

"Soaking," I squeal, readjusting my grip around his neck. "Sopping and soggy," I cry out in between chuckles. He runs into the cool water and takes us down into the water. It's pitch black but for the moonlight and his blue eyes search mine. His mouth slants up. "Soggy isn't good. What about slick?"

"You are slick, you know that?" I return. He pulls us into shallow water, and sits, bringing me on top of him—his huge, hard dick thumping my stomach anytime a wave rolls over our bodies. He eyes the shore, and his condo. "I left my work phone inside," he says. "Does this count as our sleepover commencement? Skinny dipping."

"I am dripping wet," I say, lifting and lowering my shoulders. "The water temperature is nice. I forgot how good it feels to be in the water at night," I admit, swallowing. It's been a long time since I've felt this carefree. I wouldn't even know how to define that word in my past. It's meant something completely different to me up until this point.

"Naked. With a man?" Leif asks, drawing my gaze back to him. The shade of his eyes will haunt my dreams. It's the shade the water is during the day. A light, crisp blue, but right now it's black. Like oil. A contrast of truth.

"Never naked with a man," I admit, hugging him closer—the heat from his body warming me. "You're special, Leif Andersson. You already know that. What about you? Ever skinny dipped with a woman out here?"

He shakes his head. "No skinny dipping with women. Not here. Not anywhere. This is a first. It is sort of nice. And you know just what to say to hook me a little bit more," he replies.

I smile. He smiles. Then he kisses me sweetly, his hands a whisper touch on my face. "I'm not a *hooker*," I murmur.

"I disagree," he returns, standing up and taking me with him. "You're a trap. One I'm still not sure fate didn't set for me. Here in this place I never would have considered living," he says, sighing. He walks back up the path slowly. "You had me in the water when it wasn't for work. That's a huge feat, for your information."

"Why? You scared of drowning?" I tease, pressing a kiss against his salty neck. "It is dark and scary out here," I deadpan.

"After endless hours of training in the cold, west coast waters, being in the water is never something I choose to do on my own in my free time. I'm not a sadist."

"Beach vacays are out of the question then," I ask as he lifts me out of the water.

He nods. "I prefer snow skiing. Or exploring new cities in different countries. A cruise ship would be my worst nightmare." He continues as he carries me up the beach.

"You live at the beach, Leif," I point out as we enter the house. He sets me down, our feet leaving sandy pools of water on the shoe mat.

"I like water sports. Jet skiing and wakeboarding and stuff. But I don't want to be in the water any more than I have to."

We do our best to get the sand off our feet and legs and then race to his bedroom, the air conditioning turning our skin frosty. "Speaking of getting in the water. And fun. Let's hit the showers," he says, waggling his brow as he scrolls both of his cell phones. It's hard not to wonder who he's checking for, or if there's someone else. That's my natural instinct as a woman in this century. That's sad. In this moment, I give all of my preconceived notions away to the trash man. Leif isn't going to hurt me. He isn't a normal man. He is good. So good.

I cross my arms. "You're a walking oxymoron," I say, rolling my eyes, approaching the bathroom. "And I think it might be what I love most about you." He beckons me with both of his hands as he cranks on the hot water, and I don't refuse. His shower is large—two showerheads, one for each of us. I spy a pink bottle of popular women's shampoo on one side and lose my breath. Don't bring it up. He has a past just as I do.

Leif steps into the shower and holds the glass door open for me, all while eying my body like I'm on the menu. The steam hits me and relief from the cold eases my chattering teeth. He stays on his side, washing his body with a handful of soap, while I rinse the salt water from my hair. "Where would you like to go on vacation? Living at the beach, it's gotta' be snow," he says.

I grab the offending pink bottle to wash my hair and realize it's full. Brand new. I squirt some in my palm and begin scrubbing my hair. "Anywhere but here," I say. "I'm not opposed to beach vacations elsewhere. No beach is exactly the same. I've been snow skiing once when I was young. I don't really remember it, though there is video of me flying down a bunny slope straight into a forest. My dad had to take off his skis to go in after me. Mom said I was pretty traumatized after that and just wanted to build snowmen at the base of the mountain." I rinse my hair out. "Probably time I try again. Maybe now that Mom is…" The words almost left my mouth branding me a selfish daughter. "Never mind," I say. "I like this shower," I say, trying to change the subject.

"You can live your life for you. That's the way it's supposed to be, you know?" Leif says, taking my chin into his hand. "Let's go snow skiing together. A vacation."

I smirk and swallow down the guilt. "She'd want me to try again after that disaster," I admit. "Even if she doesn't remember it now." I grab Leif's soap and start washing my body.

"I had the bathroom and kitchen redone when I moved in. It looked like the 70s puked all over everything. I'm glad you like it." Leif clears his throat. "They told me that was the shampoo you used at the store. I wanted you to have something other than Old Spice man wash for your hair. It's so…long and girly," he rambles.

Grinning uncontrollably, I point a soapy finger at the pink bottle. "You bought that for me?"

He nods, not meeting my eyes. "Figured at the very least we'd go to the beach together and end up here. No one goes to bed without showering first." He shrugs. "You have to wash your hair after the beach."

"True. That's very thoughtful, though. Almost too thoughtful. Like you were planning on me spending the night." I quirk one brow. Leif looks off to the side wearing a guilty smile.

"I get what I want," he replies, licking his lips. "Wasn't a matter of if, just when."

I can't argue with that logic. "Well, thank you. I bet their heads popped off when you asked what shampoo I used. I'm surprised I didn't find out you were shopping for me via the Bronze Bay gossip hotline. You'd be surprised how quickly news travels."

"I may have threatened their lives," he says.

Turning off my water, I eye him. "Liar."

Sighing, he pulls me in for a wet, hot, hug—our skin the same exact temperature. His lips are against my hair. "Plus, I love the way this shampoo smells so much I might use it on myself."

"So you can think of me when I'm not around?" I fire back.

He grunts. "Maybe."

Leif wraps me in a fluffy, white towel, then snatches it away when I am mostly dry so the naked sleepover can resume. I bump off the air conditioner and open the windows to let in the warm night air. The waves echo through the living room as we alternate between looking at each other's naked body to talking about everything. We talk about his family and upbringing a lot and I find myself wistful, yet happy. Happy he had such a happy childhood because it made him the man he is today, and wistful because it's obvious I missed out on so much. I was forced to grow up so quickly and fully that perhaps skipping it made me who I am. When he finishes a story, I'm no longer afraid to meet his parents, nor will I ever be intimidated by his sisters again.

"There's a game I like to play," I say when there's a lull in conversation.

"Let's play it," he says, biting his lip.

"It's not sexual," I explain. "Sometimes when I

can't sleep, and I'm too tired to read, I ask myself silly questions. It's an imagination game. When I was little, I'd ask myself what I'd buy if I had twenty dollars. It was usually whatever toy my friends at school had that I didn't. Then I got older and the questions turned into, 'What would my perfect boyfriend look like?' or 'What would I do with a billion dollars?'"

"Oh, this is my favorite kind of game. Ask me anything," Leif says, excitement lighting his eyes. "I'll win this game every single time."

"There aren't winners and losers." We're stretched out on a cotton blanket on the floor, the television playing lowly in the background. The movie was whatever came up first on his queue, it is over now and some random show is playing as background noise. There was never any question of if we would actually watch it, we just wanted the sound to help fill the silence while we stared. Our eyes are only for each other. "So, what would you do with a billion dollars? Would you quit your job?"

"First off. We couldn't tell anyone. Not our family or friends. We'd live off the interest. No ostentatious purchases. That's where people fuck up when they win the lottery. The money clouds their judgement. I wouldn't stop working. I love my job, but my hobbies would be way cooler." He folds his arms behind his head. "We'd gift some of the money to our family and friends. In small increments, though."

"That's smart," I remark. "Also, you're saying we. Not I."

The dreamy smile drops from his face. "Oh. Well,

I thought you asked what we would do with a billion dollars."

"I like being a 'we' with you," I reply, tracing his chiseled jaw with my finger. Leaning in, I kiss his lips. He deepens the kiss, leaning into me. The news anchor on television breaks through our perfect moment. Something about a terrorist squad mobilizing. It's just enough to remind us we don't live in the same world we did as children. Leif pauses, listening, but keeping his lips against mine. His body goes rigid.

"What does your ideal boyfriend look like?" Leif asks, distractedly, lips still pressed to mine. It's obvious his whole demeanor changes when his work is brought up. It's not just his work, though. It affects everyone. I kiss his jaw. His neck. The swell of his chest, where his muscles begin. His body relaxes under my touch. Maybe this is what I offer him. Peace inside his world of war and unknowns.

"You're fishing," I murmur against his skin.

"Well, you're hooking. Makes sense, right?"

"I didn't realize what my ideal man looked like until I met you," I say, meeting his gaze. "You."

He peers down at me through his thick blond lashes. "I want to change my billion dollar answer," Leif growls.

"No changes," I say, smirking.

His face is stoic, severe, as he whispers, "If the only thing I own is your heart I'll be the richest man in the world."

I don't know how I can tell from just a look, but that seems to be a trend with Leif, and I'm pretty sure we both broke a couple of rules. "Consider yourself a billionaire, fine sir," I say, bringing his face to mine in a kiss, the news once again becoming background noise.

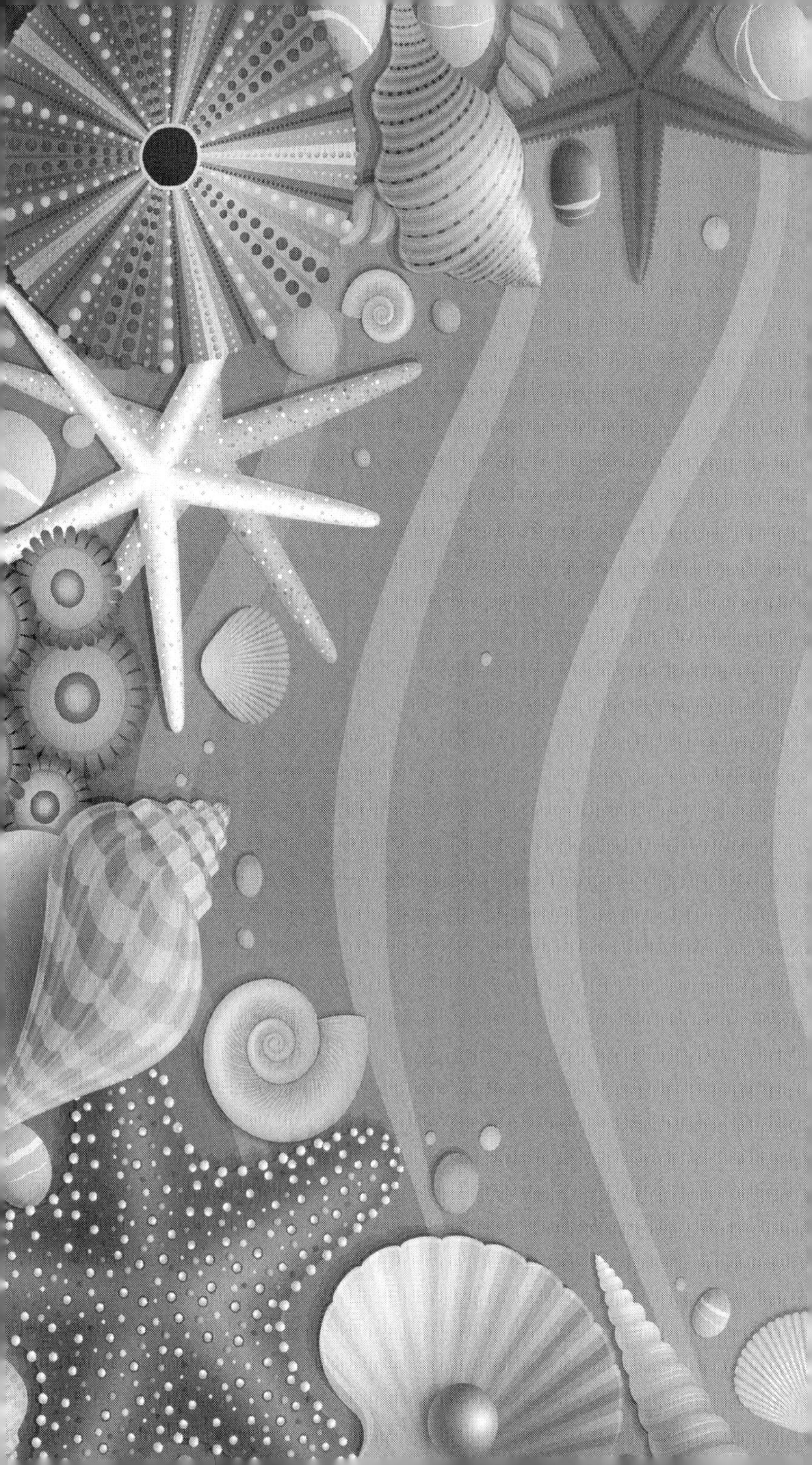

Chapter Eleven

Leif

"The night is clear. It's going to be awesome. You can't tell Aidan," I mutter to our pilot who just agreed to the biggest favor I've ever asked of anyone before. After a day of skydiving, I'm dog ass tired. The adrenaline rush causes a crash akin to a three day alcohol bender. I think it's from doing something that could possibly cause death, over and over, that does it. I could be wrong though.

"What time," the pilot asks, looking at his watch. "I'm going to grab something to eat, refuel, and I'll be back."

I tell him to meet me back here at the airport in two hours and then try to sneak out of the airport without Tahoe or Caroline seeing me. I don't even know if Malena is going to agree to this, but I want to give her the experience. I've fallen for her in ways I didn't know I was capable of. Might as well fall with her, hurdling down to earth above the town that has become my X marks the spot. The place where I found her. The one. My person.

Driving to her house on my moped, I think about waking up with her this morning. Her warm body splayed across mine, her hair in my face. That's when it wasn't a sleepover anymore and we fucked twice before I had to peel myself away to get to the airport on time. Thinking about her naked body underneath mine, our sweat mingling, the sounds of our breaths and skin slapping makes me harder than stone. Swallowing hard, I park next to the palm tree, take off my helmet and ring her doorbell.

Malena opens the door before the doorbell is finished ringing. "Hi," she says, jumping into my arms. "I missed you so much." I fold her into my arms.

"You took the words out of my mouth. How was your day?" I ask.

Malena tells me about an event she worked, and her short shift at the store. She doesn't spare details. I get everything. I love that about her. I'll never wonder, that's for sure. I'm glad she's getting to do what she loves. Event planning might not make a lot of money in the big cities when there are several hundred people vying for the same jobs, but here? Malena has the corner on the market. It's just her. Weddings are extremely popular because of the picturesque scenery and small town feel.

"Enough about me," she says, smiling. There's an ease about her now. This carefree beauty that wasn't there until I helped her mother. She is stunning. So beautiful I worry about other men going after what is so obviously mine. "What's this surprise you were talking about?" she asks.

It brings me back into the moment. Grinning, I release her and cup her cheek. "I'd rather show you how my day was. If you're brave enough."

"What's that mean?" she asks, furrowing her brow. Realization dawns a second later, as her mouth opens to form an O. "Skydiving?" she croaks.

My stomach flips as I remember the first time I jumped out of an airplane. It was after BUD/s training. You have to go tandem, attached to an instructor until you get enough jumps and training under your belt. I loved skydiving so much that I went on to be Jump Master. Now I am able to jump with people, dogs, equipment strapped to my chest. Aidan and I are the two jumpmasters at our current command. "With me," I say, palming my chest. "I have the pilot waiting for us." "I'm going to puke," Malena says, eyes wide. "This is something I've always wanted to do, but I'm not sure I'm made for it. I'm a scaredy-cat!" Her words don't match up with the excitement in her eyes. They're glowing with adventure, the chance to take life by the horns. Literally and figuratively. Technically, I'll be in charge of her life.

Swallowing hard, I say, "Do it now. It will splash in my face if you do it when we're in the air."

"Has that happened?" she wrinkles her nose. "I'll go

with you? Strapped to you?"

"Yes. That okay?"

"Totally." Her tone is gleeful. "Let's go."

There's a black glittery helmet in the basket of my moped for her. She puts it on and slings her leg over the back. "What I'm wearing is okay?" she asks, on a second thought. Small jean shorts and a backless top that makes my mouth water are perfect I think, and make me recall just how sweet her ass looked in the reflection of my mirror this morning while she was riding my cock.

"Perfect," I say. Starting up the moped and turning onto the road. I hear her laugh anytime I turn, and it sends a pang to my heart. That organ that has been dormant but for keeping me alive until now. Until Malena. The sun sets completely leaving us in dark but for my headlight guiding the way. I make the turn onto the dirt road that leads to the airport.

"I wonder if Caroline will be out," Malena says once we've parked near the hangar that houses our gear and small aircraft. I tuck the moped inside. Not because I don't want anyone to know I'm here, but because I'm not quite ready to share Malena with the guys yet. "I bet Tahoe is here. She's been talking about him non-stop."

"Tahoe is far gone in Caroline land, too," I say. "I didn't tell you that, though."

The pilot rounds the corner and halts when he sees Malena—his eyes darting up and down her body. "Hey man. Let me know when you're ready. I'll be in the plane double checking everything and getting online to comms."

Meeting his gaze, I make sure he sees my irritation. "Good deal," I reply.

Malena bounds over and offers her hand. "I'm Malena. I'm so excited. Thank you so much for this," she says to him, then turns to me, "This has to be some after-hours stuff he doesn't have to do."

The pilot shakes her hand and backs away. "Don't mention it," he replies, ignoring my heated stare. "See you on the other side." He disappears into the black night.

"I thought you were scared," I say to Malena while gathering the harness and parachutes we'll need. When I jump by myself, I can use a chute with a smaller diameter. When jumping tandem, a larger chute is required to balance our weight. "There's nothing to be scared of, though. I've done this hundreds of times. Thousands by myself."

She blows out a long breath. "I am scared. I can't let him know that though," she explains. "I'm trying to be brave through falsification."

I laugh out loud, my voice a booming echo in the hangar. "Is that even a thing?"

"Easy for you to ask. You're not scared of anything. You were born without fear or the ability to be scared."

Shaking my head, I say, "I'm scared all the fucking time, Malena. I use it differently than most people though. Some let it cripple them. I harness fear as power

tossing it

and make myself better for it."

"Okay, well the only harness I'm interested in is the one you have in your hand. Give me the lowdown." Shaking my head, grinning, I give her the basics of skydiving, the harness she'll wear that attaches to my chest, and what I'll expect of her when we're in the air. I tell her what I will do and how everything will happen. It's a step-by-step process that makes her more comfortable the more I speak, so I continue on, giving her details that are meaningless unless you do this on a regular basis. I keep talking as we walk toward the plane, a small flashlight lighting the pavement in front of us. She nods her head and asks questions every so often. A little v forms between her eyes when she's deep in thought. Though I can't see it through the black night, I know it's there. The fact scares me, but I'm not harnessing it as power. I lied. It's something completely different when it comes to her. Love. Love. Love. Love. That's what my subconscious screams at me anytime I try to make sense of my feelings. When I agreed to not fall in love with her last night, it was easy. What I didn't tell her was that I already was there, I love her.

The pilot has the engines running. He saw us approach from the hangar. It's a smaller plane, not the bigger ones we use when we're flying anywhere a long distance away. It will be harder for her to hear me when we are closer to the engine so before we board, I halt her, both my hands on her shoulders. The smaller lights on the plane illuminate her face. Grinning, I say, "You're ready." She nods, her face a mask of horror.

"I'm ready!" she shouts out. "If you were a serial killer this would be the perfect time to kill me!"

Tipping my head back I chuckle. "Serial killers are narcissistic. I'd never kill myself to kill a victim. That doesn't make any sense. Come on!" I cup her face, lean down, and kiss her. My stomach tilts as my eyes meet hers. Her arms lock around my waist, under my harness. "Don't fuck with my harness, Black Widow." My joke quells her nerves, her smile more genuine as each second passes.

Both of our nerves steeled, we board the plane. I connect her harness to mine. Her back to my front and sit on the bench along the wall. She sits on my lap, her rapid pulse evident in her stomach where my hands are placed. The flight up to jumping altitude is the worst part. The pilot gives me a thumbs up once we're where we're supposed to be altitude and landing zone wise. There's a lit field to the left of the airport we use for night jumps so we know where to safely land. I lean into Malena's ear and tell her we're going to walk to the door. She nods once.

The pilot gives me another signal that we're good to go. This is it. The adrenaline hits again but different this time. A life is in my hands that is not my own. I have to go into business mode because it's my autopilot and that's where I perform perfectly. There's no room for

tossing it

error right now. The cabin is lit so I check everything I can see.

"Toes on the edge," I command, calling it loud enough for her to hear over the air and engines. With both hands on the sides of the hatch door and Malena's tiny frame in front of me, completely at my mercy, I start the countdown. To keep her calmer, I count three and two in my head. "One," I shout and launch us out of the door. Her scream pierces the darkness of night. I bet she doesn't even realize she's screaming. Once I adjust my arms and legs after the initial tumble from the aircraft, we're steady. "Open your eyes!" I yell, using a deep tone she'll be able to hear. I already told her that when I was explaining everything, but it's the one thing most forget when they're terrified. The ocean is visible off to the side, the bioluminescence lighting the deep ocean a neon blue. The landing zone is lit with lights, forming a circle. You can see the town from up here, the lights shining like little ants.

I move my arm methodically to check the altimeter on my wrist. We're almost to the proper height to pull the chute. I don't hear anything from Malena and I wish I could see her face, wish I could see if she was loving this as much as I do. There's a freedom up here. A recognition of how small we really are in this big, wide world. How impossible is it that one person actually finds the other one they are meant for? How impossible it seems. Except, at this moment, that one human, is strapped to my chest. A part of me.

I pull the chute and silence follows, the wind of falling changes to a soft whooshing as we begin our descent under the chute. Malena's giggles cut through the quiet.

"I'm not dead!" she squeals out. "Do you see that?" She points to the ocean, and then the town, and the horizon where we can see the next city over.

My hands are busy holding the toggles to control where we glide. "It's beautiful," I call out. "Remember what I said about landing. It's the toughest part of tandem. Feet straight out in front of you. Just let me do the landing."

Her reply is another burst of laughter. I pull the left handle hard to spin us toward the lighted landing zone, the spotlights surrounding the grassy circle like an alien spacecraft imprint.

"Brace," I tell her. Her body tenses, and we glide into the center of the circle far faster than anyone ever expects. I try to protect my knees by waiting until the last possible moment to place my feet on land. It's smooth. Easy. The way every landing is supposed to be. I unhook her from my chest as quickly as I can. She turns to look at me. The lights lighting her smile like she's some Hollywood star on stage—ready to give her acceptance speech.

"I can't believe you get to do that for work. That is so unfair." She bends down and hops up and down, as if she's testing the earth's solidarity.

I grin. "Safe to say you enjoyed yourself. I love doing

it at night. You can see so much. The lights are always amazing."

"That was surreal," Malena says, shaking her head. "Nothing will ever compare to that feeling. I…I…It was the greatest, the freest I've ever felt in my life. That view. The rush—falling."

Her lips are still calling to me—shining in the dim glow. "I need to kiss you right now."

"Because I love what you do for work?" Her brown eyes turn an amber color with the way the light is reflecting on them. Her white smile the shade of I'll-never-fucking-shake-this-woman-in-a-lifetime.

This isn't adrenaline I'm feeling. My breaths push through my mouth fast—harried, irrational. "No." I shake my head.

Malena tilts her head to the side. "No?"

"I need to kiss you right now because I'm so fucking in love with you that I need your kiss to breathe."

Her mouth pops open, and I take that as my sign from God. Taking her face into my hands, running my hands into her wind-blown hair, I press my lips to hers, my tongue taking hers, my heart pounding against hers. Her hands wind up and around my neck. It's comforting.

I imagine what we look like from where we just were high up in the sky. A bird's eye view of us kissing in the middle of this lit circle. All signs pointing to what is so now blatantly obvious to me. I love Malena. And I'll love her for as long as she'll let me. The kissing turns into a frenzy of tossed clothing and our bodies colliding. I make love to her on top of the parachute that guided us safely from the sky.

Her skin against mine is the only feeling I've ever craved in such a perilous degree. Like I may die if I go too long without being inside her. When Malena comes this time, she doesn't call out my name, she whispers three sweet words into my ear. Over and over.

Over and over.

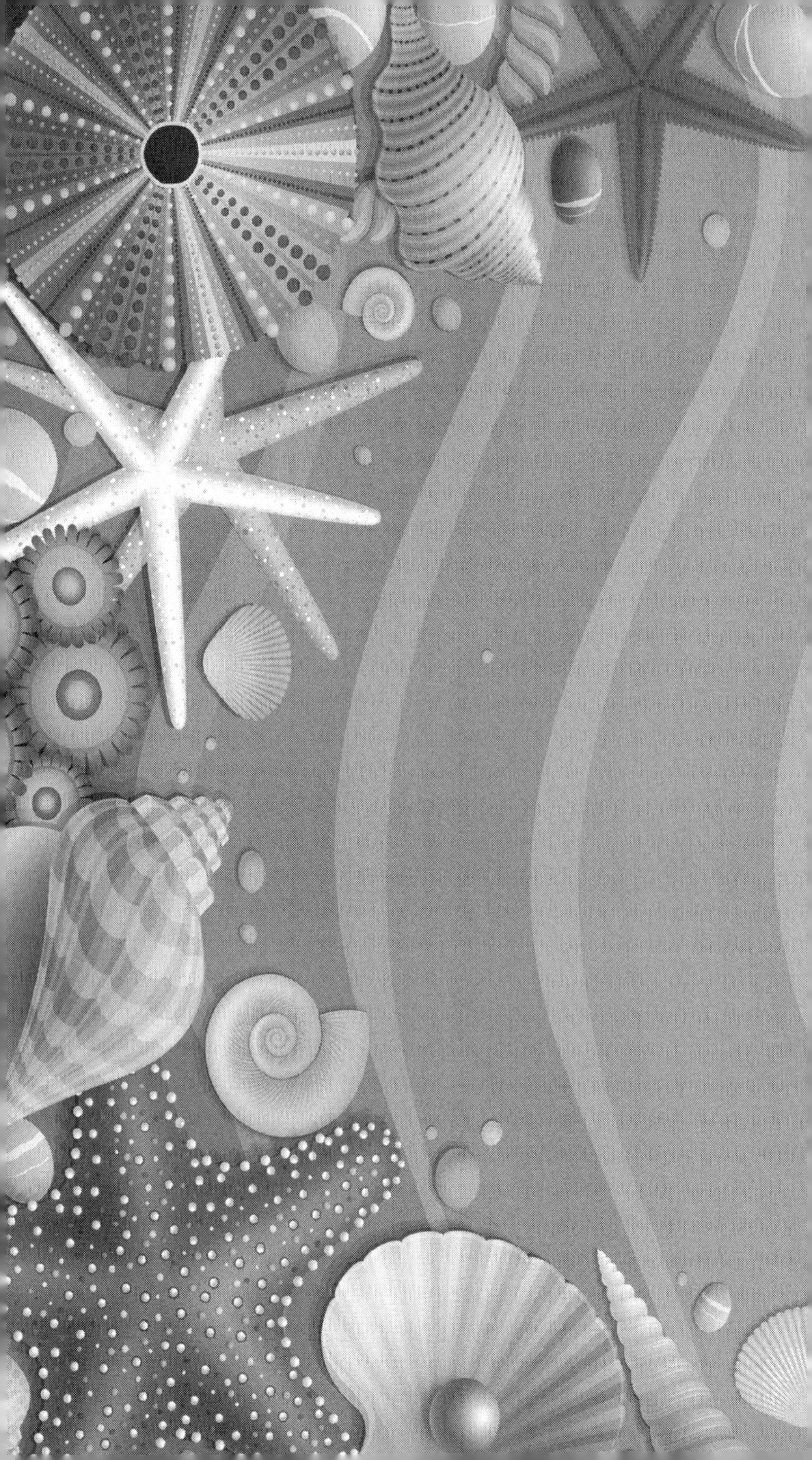

Chapter twelve

Malena

Months passed in an unbearably blissful pace with Leif at my side and involved in every facet of my world. He's entwined himself into my group of friends and has been there for me in every single way a man in love is there for his woman. When I'm upset and missing my mother, he offers to drive me to Garden Breeze to visit her. When I'm stressing out over deadlines now that my event planning business is in full swing, he makes sure I have pints of ice cream waiting for me when I get home. Weddings are hopping, and I left the General Store as soon as humanly possible. I am the most fulfilled as I've ever been in my entire life—surrounded by love from all angles.

We went to N.Y.C for Tahoe and Caroline's joint bachelor/bachelorette party, which I planned all on my own. Dating Leif in a new setting was something that I never dreamed of. Don't get me wrong, seeing him in a T-shirt and board shorts does indecent things to everything below my waist, but seeing him in a suit and tie, his hair coifed, and his shoes shined makes my mouth water. In any situation or circumstance, he's ready for whatever—a chameleon in a human's body. I took my party organizing duties seriously, but when we retreated to our hotel room at the end of the night, it was nothing but him and I and our explosive connection. It's been like that for months, an undying spark that usually only exists in a new relationship.

My friends felt a little neglected as I steadied my footing in a real relationship for the first time in a long time, but I eventually figured out the balance. This is the first time since Dylan—the marriage that crashed and burned in ways no one should ever have to bear witness to, that I'm committed to a man. Thinking about Dylan brings forth a searing guilt. Leif doesn't know much more than Dylan was a failed relationship. Do I owe him more than that? The deeper in love I fall, the more I think I do. I'd want to know if the roles were reversed and Leif had a botched marriage, founded on a family that he couldn't create. Now I'm in a serious relationship founded on the exact opposite. I'm afraid of what it will label me if I admit to the gruesome failure. It failed for legitimate reasons that were out of both of our control, but that's an excuse.

Leif doesn't like excuses. Or lies. A fact made blatantly clear anytime I try to give reasons why I haven't accomplished something. Be it a daily task or other loftier life goals. He is a cheerleader for every aspect of my future, and I feel like I'm cheapening it by not telling him about my past. I like to keep my secrets in the vacuum of my mind—where no one can use them against me. Where no one will label me. It's already a freaking miracle no one has mentioned my divorce to Leif in passing. I think enough time has passed that it's considered old gossip and not worth sharing. There are far more scandalous things to talk about these days. Things such as the war raging in our country.

Shirley shifts in her seat in front of me at the diner. She's taking a break, guzzling coffee like it is her oxygen. Our friend Caroline's mother owns this diner. When Caroline married Leif's friend, Tahoe, she began spending more time running their Bed and Breakfast on the water instead of waitressing here at the family restaurant. Shirley picked up the slack and now she's so busy she doesn't have time to annoy her friends.

"What time are you going to the spot tonight?" she asks, pausing her coffee assault.

"Oh, I don't know if I'm going. I have a ton of work to do," I reply, tapping the keys on my laptop responding to an email. "It's always the same thing. Everyone gets drunk. At least one couple gets into a public fight, another gets caught having sex, and someone ends up in the E.R. I'd rather hang out at home and read," I say, knowing full well she won't accept it and also knowing I'd rather be naked with Leif.

She cracks her neck, and the sound jolts my attention from my screen to her. "You're going. We don't hang out anymore. I don't get days off anymore. You start your fancy business and spend the other remaining hours humping your mastodon boyfriend. Friend time. You're going." Shirley runs her hand through her hair. "And we need to swing by the store. I need a box of hair dye, and you're going to help me turn my black roots white. You understand?" Shirley clicks her tongue and sighs. "Caroline is all wifed up and my boyfriend never leaves the kitchen back there." Turning, she looks back toward the counter where Caleb, her on-again boyfriend is wiping the counter. "What do you say?" She closes my laptop slowly, until it clicks all the way.

"I was emailing someone back, Shirley. If that didn't save, I'm going to be pissed," I deadpan. "Aren't we too old for parties at the spot?"

"It's *your* spot, Malena. We will never be too old for parties at the spot. Keg beer. Canoes. Toes in the sand. Bonfires. It gives me life." This debate is over before it really got started. I can tell.

"Let's go then. You're finished for the day?" I slide my cell phone from my purse and send a quick message to Leif. He was planning on stopping by my house after work. He's been at work more lately. He told me he likes to be in the office when updates come in. I get it. Even if it means he's spending less time with me. The commitment he shows to his job is a turn on. Basically, at this point, I haven't found anything about him that isn't a turn on. Even as I hit send on the message, I hope he'll still swing by if Shirley is there. I send another message letting him know I'll be at the spot and what time in case he'd rather meet me there instead.

The spot is a place down by the water that's secluded by wild forest on each side. No one remembers, but my dad bought it when we first moved here. He was going to build my parents dream home on the land. He left without selling it, which in a way, does make it mine. Most people think it is a distant relative that owns it, and I don't correct them. It has picnic benches, and over the years it's turned into something awesome and civilized. When we were teens, it was a patch of prickly grass where we came to get drunk. Everyone left with sand spurs in their ass and ankles covered in fire ant bites. Now there's poured concrete and a lit path guiding us down to the water and dark stained docks. A few of the guys who own the construction company in town made it what it is today. Mostly because they wanted to have somewhere to drink on the weekends other than Bobby's. I have enough positive memories of the spot that I sometimes forget it is mine. My father wasn't able to taint this spot with his abandonment.

Leif doesn't text me back right away and my mood falls even though I know he keeps his phone in a bag at work. It's unreasonable morose, but I sigh anyways. That's what he does to me. Shirley confirms she's ready to leave after talking to Caleb who offered to cover for her so she could have a break, and we set off for the General Store.

"Is it weird coming in here after you quit?" Shirley says, eyeing the shelves filled with hair dye trying to find the proper platinum shade. "Like do those bitches scowl at you? I would if I were them."

tossing it

Laughing, I shake my head. "It's not even…anything. I never felt a part of this family. That's what it is, you know? They've all been here so long they know the passers-through right away. I only worked here to help pay the nurses," I say, swallowing hard. I miss my mom. I lay awake some nights trying to remember the last time she remembered. It makes my chest hurt and my eyes leak, and it never gets any easier. Time, I tell myself. It will get better with time.

Shirley notices and lays a hand on my shoulder. "You got the world by the tits, Malena. A hot guy is paying for her to be in a safe place. He cares about you so much. You're like the royal princess of Bronze Bay."

I shake off the memories. "Caleb cares for you, too. You're here because he's waiting your tables," I remind her.

She smiles. "He's good people. I know that. You know Leif is good people, too, right?"

I nod. "I mean, I would still be having sex with him even if he wasn't paying for Mom to be in Garden Breeze," I explain, grinning. "I hope it lasts. That's what I'm worried about. I'm so in love with him I can't imagine being without him." A lump forms in my throat. Shirley picks up a box of dye and flips it over to see the photos. "Can I ask you a question? Between you and me?"

"Oh, fuck. What did you do?" Shirley replies, focusing her gaze on mine.

I roll my eyes. "Stop it. I didn't do anything. Well, it's something I didn't do, I guess you could say."

"Go on," she says, looking down the aisle to make sure we're out of earshot of anyone. She sets the box back on the shelf without looking. "I'm waiting."

"Dylan," I choke out. "He doesn't know about the divorce. He knows about my infertility which was my biggest concern. He didn't bat an eye at that. Leif even knows I was in a long-term relationship with a man named Dylan, but he has no clue I was married. Do you think that's a big deal? How do I bring that up?"

Shirley blows out a long breath through pursed lips. "Is he the jealous type?" she asks like it's the only logical question.

"Aren't all men jealous?"

She lifts one shoulder. "Some more so than others. If I was a betting woman I'd guess Leif is a very jealous man. Beats on his chest, marks his territory with piss and all that. If he knows you were with Dylan, I'd just leave it at that. It's not like you were married for a decade and made a billion sweet memories together. It was mostly awful. And he took off when you didn't deliver on your promise to repopulate Bronze Bay and give him his football team."

Folding my arms, I say, "You put my medical condition so eloquently."

"I get something wrong in there? Just gave you the facts," she states, grabbing the box she's already picked up twice. "Got what I came for, you need anything?"

There's a blueberry lip gloss hanging on a display, and I snatch it up. My mouth waters. "You got it all right, but you're so blunt about it. I shouldn't expect anything

tossing it

else," I growl

"No. You shouldn't. Real friends give real facts. Always."

I tamp down on my annoyance about my friend dredging up old memories and realize she's given sound advice. I don't have any feelings for Dylan. I realize that what I felt at the height for Dylan, is not even a drop in the bucket of the overflowing, cascade of love I have for Leif. Telling him would do nothing. If it comes up, or he hears about it from someone else, I'll tell him Dylan was so inconsequential that he wasn't worth talking about. That's it. This is the last time I'm going to worry about it. Shirley checks out, and I follow, trying to make small talk with the checkout employee, but it comes out all wrong and I'm sure she thinks I'm insulting her job. Floundering I try to say something nice and fail again. "Have a good day," I mutter, and grab my lip gloss off the counter.

"You're a real mess today, Malena," Shirley says, laughing under her breath as we exit. "You need a night out more than I do if that little exchange has anything to say about your mental state."

"You talk to people all day long, Shirley. Plus, you're just mean," I say, checking my phone. Still nothing. Sometimes Leif will check it if he has a spare second and get back to me. It's the last time I look at the damn thing without being prompted by a ringer.

Shirley and I make brownies while we wait for her roots to turn blonde, and then we spend way too long doing our makeup and selecting what to wear. It's like we're teenagers again getting ready for a party in secret, except now I have this whole house to myself, an entire life that I never thought was in the cards. I settle on a backless tank and a pair of shorts. Shirley borrows one of my black dresses and makes light work of uncorking a bottle of wine. We're riding our bicycles down to the spot so we can have a drink or two before we set off.

Cleaning the kitchen, I carefully package some of the brownies to take to my mom tomorrow when I visit. I put the container in the bag which contains a few photo albums. The nurses told me that even if she doesn't remember who is in the photos, she'll enjoy looking at them, and they might help her. I do anything I can to be helpful now that I feel so useless with regards to Mom's care.

"You handling everything okay? Seems you are, but I'm not sure if it's the orgasm haze. Are you really handling it, or are you distracted?" Shirley says, sneaking up behind me as I load the bag.

"I'm okay," I say, nodding. I tell her I know it's been coming for a long time. "The real kicker is sometimes I wonder if it's going to happen to me. I look at these albums and can't imagine not remembering my life. It's scary."

She puts her arm around my shoulder. "You know they told you it may not happen." "But it might," I say, shaking my head. I tell her what her doctor told me about statistics, and she poo-poos them by trying to convince me doctors only say things to cover their own ass. When the wine-fueled conversation turns to something happier, we mount our bikes, turn the headlights on, and peddle toward the ocean. It's an easy ride, the sidewalks are wide, and the traffic nonexistent. The salty air turns my hair into a wavy mess, and the humidity covers my skin in a dewy glow. There's no point in trying to go for a matte makeup look in Florida. It's impossible. I grab the half-empty wine bottle from my basket and my cell phone as we park our bikes at the long bike rack adjacent to the field that everyone uses as a parking lot. Shirley has a head start, walking toward the path down to the spot.

I'm momentarily distracted by the wine buzz and making sure my bike is secure when he sneaks up behind me, wrapping his big arms around my waist. I jump and let out a tiny yip. "There you are. You're late," he rasps at my ear, the heat from his body enveloping me fully.

We are late, but he never messaged me back, so I didn't know if he was coming. "Shirley and I got caught up at home. How was work? I missed talking to you today," I reply, setting the wine back in the basket.

He kisses my cheek, and then spins me to face him and plants his lips firmly on my mouth. It turns scandalous fast, his tongue invading my mouth as his hands trace lazy circles on my exposed back. "I missed you too," he says. "So much I had to do that so you would know just how much."

"You could have just said it, but I enjoy kissing you," I reply, my lips brushing his as I speak.

Leif licks his lips, pulling me closer. I exhale every pent-up worry and relax into his strong frame. "Work was crazy today. Lots of meetings. The thought of seeing you tonight was what got me through. Can we go somewhere?" he asks, tilting my chin up to take my mouth again. "I need you now." His hard-on is pressing against me, in an unbearably noticeable way. "Any which way I can have you. As soon as possible."

He's not usually this forthright or savage in his need. Don't get me wrong, if he catches sight of me naked, it's over. We're having sex. If my shorts slide up when I bend over, we're fucking as soon as an opportunity arises. If skin touches skin, he's touching me, kissing me. The attraction is unlike anything I've ever experienced in my life. Leif looks at me with dark, hungry eyes, and I know he's not just talking.

"Where?" I reply, the bundle of nerves between my legs pulsing from his heady gaze.

He looks around frantically. "Follow me," he whispers, tugging my hand and keeping me close. The wine makes me a little slow and cumbersome on my feet. The peddles on my bicycle were easy compared to walking. There's a lifeguard stand in the distance, at the beach nearest the spot. It's illuminated by a domed beacon on the top and after a few seconds, I know it's where we're headed. Leif picks up the pace and at this point, I'm running to keep up. We kick off our shoes, leaving them where pavement meets sand and rush the white ladder. He hoists me up and climbs up quickly himself, using every few rungs because his legs are so long. It's unlocked because no one locks anything in Bronze Bay. That's the best part of staying in this small town bubble. I can pretend that life outside it doesn't exist.

There's an old lamp, a pair of binoculars and a system that must be a radio for communication purposes. There's also a small stool that swivels. We're both eyeing that at the moment. We can hear the party raging on the other side of the tree line. I take a seat on the red worn out stool. "So, you had to have me. Here I am," I say.

Leif swallows hard, his neck working. "Malena," he says, eyes darkening even further. A crease forms between his eyes as he appraises me.

I nod, waiting for him to make the first move. "Leif," I toss back. "Mr. Andersson. My hero. The love of my life." Smirking, I try to gauge his reaction to my words, but he's a blank canvas. His chest works as he breathes heavily and he runs both of his hands through his hair and down his face. Shaking his head, he grasps whatever resolve he's searching for and confuses me even further. "Come here, Leif. Tell me what's wrong." I rise to my knees on the stool so I can reach around his neck instead of being eye level with his dick.

He obeys, letting me circle my arms around him. Leaning down, Leif inhales my hair. "I need you," he says.

Looking up at him I wrinkle my brow. "You have me." No one else has ever had someone so completely in the history of time.

He shakes his head. I don't have long to ponder what that means because he's kissing me, his large hands stripping me down until there's nothing left but skin. I help slide his shirt off and he drops his shorts and steps out of them. He doesn't take his eyes off mine. There's a desperation that I've never seen before. A wicked gleam of something sharp, painful.

As he runs his hands down the sides of my body, I ask, "What's wrong, Leif. Talk to me. I can tell something is off."

He silences me with a kiss, tilting my head to the side and running his hands through my hair. Picking me up, he steps forward until my back is against the floor to ceiling window that overlooks the ocean. We're like fish in a tank. Anyone looking up has a view of my ass. He enters me the next second, and I wouldn't care if the whole world was watching. Crying out, I tuck my face into his neck and ride the thrusts as he pumps, hard juts, as deep as my body will allow him.

"You're mine," he says, teeth grating along my shoulder. "Always."

The act of forming coherent words isn't something I'm capable of when Leif is this wild with lust, or I'd confirm his sentiment. My skin makes squeaking noises as he fucks me against the clean glass. His grip is firm on the sides of my thighs as he uses that as leverage. The noise intensifies as he brings both of us closer to orgasm. My stomach tightens and my arms feel limp as the pressure at my core builds to a fever pitch. We come at the same time, him letting out an exasperated sigh as I sink down on his shaft when his grip loosens a bit with his release.

The high is always intense after we make love, my body craving his touch, his warmth, all of him. "I love you," I say, tracing the edge of his ear with my lips. "That was amazing. It's always amazing with you."

He breathes heavily in favor of replying. He needs a few moments to collect himself. Almost as if his brain needs to switch from one mode to another. He lets me drop to the ground, disconnecting our bodies as he goes. My back is sweaty and has left an imprint on the glass, a lovely heart shape where my ass was just pounded. "Malena," Leif rasps. Different this time than when we first began this tryst.

"Look at me," I order, placing my hands on each of his shoulders. "You have me." I reach between my legs and draw my hand back when it's coated with his seed. I hold it up. "Yours," I say, wiggling my fingers. "Always yours. Why are you acting like I'm going somewhere?"

Then it hits me. This has nothing to do with me going anywhere. My stomach sinks and my legs shake a bit. A little from my intense orgasm, but mostly from the knowledge that he's about to tell me something I don't want to hear. Bad news. It's something I can sniff out. "Spit it out," I prompt.

He finally lets his gaze flick up to meet mine. It's pained. "I'm leaving, Malena," he whispers. "And I shouldn't be upset because this is the opportunity I've been waiting for. I'm going to get the bastard this time. But that means I have to leave you. Here. For a long time."

I stutter, try to begin a sentence, but close my mouth and think for a few more beats. "This is your home," I say, narrowing my eyes. "You said you weren't moving away from here."

He shakes his head, placing his hands on my cheeks. "I'm not moving from here. Think of this like a deployment, Malena. Back before the war, I'd go overseas for months at a time. Now I'm heading to place here in the states…and I have to be there for a while. I'll come back. I'll always come back to you. Here. To Bronze Bay."

I shake my head. "How long?" In my fucked up fairytale, I think he's going to say a few weeks. Maybe a month. I should know better.

"A year." His voice shakes.

My eyes must look incredulous—scary, because he takes a step away from me. "It's a lot of reconnaissance to prepare. It's the largest mission the Teams have done yet. It might be the mission that stops the war for good. The end of it. No more attacks. No more terrorists lurking next door. Malena, you have to understand." Leif steps toward me, reaching a hand out, but I take another step back, the sting too encompassing to let him feel it. "This is why I chose this career path. Why I'm a SEAL. This is how I make a difference. How I rationalize my life choices. We can end the war," he repeats himself.

How do I tell him that I don't care about the war? What about my heart? What about the promises he's made to me? The war isn't in Bronze Bay and maybe that makes me out of touch, but I'm not thinking clearly right now. "I understand," I whisper.

He shakes his head, looking toward the low ceiling. "We can talk every day. Or, most days. This isn't me saying I'll never see you again. I'll be back."

I drop my head and cover my face with one hand. "A year, Leif. Do you know what happens in a year? Everything. You won't be able to visit me? You're not going overseas. It's not like a real deployment. You'll be a quick flight away."

"No," he says, taking my hand from my face and capturing it between both of his hands. "It's more important than a real deployment. Once the ball gets rolling and we involve ourselves, no one in our lives will be safe. I'll have to stay away. That said, there are ways we can communicate." His face changes, a scowl piercing all the way to my soul. "You won't wait for me then." It's not a question.

"Of course I'll wait for you!" I yell. "That's what makes this so bad! I'd do anything for you Leif and this is breaking my freaking heart. Sure we can communicate ,but we won't have this," I say, motioning between our bodies. "That's painful. I've had a taste of it and I've fallen so madly in love with everything about you that I'm not sure what is going to be left when and if you finally do come back to Bronze Bay."

"I'm coming back," he states. "I love you, Malena. I. Love. You. There's nothing that can keep me from coming back."

I slide my panties back on and sit on the stool. "Except war. That can stop you from coming back home to me."

I watch his neck work. He's deciding the best way to lie to me. "I'm coming back," he says.

"In a body bag?" I fire back. I regret it the second I

say it.

He winces and looks down to the floor. "I'll do everything in my power not to."

I spin on the stool and look out to the water. It's a smaller beach, with tree lines on each side of it. When I was small, my father took me here. Another memory tainted by his abandonment. "When?" I whisper.

"I leave in the morning," Leif says.

I nod, a sardonic gesture. "A year," I repeat, trying to wrap my brain around that time frame. It's not a week-long business trip. It's an ocean of time that can change so much. Hearts. Minds. Bodies. Personalities. One can change completely in a year. My mother's mind was stolen in half a year, a little going each week. "I'll wait," I tell him, spinning back to face him. "You really think you can end the war?"

"I fucking hope so," he says, voice brightening now that his bad news is out of the way. "They said this is the last line of terrorists and we're going to attack them full on, as quickly as possible."

I want to say a year is not a quick timeline, but I don't want to sound like a catty woman. Supportive. That's what I need to be. He's done so much for me. In the big scheme of things, don't I owe him this?

"When did you find out about this?" I ask, trying to search for the answer from his gaze.

He puts one hand behind his head, his bicep bulging at the slight motion. I try not to let it affect me, but it does remind me of how much I'm going to miss out on. "This week the wheels were spinning, but today it was confirmed. I was sort of ignoring my phone today because I wanted to tell you in person."

"You mean you wanted to have sex with me first," I counter.

He smirks. "That too."

"San Diego?" I ask.

"The west coast." It's almost as if he's just now realizing how far he's going to be from me. Leif pulls on his shorts and leans against the desk. "I'm fucking scared."

That gets my attention. "Like you said, it's what you've been waiting for. Training for. You're ready for it, Leif." I take his hand in mine. "There's no need to be scared." I hope I sound like I know what I'm talking about. This is me trying to be supportive even if it destroys every shred of my heart. Because that's what you do when you love someone. "You're going to come back all decorated with fancy pins and ribbons. Even hotter than you were when you left." I've only seen photos of Leif in full uniform and it's almost a good thing because of how delicious he looks. Like he fell out of a fundraising calendar.

He raises his eyes from our entwined hands to mine, a smirk on his face. "I'm not scared about doing my job. I'm good at that. That's like breathing for me. I'm worried about…you. Leaving you. Not having you. Not seeing you. Not coming home to you. Leaving you isn't something I'd planned on and the mere thought of it makes my chest hurt."

Now his voracious declarations make sense. I smile. "You'll still have me," I say, putting the rest of my clothes on while he watches my every move. "Just via video calls and letters. It's a foregone conclusion. I'm not going anywhere."

He leans in and presses his lips against mine. "I'm going to love you forever."

My heart skips a beat, and my stomach flips. "Absence makes the heart grow fonder. Isn't that what they say?"

"And punishes the dick."

Something pings. "You're not going to see other people while you're away, right?"

He pulls away, one brow raised. "Are you seriously asking me that? After everything? I don't want anyone else. I've never wanted anyone else. You're it for me, kid. You're it."

Grinning, I reach up and hug him laying my ear on his chest. I let the thumping of his heart calm mine. As long as his is beating, mine has a reason to keep going as well. I didn't plan on falling for a military man. The sacrifice on both sides wasn't something I ever considered. Sure he's off at war doing battle against those that wish ill will against innocents, but what about everyone they leave behind in their wake?

He whispers things to me. Details about the time he's leaving and what he needs to accomplish by morning. There's a laundry list of things I agree to take care for him. It's all business for a couple hours as he lays it all out for me—delivers my worst nightmare like it's an everyday occurrence. I don't miss the excitement in his voice when he talks about the mission, and the particular bad guy he's been after for a long time.

My heart starts hollowing in a Leif sized space at that moment. Setting him free. Paying the price. Getting what I deserve—what I always knew was coming. He's leaving me.

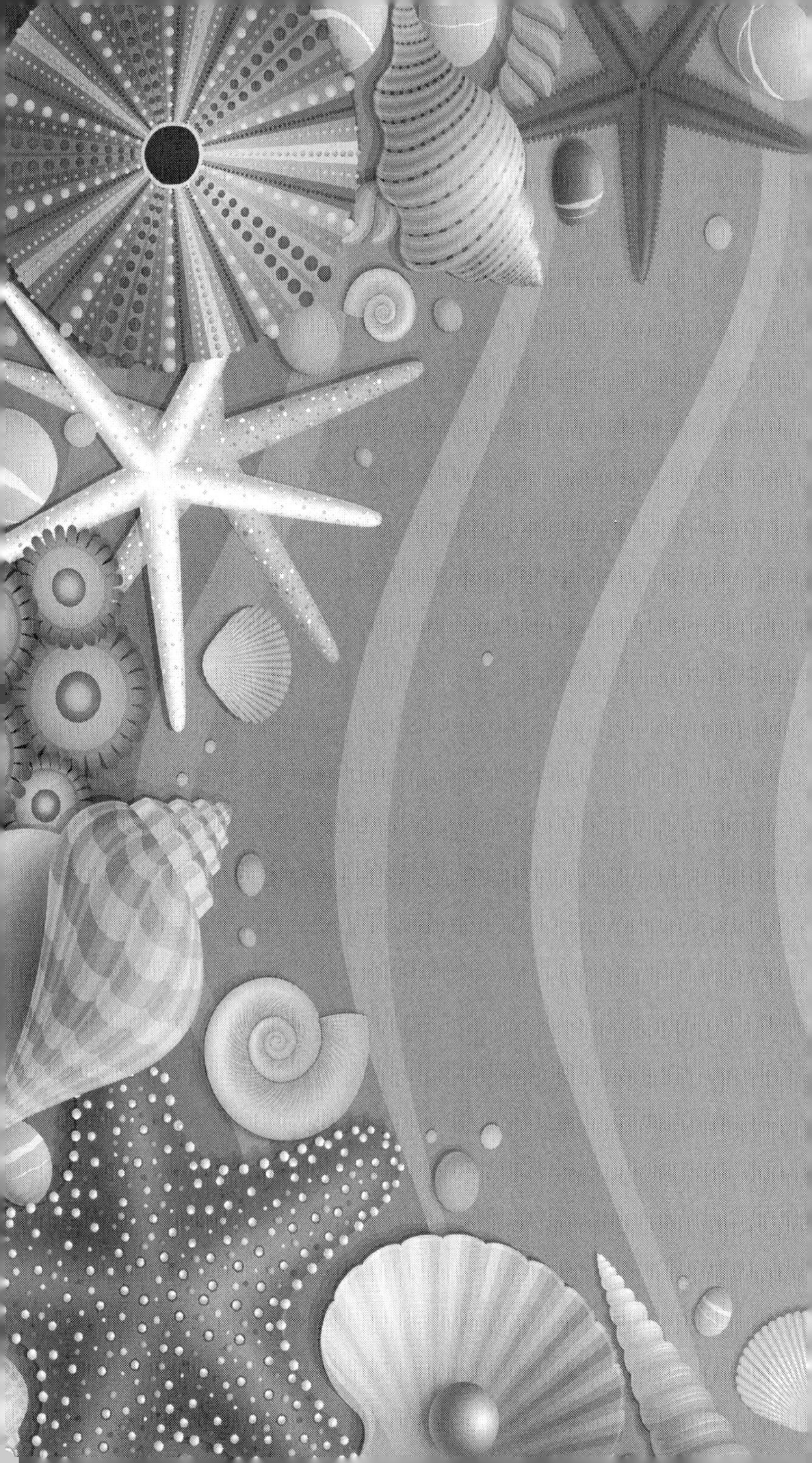

Chapter thirteen

Leif

The loose ends tie seamlessly with Malena holding the fort back in Bronze Bay while I'm gone. I've given her everything she'll need, access to my bank accounts, keys to my house, every piece of information I thought she may need. I added her to my will as the sole beneficiary last week. She doesn't know that yet, and hopefully she'll never have to know. She would have freaked. There are those that get it, and then there's everyone else. Malena is too new to the military life to understand the sacrifice quite yet. She's getting there. I was surprised at how well she took the news of me leaving. I expected a blowout—a fight so large, I'd end up leaving without closure. Instead, she showed me her strength. Proving again without a shadow of a doubt she's the woman for me.

Her sun-kissed body is sprawled in my white sheets, one leg out, her skin glowing in the early sunlight. I won't

tossing it

wake her. That would be too hard, too costly a mistake for a man trying to leave everything behind. My mind needs to be clear, eye on the prize. Finishing this fucking war and getting back to my life. For the first time in my life, I get it. I understand how much another person can mean. Why I'm fighting so fucking hard. I realize what life is truly about.

I swallow hard as I gaze down at her chest rising and falling softly. Her eyelashes flutter and a smile creeps to one corner of her mouth. I wonder if she's dreaming of me, thinking of us. Will she remember me? How my touch causes an immediate reaction? What it feels like when I'm deep inside her? How quickly will those new memories fade into distant memories? I shudder. A painful realization. Her life will go on without me and I have to take it on her word that she'll be here when I return. If I return.

I didn't tell her how dangerous this year would be for me. A no-fail mission means I'm willing to go down with the ship to make sure this ends successfully. I'd give up my life to make sure she's safe. Forever. Saying goodbye to my parents and sisters was easy. They're used to this. It's an old hat gesture to send me away. I think they knew it would be hard for me to bid Malena farewell and let me off easy with a quick breakfast sendoff last weekend. Celia promises to continue to make sure Ms. Winterset is doing well, and Eva deems herself responsible for keeping Malena occupied. I tell her that's not necessary, but I know she will do what she wants regardless of what I say.

All of these months of dating and I've never given Malena any sort of significant gift. Nothing tangible to remember me by. I found a ring last week at the only jewelry store in town, a pawn shop, it made me think of her. It can mean whatever she wants it to mean, and the fluidity in that makes me happy and terrifies me at the same time. I want to keep her. Forever. The ring is simple, a gold band with tiny diamonds sprinkled into it with no real pattern. It reminded me of little clusters of stars in the sky and what they look like during a jump at night. The guy behind the counter asked if I needed it engraved and I didn't have much time to think of what I wanted but decided on the first thing that came to mind: *You are my night sky*.

I have to go or else I'll be late for the flight and I don't want to be the asshole holding up a plane. Usually that's Aidan because he's been out all night fucking. He's coming with me for this mission. I set the ring and a letter on the nightstand. With a pain deep in my chest and tears threatening, I turn from the room and exit my house, locking the door behind me.

Mr. Olsen is out in his chair. When he spies the big bag I have slung over one shoulder, he nods at it. "Gone for a while?"

Sighing out the pain, I nod. "Yeah. Too long."

He smiles, a twinkle in his eye. We both know he will be gone before I return. "I'll see you when I see you. Get them assholes, son. Get 'em."

"I intend to, sir."

Mr. Olsen nods to the door, his pallid face and gaunt eyes on display in an errant ray of sun. "She's a good one. Better come back for her."

"I intend to do that as well," I reply. "Take care of yourself. Malena will help you out. Don't be afraid to ask her for anything you need. Eva and Celia, too. Anything. You hear me?"

"As long as you aren't afraid to ask for what you want," he replies.

It's a loaded statement. "I'm not afraid of anything. You know that." I grin.

"Everyone is afraid of something, even big muscled SEALs. If I can give you one piece of advice before I go," he says. We both know he said I instead of you, and it stings. The bite of death knocking when you have no control. I nod. "Nothing is more important than family. I lost mine and I thank God I got the cancer so I can be with them sooner." He looks up to the sky and it's a revelation. A fucking pang resonates because I know he's right, and maybe no one has said it before, or I didn't listen. "Everything in this life is fleeting. Make sure you use the time wisely, son."

I agree, give him a hug, and make sure he has phone numbers for anyone who I think may help him if need be. I'm feeling like a morose asshole when Aidan picks me up. He makes a sex joke, but catches onto my bad mood right away and shuts the fuck up. Should I have said goodbye? Should I have turned down this mission? I'm not even sure it would have been an option. I know the most about the target, this is basically my mission now. Aidan parks at the airport and we grab our bags from the back of his truck. One of the other guys will grab his truck and store it for the time we're away. Our plane is waiting and ready as we approach.

We board, take off into the morning sun, and circle around to the west. I hate everything about it. I keep my eyes peeled for my house from the air, but by that time we're too high up to see people. Just shapes. The shape of my roof. The shape of the ocean, the bay. The shape of my fucking heart vanishing beneath me.

I throw up into a barf bag.

Aidan chuckles, but I merely shake my head, still in no mood for his bullshit. I open my computer and start working, start scouring the reports and my emails for new information. I begin talking to the SEALs on the west coast. This is war.

And it's my job to finish it.

It's been two months and it's a constant stream of work and meetings. We're on the large San Diego SEAL compound so we have all of our training facilities at our beck and call. In between planning, we're shooting and working out, honing the skills that may have been pushed to the back burner while in Bronze Bay. It's a whole different world here. One that I'd forgotten. The breakneck pace. The falling into bed at night so tired I'm not sure if I pass out or fall asleep. My limbs are sore and my arms are full of holes from the doctors poking and prodding to make sure I'm in top-notch condition. My body is in fine shape compared to my emotions. I fucking miss Malena so much it's hard to talk to her on the phone. When I hear her voice, I want her.

Wanting her turns into a haunting reminder of everything I won't have for an entire year. I tried to be honest. Tried to tell her talking to her makes everything more difficult, but she said I need to get freaking used

tossing it

to it. I won't, but I'll pretend for her benefit. She is busy with her work and friends and seems to be doing well. It's all so superficial. Not like those deep thought provoking conversations we'd have when we were together, lying naked in bed, staring at the ceiling, together. The quiet, poignant moments are gone and in their place are conversations about weather and Bronze Bay gossip. It would be horrifying if it wasn't Malena. But it's her, so I gobble up every single syllable she utters, harboring the desperation deep within.

She emails me once a day and tells me everything. Some days she'll attach photos of us. Other days it's photos of her and her friends at the beach. It's strange to feel homesick for a place that was never truly my home. I have learned that home is a person. Home is Malena. Home isn't where I'm at. I try to email her back, but my schedule and the time difference makes everything that much harder. She'll stay up late some nights so we can video chat, and I'll wake up early other days when I don't have meetings or obligations, but it doesn't happen very often.

I have a secure phone line and safe internet access that blocks out everyone who isn't on an approved list. My inbox has a few new emails. Two brand new from Malena, one from Garden Breeze, and one from Eva. I don't have time to check them right now because I'm due in the office for a meeting and then a workout. My body has already transformed back into the peak machine it was before my life slowed down. My nutrition is monitored and my daily workouts tailored for my body. There are cryo tanks that soak our bodies to help our muscles recover faster, and hundreds of highly trained support staff on hand for any desire or concern. A lot of distractions on top of the main facets of tracking killers.

"You ready?" Aidan pops his head into my room without knocking. We have nice quarters on base—a house we share. Our schedules are so busy we rarely see each other at home except for early mornings before the full day begins.

With the mouse hovering over Malena's email, I close the laptop and ask him if he wants a banana instead. I toss him one and we head out, locking the door behind us. "You have your workout first today?" he asks.

I shake my head. "Meeting, then workout. Then I have to go take a piss test," I tell him.

He laughs. "I'm taking my piss test first. I'll be happy when this is over," he says, breathing out.

It's surprising. "You want to go back to Bronze Bay?" I say, my tone mocking. "Too rough now that you're an old geezer?"

"Fuck you," Aidan says. "It was supposed to be a permanent switch. It's a big change. Admit it. I see you limping," he tosses his words over his shoulder.

Sighing, I look left and right as I step into the street. "I'm fucking perfect," I exclaim. "Ready for it to be done as much as you, but I have something to go back to."

"Maybe I do too," he quips.

He's such a liar. He has everyone else's chicks to try and steal. That's what Aidan has. "Did you see the last intel brief that came through? They're on this coast. It may happen sooner rather than later. I wish I could go right now and blow the motherfucker into outer space."

Aidan nods. "It's never that easy. Come on, bro. You know better." I do, but wishful thinking never hurt anyone. "See you at home, honey. Better have my bourbon waiting when I walk through the door and crotchless lace panties under your dress," Aidan rasps, splitting away from me as he heads to another building.

Shaking my head, I grin. No one else is around to hear him which only makes it that much more disturbing. The base is usually bustling at this time of day, but since the mission planning began, they've closed it down to everyone except SEALs and required support staff. I haven't left the gates since I arrived, and I'm itching to go beyond, back into the real world. I decide right now that I'm going to put in a request to leave base and go out to eat at a damn restaurant in town. I won't talk to anyone, and I'll find something that follows my diet, but I need to feel the buzz of life to level my head.

The Navy isn't granting leave to any of us. We're trapped here until it's go-time, unable to visit friends or family. It's supposed to be for our loved one's safety, but this is the first time in history there's been this kind of a full-scale hunt in the states so all of the rules have changed, and I'm not sure anyone knows what exactly to expect. I scan my ID card and press my thumb into the reader to open the heavy metal door, making sure to close the door all the way behind me.

Inside the building there is life. Lots of it. People in military uniforms litter the hallway from every branch imaginable, even foreign service members who are here to watch us operate for their own training regimes—taking our tactics and applying them to their own countries and problems. Nothing brings a world together quite like one common thread: the same enemy. I nod at a few men I recognize and bang a hard right into our wing and scan my ID again to get inside. It's a little more lax in here, some SEALs are wearing uniforms, and others are in PT clothing, black running shorts, and a brown tee, depending on what they have on their own schedules. We have relaxed grooming standards among dozens of other privileges that aren't granted to big Navy, it is most evident in the hairstyles we are allowed.

"You ready? We've been waiting for you. Twiddling your diddly again?" A SEAL in my group rasps, nodding his head toward my empty seat.

I chuckle, taking my place at the conference table and grabbing the tablet in front of me. "I'm only late because your mom likes to watch," I hiss back, glaring at him with a smirk.

"Mom jokes are out, Leif. You'd know that if you weren't so busy tanning your ass cheeks in Florida instead of back here with the *real* Teams working like a man."

The screen turns on and lights dim, and he has the last word…for now. The commander's red, irritated face flashes on the screen and the meeting begins. We get the notes on our tablet screens as someone gathers the important points during the exchange. My heart starts hammering as the facts trickle into my awareness. We're getting closer. I'm not thinking about zings, mom jokes, or anything other than what's in front of me. The familiar hatred creeps into my awareness, the power that thrums through my body to destroy.

I won't miss this time. I don't care what it costs me.

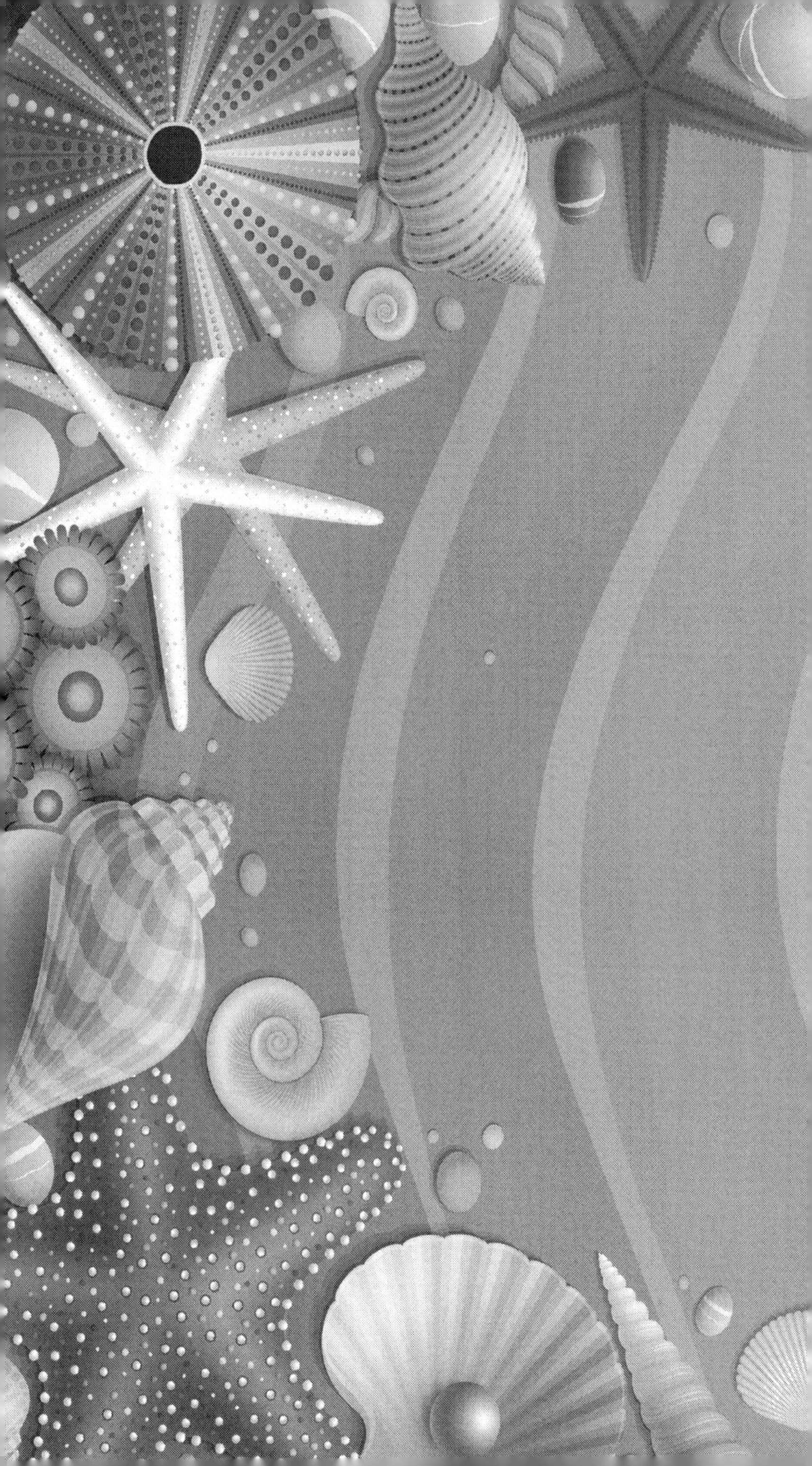

Chapter Fourteen

Malena

My mom has pneumonia. The doctors are in and out of her room regularly. They say she has the same care at Garden Breeze as she would have at a hospital. There are monitors beeping and saline bags dripping into her frail body. It came on quickly, a common cold morphing into this threatening monster overnight. Her coughing and wheezing make it seem she's on her deathbed. They reassure me she'll pull through, but there's this nagging feeling in my chest that tells me otherwise.

This, a mere hour after a doctor's appointment where I discovered that not only am I pregnant, but I am three months pregnant—a basically all the way formed baby in my still flat stomach. My shock and stymie are still there, but now I'm contending with my mother's life. I feel like in a matter of a few hours I've lost everything, including my grip on reality. With my head resting on the edge of her bed, I clutch Mom's hand, the one not drowning in tubes and needles, and sob. I pray. I ask God to let her remember everything. For her to wake up and remember I am her daughter, that she loves me, because I need her right now more than I've ever needed her in my life. I need the warm hug that tells me everything is going to be okay. The one she would give when I skinned my knee or had a fight with my best friend at school. My mom is the only person I have.

With my hand on my stomach, I acknowledge the life that will steal Leif away from me. The irony that this relationship will fail because of a baby, when another relationship ended when a baby didn't arrive, is too freaking much. Her door is closed, so her room is shrouded in a morbid darkness. Tears streaming down my cheeks, I walk over and throw open the door. A nurse comes in and checks her vitals and does her best to ignore me, but I see her gaze wander to the crazy woman clutching her stomach.

"I'm sorry," I say, manners dictating I should be presentable at any given time while in public. That's the southern way, and I am breaking that custom all to pieces in this moment of weakness. "I need a second or two. It's a lot. She looks so bad. That's all." My explanation must work because the nurse closes the door after she writes down notes on a thick file.

"Mom," I say. "I need you to hear me." My throat clogs with emotion as I sit back down in the chair next to her bed. "I'm having a baby and I need you to be here for me. Like you used to be here for me."

Her eyes flutter, her mind in deep sleep. A spluttering, horrible sounding cough breaks the silence. "Because you owe that to me!" I yell. "I never had a chance," I say, wincing. "It's your fault. It's all your fault! You got sick," I say, losing my breath. "He left because you got sick. It's all your fault!" My breaths are shallow now, my anger controlling my words. "Come back to me. Be here. For your grandbaby."

She doesn't move. Doesn't stir. Won't wake up and be my mother. "He doesn't want this baby, Mom. I'm going to do it by myself. I have to," I say, tone calmer. "I don't know how I'm going to do it. It's going to break me."

The doctor comes back in and sees my red-rimmed eyes. "Visiting hours are different for sick patients, Malena. I have to ask you to leave. She needs her rest. We will take care of her. I promise." The nurse must have sent him in, afraid of my apparent anger.

The need to bargain with the doctor for her life arises, but I squash it. He can't do anything more for her. No one can bring her back to life in the way I want. I thank the doctor for his time and flee Garden Breeze without a purpose, my mind a disaster. Do I tell Leif? How do I break up with him? There's no possible way I'd ask him to stay with me because of the baby. No one should be presented with that kind of pressure when they don't want a family. I think he may stay with me because of it, but that's not the kind of forced love I want, and he deserves to have a life of his own choosing. The life he thought he was getting with me.

I pull into a random parking lot and take out my phone. I fire off an email to Leif because I haven't done it yet today and I have expectations to meet regardless of my mental state. Especially if I want to hide this secret

tossing it

for any length of time. I need time. More time. I try to sound happy and write about the nice weather and the job I'm currently working on. I hit send in a blind, manic rush. On a second thought, I write up another email and tell him that my mother has pneumonia and tell him to call me as soon as he can. This pregnancy will label me a liar. It breaks apart the foundation our love was built upon.

The anger and terror slices deep, and I don't know who to call or who I can trust. Shirley. Shaking my head, no, I realize I can't talk to her or to Caroline about this. I need someone who is completely removed from my life. Someone who has no stakes in my failures or successes. Maybe it's the bitter resentment, or that I'm grasping to find some sort of positive in this, but I know who I need and want to tell. With tears in my eyes, I pull up the internet browser on my phone and begin searching. It doesn't take long to locate the information I need.

The name and address stares at me from the screen like a dirty joke no one finds funny. This is what I have to do. I head for home to change and shower off the doctor's office scent. Then I go to war.

I pull into the dusty side access road and park my car in one of the free spaces adjacent to the garage. Maybe it's because I'm still shocked, but I have no problems pushing open the office door and walking directly up to the tattered desk covered in flyers reminding people to get their oil changed. It smells like grease. It's a scent from my past. One that used to soothe my worries. How time changes things. Everything. "Where's Dylan," I ask, glaring at the bleached blonde receptionist with a swollen stomach. She ushers a little girl who can't be more than two to the waiting room with a fenced in area. It has a few broken toys and an old-fashioned box television tuned in to a kid's channel.

"What do you need done?" she lilts, leaning around me to try to glimpse my car. "He's finishing up a grease job, but can get to you next." *He got to you next*, I think bitterly.

I almost feel bad for her, but I can't. Nope. Today is the day the world will feel my wrath after years of never getting a break. "I'm Dylan's ex-wife. I need to speak to him about an important matter."

Her big blue eyes widen. A deer caught in headlights. She opens her mouth to respond but closes it again. "Let me get him," she says, rounding the corner again to pick up the toddler and uses a side door to walk into the garage area.

Closing my eyes, I breathe out. This could be my life, and the thought makes me want to be sick. Dylan comes through the door, eyes just as wide as the woman's was. "Malena, what in the hell are you doing here?" He doesn't say it in a mean way, he really is shocked and wondering what in the hell I'm doing here. I'd feel the same way if he popped into the General Store at any point in time that I was working there. Especially after all of these years of no contact.

I feel absolutely nothing when I look at Dylan. I wait

for it—the feelings I used to have for him, the feelings I have for Leif, and they don't come. Nothing except a blind numbness and a huge heap of regret. I needed this more than I would have ever thought. Swallowing down the horror, I whisper. "I need to talk to you outside."

"Is everything okay?" he asks me. The blonde slides through the door but doesn't put the girl down this time as she eyes me down suspiciously. "I'll be right outside if you need me, okay?" he says, kissing the woman's cheek. She looks pleased, victorious that she's won this prize of a man. It's laughable. Insane. Sad. I don't say so though. I would never go that far.

I lead him outside, to my car, and cross my legs at the ankle. "I'm fine," I say, shielding my eyes against the sun. "I came here to tell you I'm pregnant."

The words spoken aloud feel freeing. "Pregnant," I say again, pleased I'm able to say this word in his presence.

"What?" Dylan narrows his eyes.

"I'd say it was your fault we never got pregnant instead of mine, but it looks as if you've already started filling a minivan in there," I point to the office. "So, I guess it was just you and me together that didn't work. Thank God. Someone was looking out for me," I say, shaking my head. "You were dreadful at the end, Dylan. And you need to know that's not okay." I cross my arms at my chest.

He stares at my stomach like a gremlin is going to pop out and eat his face off. "Fuck, Malena. They said you couldn't, that it was doubtful you could ever have a baby." I remember the words. I lived by them. Our marriage died by them. "What was I supposed to do?

You knew how much children meant to me."

I shrug. "They were obviously wrong. Or things changed. I just wanted you to know that I'm pregnant and I'm glad it's not yours." Why? Now I'm pregnant by a man that doesn't want the baby. The juxtaposition of the two scenarios is laughable.

"I loved you, Malena. Wanted this life with you," he says quietly, motioning to the building with his first name emblazoned across the top in juvenile script. "More than anything in the world." Dylan must be on autopilot, because he kneels in front of me, and hugs my waist, the side of his face pressed against my stomach. My car is behind me so I can't back away. Too shocked to say anything, I freeze. "I'm sorry," he says. "I didn't treat you right."

Swatting his hands and face away, I step to the side to juke his grasp, disgusted he's apologizing now after everything we went through. "I was never enough for you," I say, shaking my head. "I came here to…"

"Let me know I was wrong," he finishes, standing and backing away. "I hope he knows how lucky he is to have you. Both of you." He takes another step away from me, his eyes shining with frustration and pain.

It confuses me even further, muddies my emotions. Shaking my head, I get into my car realizing what a lunatic I look like right now. How desperate for acceptance, that I've come to the one person who I thought would give it to me. "He gave it, Malena," I whisper to myself. "You got what you came for." I pull out of the spot and drive the fifty miles back to Bronze Bay with tears blurring my vision. I'm not even sure how I made it back home safely, forgetting the drive completely as I fall into my bed.

I twist the gold band on my right ring finger, the beautiful gift Leif gave me when he left. It's a reminder I don't want or need, so I pull it off and toss it across the room. I lied to my mother earlier. I'm not by myself. Nope, I have my baby, and I need to pull my shit together if I'm going to give it a beautiful life. I'll give myself a few days to be upset and then I will rally, regardless of what happens. The world is crumbling down around me in every single direction and without a lifeline, I'll have to do the best I can.

My cell phone rings from the dining room table. Finally. By the time alone, I know it's Leif. I answer the video call. "Hi," I say, my stomach tipping when I first glimpse his face. Love. Painstaking, soul-searing love.

"Hey," he says. "I'm so sorry about your mom, Malena. I got your email. She's going to be okay. How are you holding up? I'm so sorry I'm not there with you." His words are sincere, so full of truth that my lying soul singes in response.

"She's such a mess, Leif. You should hear her breathing. It rattles. Her cough," I say, but get choked up. "I don't want to upset you. I'm sure you have enough to worry about without adding this to your list."

"Malena, stop. Let's try to talk about something happy. Brighten the mood a bit," he says, face firm, no smile. "You know I don't mind anything that has to do with you. That includes your mother."

"I just…miss you," I say, crying. It's not pretty, it's jagged and steals my breath. "I wish you were here to hug me."

"I'd do a lot more than hug you if I were there," he counters, his lips tipping up in the corner. "Time is flying by. I'll be home before you know it." I want to tell him right now. He can make plans to stay in San Diego where he's happy and unhindered, but my pride won't let me quite yet.

"Listen, I wanted to call you to tell you I love you and that your mom is going to be okay. Eva emailed me today and told me I needed to call her as soon as I got her note and it's late, and I want to give her a call and make sure everything is okay before it gets even later. I will call you tomorrow." My heart sinks. "That's fine. I love you too."

"Chin up," he says. "Better yet, tits out."

I laugh, shaking my head. "I'm not in the mood for that right now."

"Fine. Fine. Malena?"

"Yeah?"

"Look out the window." I wander to the front door and open it up as far as it will go. The wind has picked up and it blows a sprinkling of rain around. "You're my night sky, baby." The stars shine bright, twinkling reminders of what I'll never have. I think about where my ring lays, over in the corner of my bedroom.

"Always," I reply.

"Goodbye, Malena," Leif says, then ends the call.

I stand outside, letting the little raindrops sting my skin like flying needles. The pain clears my foggy mind, and I subconsciously bring one hand to my stomach.

Goodbye, Leif, I think.

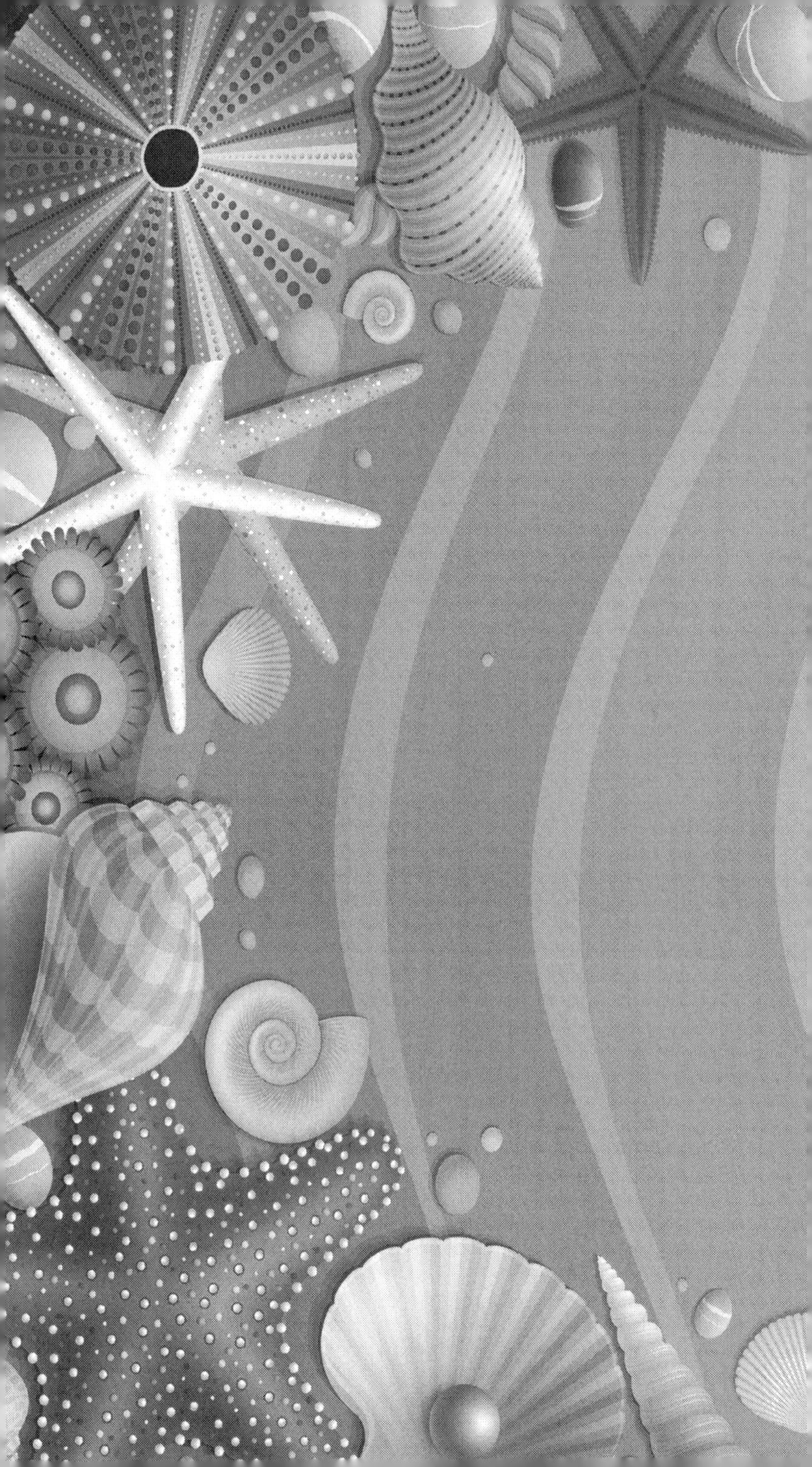

Chapter Fifteen

Leif

"Are you on your computer?" Eva asks. "I refuse to tell you anything until your sitting down and looking at your computer."

"Alright, alright. Don't be such a bossy bitch."

She sighs. "You're going to be eating those words in mere seconds," she says, her tone strained. "Pull up your messenger. I need to send a few things," Eva adds.

Irritation is all I feel at having to cut my phone call short with Malena for whatever trivial bullshit Eva wants me to see. Her screenname is darkened signaling she's sending something and an image pops up in our message on the secure server. I double click to open it.

And lose my breath. It's Malena, clear as day, as beautiful as I've ever seen, except there's a man hugging her around her waist, kneeling on the ground. It's obvious Eva took this photo while on some sister reconnaissance mission because of the angle and the distance. Another photo pops up on the screen and it's an image of Malena and this asshole talking, their faces close, and emotion spilling into the air between them. My throat feels full as my heart begins to hammer. A blind red rage clouds my vision.

"What the fuck Eva," I say into my phone.

Eva makes a little noise and I think it might be because she regrets what she needs to say, and that says something because Eva regrets nothing. "Celia called me to tell me about her mom being sick, Leif. You have to understand I didn't plan on following her. She was pulling out of her road. I could see she was crying and I followed her because I was worried. Okay? It was about forty-five miles to some bum hick town in the middle of nowhere."

My heavy breathing is the only response I give her.

"I parked across the street at a little gas station to fill up my car, assuming she was getting her car fixed or something because it was a mechanic shop. It seemed weird to drive that far away if her car was broken, but she came out right away, this guy behind her. They had this heated conversation and I…" Eva trails off. "Just knew something was between them. Body language and their facial features. Everything. It was intimate in nature even if Malena seemed upset."

I enlarge the photo and confirm everything she's saying. It's awkward, like I'm looking at someone else's love story. "Who is he?" I ask, only because I know Eva wouldn't come to me with just photos. She is a fucking FBI agent when it comes to shit like this. I think it's why she gets on in Bronze Bay so well. "Dylan Bowers," she says. "Leif." "What?" I ask, running a hand through my hair as I remember the first time I met Ms. Winterset and she called me Dylan. "Stop beating around the bush. Just fucking say it out loud. What else do you know?"

"They were married."

All the air leaves my lungs. Every moment between Malena and I tainted by a singular, nonnegotiable lie. "Married? Are you sure?"

She sends another photo and it's the marriage and the divorce certificate in one PDF image. "I'm positive," she says after giving me a second or two to review the photo. "I asked around after I pulled the information online and I guess it was a huge scandal. They were high school sweethearts. The type of couple who everyone says was destined to be together. Word on the street is Dylan never got over Malena and he's been trying to woo her back into his graces. Maybe with you being gone," Eva stutters. "It's a lot. The separation. I'm sure it's a lot for most people to deal with. Maybe it was a weak moment, Leif. It could be nothing."

"Or it could be everything. Thank you, Eva. Even if you just ruined my fucking life."

She scoffs. "I'm just as surprised as you are. You guys were it. I'm done. I'll leave her alone now. Okay?"

Or do I have her follow her around like an insecure dog? That's not me. It can't be. It's never been me. "I need a bit to sort things. I'll talk to you later."

We end the phone call, but I continue staring at the computer screen and the images that tell a story I'm not a part of. His face. It's almost more than I can bear witness to. This was a private moment never meant to see the light of day. I'd feel guilty if this didn't change everything for me. I thought I meant more to her than this. I could get over the omission of the marriage and divorce, I think. With a ton of time and soul searching, but I'll never get over these photos and whatever the fuck they mean. I want to kill him.

It's too late to call Malena so I do what she does every day. I write her an email and I tell her about the weather here in San Diego. My words convey a bland temperament of someone who is distancing themselves from a situation or person. Maybe that's what she's been doing over the course of these two months. The emails formed as her easy way to get out of a relationship with me to be with him. A man who she used to call husband. Shared a bed with. Shared a life with. I close my eyes when the sting in my chest becomes unbearable.

In the last paragraph, I ask her to explain herself and the photos. I also attach the marriage and divorce certificates and ask about those as well. I tell her what I think the photos mean in the most concise manner I can manage without hurling every single curse word in the English language. I tell her to confirm I'm right and to walk away if I am. What I don't do is give her any indication of how these photos and her lie make me feel. I'm not giving her that power over me. The reason I feel like a gutter slum right now is because she had that power to begin with.

I'm blindsided.

"Time to go! Our leave request was approved, fucker. Let's go eat tacos and drink beer!" Aidan roars from the other side of my bedroom door. An off night. A rare pleasure. I pause for a moment or two wondering if I'm approaching this in the correct manner before hitting the send button. Fuck it. She wasn't thinking about me when she was visiting this guy, didn't have a thought of me in her mind. One time she said she'll always be the one who needs me more. Such bullshit.

Closing my laptop, I call out, "Yep." Then head to open my door.

"You okay?" Aidan says. The dude might be an asshole superb on most days, but I can't deny he knows me well, and vice versa. That's what's best about our brotherhood. We can move from razzing each other to supporting each other in a way no other friendship can. Not until you've fought side by side, for your life, saving each other's, can you understand how deep the brotherhood goes. We've earned our right to be assholes to each other.

I think about showing Aidan the photos, but then I think better of it because of the emotion on their faces. It's that embarrassing—that telling. "Yeah, man. Woman problems," I say, hoping that will suffice. "I need this night out more than ever."

"What happened? Malena realized what a tool you were and changed her cell number?"

"Ha-ha. I wish," I say, sighing. Aidan picks up on the shift immediately. "Way worse."

"Oh. Let's get out of here, and you can tell me about it at the bar." His eyes shift from mine and away just as quickly, also a telling sign.

I laugh a little. "You're really going to drink beer? Just because they granted us leave for tonight doesn't mean we'll be alone. I bet they have people trailing us all night. We're in deployment status, dude. I'm going to mind my manners like a good boy." I try to change the subject, but the words left unsaid hang in the air.

"Well, I'm going to have to pretend no one is watching

because they have us trapped on this base like a prison. It's never been this bad before," he remarks. "Remember the good ole' days? There wasn't war in the states, I suppose. It's hard to get used to."

"It hasn't been this bad before," I agree. Before the attack that changed the world as we know it, we were just a part of the Navy. Yes, a special operations part of the Navy, but now they treat us like a nonrenewable resource. They aren't allowing people into BUD/s like they used to. You can't trust anyone these days. Moles are everywhere and to prevent them from infiltrating the very heart of our military, they put a kibosh on accepting candidates until we have a more thorough way to screen individuals. The technology is coming, I've seen it, but it's not there yet. In the meantime, we wait, atop a golden throne of stay the fuck away from everyone during this mission, and pray no one gets hurt. "It could be the end," I say.

"That's ominous. What exactly is that in regards to?" Aidan says, opening the door to a black pickup truck. They belong to the base and we use them to get from one side to the other of the expansive compound. My stomach sinks as I conjure the different meanings of the end.

I get in the passenger side as he starts the engine. "Everything, man. Just fucking everything," I reply. "I'm going to tell you the whole story and without being a douche canoe, I need you to tell me what your take is."

"Without joking once?" he asks, pulling onto the road that will lead us to freedom.

"Not once," I confirm.

We have to scan both of our ID cards to open the gates

and the guards make note of the time and license plate number. Aidan sighs as the process takes longer than it should. "Fine. Tell me everything. I'll probably make jokes about it tomorrow though." "That's fine," I say, grabbing my ID from his hand after the guard hands it to him. I nod my chin at the man in uniform, making sure to give him eye contact. Aidan does the same. It's tense. It wouldn't have surprised me if they'd started laughing while saying, "Gotcha. No night out for you! Get your asses back home." We pull into traffic—free.

"Head down the strand," I tell Aidan. "I don't feel like doing Gaslamp tonight."

Ne nods. "We need that much time, huh?"

"More than we have tonight," I say, sighing. "Unfortunately."

"Don't dick the dog. Just out with it."

It makes me sick as I tell him the whole story, not leaving a single detail out. I try to keep the narrative positive, because even subconsciously I'm trying to protect Malena from any back blow. Even when she's as fucking wrong as they come. Aidan keeps his face neutral, wincing when I describe the images Eva captured. His eyebrows shoot up when I tell him the tidbit about her failed marriage and I remind him not to crack a single joke unless he wants me to crack his face. He nods once, compliant as a friend can be in a moment like this.

"I gave her a ring before I left, man," I say, swallowing hard. "There was no question in my mind what she meant or how far I'd go to keep her. No other woman compares and it makes me sick to think I'm just some dude she can toss away so easily." *When you say you're the kind of guy you toss? What exactly does that mean?*

tossing it

Malena asked me. I defined it for her so very clearly, and here I am surprised by the outcome. Like a sign that says IDIOT should be flashing over my head, signaling how I botched this from the word go. Maybe Dylan is her keeper, the man I've been preventing her from going back to until now. Banging a fist on the dash, I let out a roar.

Aidan swallows hard. "You haven't straight up asked her what the deal is? Face to face, or by video chat though?"

I shake my head. "This is fresh information. Just the email." Now it seems a little immature. I should have called her. "I wasn't thinking clearly. She does that to me. It's unnerving," I explain. "You wouldn't know the feeling, man."

"Sounds like I don't fucking want to know that feeling," he says. "Sounds like this is a bunch of horse shit and drama that I'd do well to avoid. This is what I think of anytime someone asks me if I'm going to settle down with a woman. This. Right here. Is it worth it? All of this heartache?"

"I guess it remains to be seen. I'll keep you posted,"

"Wait. This is the first time you've...cared for a woman before?"

"Yeah," I say, shrugging. "Without a shadow of a doubt." All I'm left with to show for it are shadows and doubts.

The strand is a long stretch of road that leads to Imperial Beach and it lays in front of us. There's sun begins to set as we talk through my messy love life. He asks questions I'm surprised by, and I give him answers that he never expects. Aidan keeps his eyes on the road, as do I, out of habit, and also because while we're off tonight, we're still on alert. You don't see the things we've seen and live a normal, carefree life ever again.

"The taco place?" Aidan asks, either trying to change the subject or giving me an out to be finished with this conversation. "Figured low key might be best," he adds.

Running my hands down my face, I say, "Yeah." And even though there are probably a thousand taco places in Imperial Beach, he knows the one. The same one we frequented when we first arrived in San Diego all those years ago. It was delicious, cheap, and fast. "You see that black car that just passed?" I add, narrowing my eyes looking at the side mirror to try to catch a glimpse of the tail end of the sedan.

"Yeah, looks like a convoy of sorts," he replies, nodding in front of us at the cars heading toward us in the opposite lane of traffic. Another sleek sedan passes with windows tinted so dark we're unable to see how many passengers are inside. The next car, exactly the same as the first two slows down, a significant change in speed, and Aidan follows suit. "What the fuck is going on, man," Aidan whispers. It's not a question, it's a statement. "A suicide bomber?" he asks, eyes cutting to mine quickly, and then focusing back on the car, now crawling toward us. There are no cars behind us in our lane, and there's one car quite a distance behind the one creeping toward us. The four cars, the two that passed going in the opposite direction and the two now moving toward us, are all identical.

My hand automatically falls to my sidearm on my hip under my T-shirt. A weapon that would have no purchase in a fight against a bomb. "No. The car is too nice," I say, letting my mind wander back to our meeting earlier in the day. This is what the war has done to us. This mentality of assuming the very worst right off the bat. Action first. Questions later. Innocent lives have been lost when we pause to question before springing to action. "The two that passed have stopped," I say, shifting in my seat. While this truck is armored, like any military use vehicle, we'd be fucked if a bomb is involved.

"Call it in," Aidan says.

"So much for someone following us," I say, regretting my earlier statement. We need backup. The phone call to base takes mere seconds as I give them exact details of the situation, I disconnect as the sleek car veers into our lane and blocks all forward movement. "Fuck," I mutter, opening the glove box rooting around for anything that might help us.

Aidan swallows hard, pulls the truck to a stop and puts it in park, his concealed carry already in hand. It will take our heavily armed backup at least ten minutes to get down this far. Underneath the seat, I find an errant bulletproof vest someone stashed after a training session and toss it to Aidan. He doesn't question it and slides it over his head, on top of his shirt, gaze focused on the imminent threat in front of us. "Wait them out," I say. "Give the boys more time to get here," I say. "They'll bring the bomb squad just in case. Staying put is our best chance if these bastards get funny." What else would they be doing? Why would they stop us? They wouldn't know who we are. Except for…the truck. They'd know our vehicle.

My heart is pounding, and my stomach turns upside down as different scenarios flit through my mind. My chest rises and falls as I watch the car door open. I check the clock on the dash. We need more time, but we also have to stay ahead of the situation. The cars behind us are still far enough in the distance that our focus should remain in front of us. "Okay, fucker," Aidan growls. "Ready?"

"Yes," I reply, the grip on my gun tight, my only weapon. A man in a dark suit steps out of the car, a casual swagger in the slight movement, sunglasses covering his eyes. He's being protected, it's obvious. "Cover me," Aidan says, stepping out of the truck, staying behind the open door. Opening the passenger side door, I repeat the movement, keeping my gun between the jamb and the truck.

The sunglasses come off. "You boys are all alone," the accented voice calls. "How explosively perfect." He grins, and two more men similarly dressed step from the back seat of the car, guns bigger than ours clutched in their hands.

"State your intentions," I demand. A verbal threat would make this easier on paperwork.

"For men so elite, you are ignorant. Why would you leave your guarded playpen?" One of the men barks at us. His voice pierces me, sets the ringing bells of familiarity into a warning siren inside my mind. It's him.

I try to keep my voice down and tell Aidan my realization. He stiffens, his whole body processing what exactly this means. "He's mine," I say, taking in my surroundings, the positioning of the other car. Aidan will start left, I'll go from the right. With limited ammunition, this is going to be a challenge. I contemplate if trying to run them over with the truck would be a quicker option, then decide against it. Explosives. There has to be explosives. This fucker's favorite game is comprehensive, small devices that create devastating damage.

"The second car is their go car," Aidan says. "Take out the tires."

"We don't have that kind of ammo," I deadpan.

Aidan chuckles. "Guess you better shoot straight." Aidan shifts his weight, leveling his aim. "Next step," he says.

"Yep," I throw back, checking the mirror to confirm the cars behind us are still as far away as they were the last time I looked.

One of the bad guys that stepped from the back seat takes aim at Aidan with a ratty looking M4 and pulls the trigger. The bullet hits the door and pushes Aidan back a step, but it doesn't penetrate the panel. First fire means fair game, and I pick off the one in the back easily, his body falling to the ground. That's all it takes for all fucking hell to break out. Gunshots resound around us, loud and relentless as the bad guys scatter. More men appear from the go car, all of them with weapons far superior to ours.

Aidan takes out a guy, a perfect headshot, just as a searing pain seethes up one of my legs. A glance down proves blood is, in fact, seeping down my leg at a steady pace, a momentary distraction. My gun disappears from my hand as a bullet picks it off, sending it flying through the air, rendering me useless, weak, bleeding, and fucking unarmed.

I fall over into the seat of the truck, unable to stand on the leg bleeding out. Aidan only glances at me briefly before leaving the safety of the paneled door to seek out my weapon, our only chance. I see the two cars in the mirror rapidly moving toward us—one in each lane.

Aidan appears in the mirror, cutting my view of the cars. He has my gun. He has it. He takes a bullet in his chest plate and I hold my breath for him, knowing how strong the blow feels when you're hit.

"Toss it," I call out to him, leaning out of the truck on my good leg, holding out my hand. "Fucking toss it," I scream, sweat dripping down my face. He does and by some grace, I'm able to catch it and pick off the guy approaching my side of the truck.

"We're fucked! Where is the backup?" Aidan calls.

Limping, trailing more blood than I'm letting myself process, I stumble toward the bastard reloading his gun. My guy. My guy. My guy. My guy.

"No! Leif," I hear Aidan say, but he's already firing toward the assholes approaching from the back.

This is the moment. My defining moment. With the black, steel clutched in my outstretched hand, my other hand steadying it, I take aim at the bastard's head and pull the trigger. A misfire. No bullet. He laughs and turns his fully loaded M4 on me.

The world goes black.

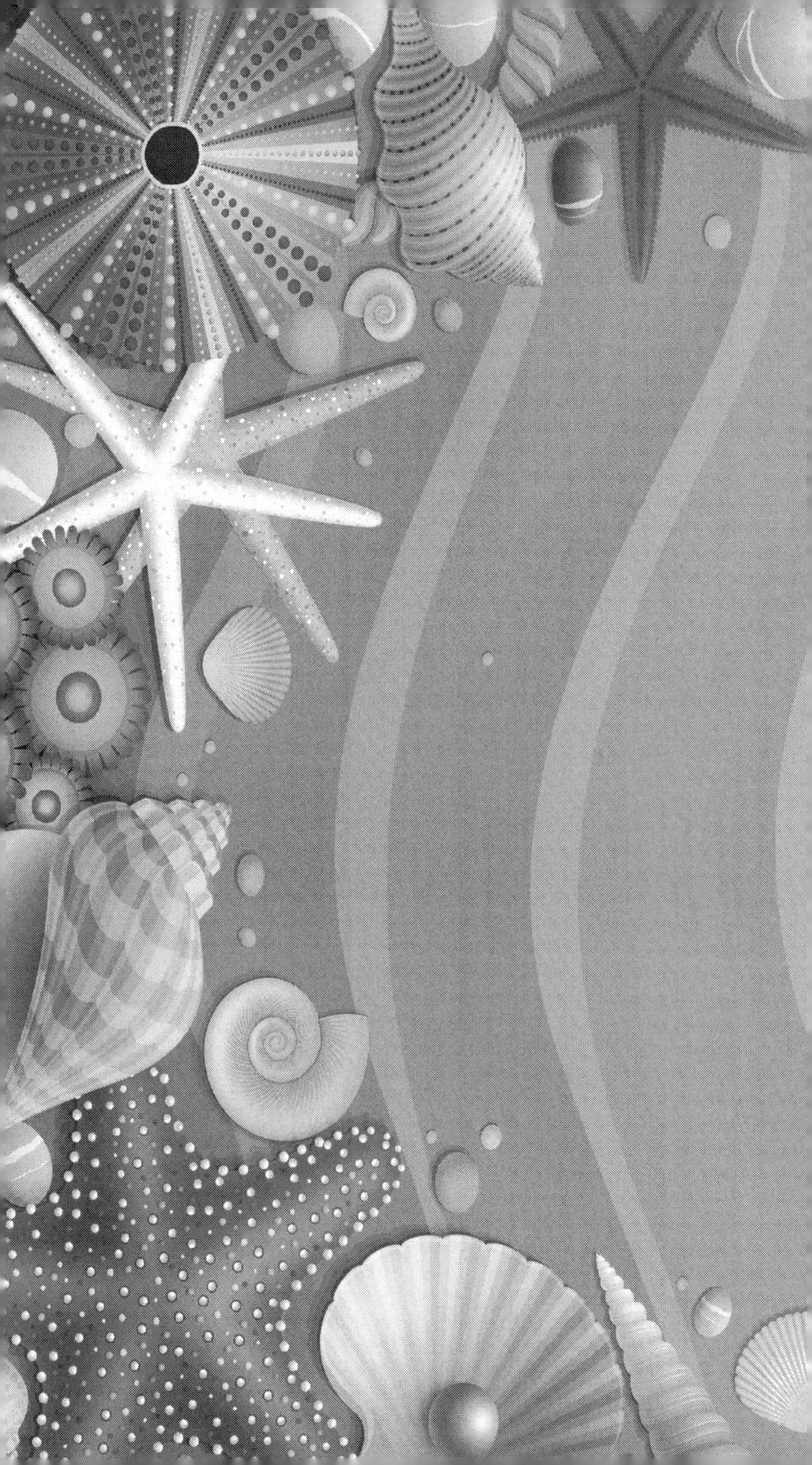

Chapter Sixteen

Malena

Nine months later . . .

She died on a Friday. About a week after I broke up with Leif. Of complications brought forth by the pneumonia. I buried her in a plot next to the Baptist church. The whole town showed up for the funeral. After she passed, I moved in with my cousin Amber, I always knew she would be there for me when it mattered. It was mostly so I could stay out of the Bronze Bay limelight when my pregnancy finally started showing. And so I wouldn't have to be alone all the time. I worked in Amber's coffee shop and kept up with my business as best I could. My friends eventually found out about the pregnancy, but I still stayed away, unable to shake the memories of my hometown. Of my mom. Of Leif.

Leif sent me an email with photos of Dylan and I attached. I still don't know who I have to thank for the

tossing it

images, but they were the perfect excuse to make an easy break. When he questioned the photos, I told him the biggest lie of my life. That I was in love with another man, my ex-husband, and never wanted to see him again. I wrote the email and nearly hyperventilated moments after I hit send. Leif never tried to contact me after that and I still feel guilty for letting him believe the absolute worst of me after everything he did for my mother.

I lost my mom long before she was buried. I grieved the memories shared ages ago. When she passed away, it was merely the last step of saying goodbye to the vessel that used to house my mother. It was closure. In a way, it was the beginning of a completely new life.

After the baby arrived, I moved back to Bronze Bay, mainly because I needed more space for all of the baby gear and supplies. She has taken over my world almost completely. My heart was hers from the second she blinked her bright blue eyes, the same shade as her dad. She has a darker skin tone, like me, but her hair is a light blonde to compliment her eyes. She is beautiful and healthy. Everything I never knew I needed. When I first looked at her, a desperate sadness took over—reminding me of the love lost, that I'll never have again. It didn't take long for me to realize how blessed I am to have living breathing proof that such a thing even exists.

Her name is Luna Winterset, and she changed everything. It's hard single parenting. It's lonely. Every tear and late night is worth it. Loving her is as natural as breathing. Caring for her gives my life a new purpose.

Shirley is cradling Luna on the sofa. I called her to come over so I can clean out my mom's room. It's time. Luna will need a larger room soon, and I've been avoiding the heartache for as long as I can. I push open the bedroom door and I'm hit with the scent of my mother. A mix of flowers and laundry soap. It's tinged with a musty, uncleaned scent, but she's still in here. My skin pricks. Rubbing my arms, I enter and head for her bed where a sealed, cardboard box sits unopened. A package Garden Breeze mailed after cleaning out her room. With the razor blade clutched in one hand, I slide it across the tape and open the box. Her robe is on top. I toss it and a few nightgowns into an empty laundry basket. There's a couple vases, the photo albums I brought her, and tucked into the side, is her notebook.

I grab that, interested in any words she might have scribbled down, but not expecting much. There's a sealed envelope, my name printed on the front in my mother's shaky handwriting. It's crumpled, almost as if it was thrown away on accident. I feel my heartbeat in my neck as I slide my finger under the flap to open it. My eyes blur with tears when I see a page filled with words. For me. Luna squeals a contented coo as Shirley sings a funny song. With my daughter's voice in my ears, I read my mother's note. It's dated a couple weeks after she settled into Garden Breeze.

Malena, my sweet baby love,

Thank you for this. For this place. With the garden and the intelligent doctors who help me. They are kind. As kind as you were all of these years to care for me. Thank you for those years, baby. I don't know how long I'll remember this, and it gets a little spottier each time, but this time you are the only person that stands out clearly. You must miss me. You must feel so alone in this world. Malena, I must write quickly, as fast as I can, because I need you to know that you don't have to be alone, that a man loves you so severely that hearing him speak of you gave me this flash of clarity. It stung me on a soul level, forced me to remember what true love feels like. Leif came to visit me today and although he kept saying he knew I wouldn't remember, and I'm sure that's why he said the things he did, and why he told me of his feelings for you. He said that when you smile, it brings meaning to his life. Leif wants to be with you forever. He said that you are the only person in the world that his heart will ever belong to. Baby, the way he spoke of you, his heart is yours. I hope that your heart is his. You'll never be alone if you have a love like that. A partner. A lover. If I don't remember in the morning, know this is what I want for you. I had it for a short time with your father, and you were born of that love. Had disease not addled my brain, I don't doubt your father and I would still have it. Please, darling. You are worthy of so much more than you give yourself credit for. Leif said you opened his eyes to loving on a different level. He wants to have a family with you and take care of you and any future children. His words brought me such comfort, a relief that there is hope for humanity. I can only assume if you've created such an effect on his heart, that you have strong feelings for this man as well. Don't be afraid to ask for what you want from him. Be truthful in your love. Don't sacrifice a life for me anymore. Don't sacrifice love for anything.

I love you so much and I am so proud of the woman you have become. You are brave and kind. Sweet baby love, if there's one thing I never had time to teach you it was that there are only two things you never let go of: love and yourself. Hold tight to both of those. Thank you for being there for me when you shouldn't have had to. Watching you grow up was a great privilege. Your life, my greatest accomplishment. I love you. I'm so sorry. I

love you.
Forever love,
Mom

Tears dropped onto the page, onto her words. Words I will cherish for the rest of my life. Truths that tear open my chest and steal my oxygen. My eyes seek out one sentence again and again. *He wants to have a family with you and take care of you and any future children.* How? Why wouldn't he tell me this? He thought I couldn't have children. Knew it wasn't ever going to be in the cards with a relationship with me. Shaking my head, I let the rush of pain inside. I push it away most days because it makes me weak and my daughter needs a strong mother.

"You doing okay in here?" Shirley strolls in, Luna on her hip, grabbing her hair. Her gaze dips to the piece of paper shaking in my hand.

I hold it out to her but resist handing it over when she tries to grab it. "It changes everything," I cry, taking Luna from her and hugging her to my chest. "I've been cruel. What have I done?" I whisper into my baby's ear, inhaling her sweet scent. She looks at me and I have to close my eyes to banish Leif's face.

Shirley reads the letter a few times, her eyes growing large as she finishes the third time, letting the knowledge soak in. "Fuck."

"Language," I bark at her. "I know," I say in the same breath.

"What are you going to do?"

I shake my head. "I have to go to him, Shirley. I have to tell him. This letter changes everything. I've ruined it, I'm sure."

"You did what you thought you had to do. For Luna. You couldn't have kids and he didn't want a family. You made a selfless decision, Malena. Don't beat yourself up over this." She holds the piece of paper up between us. The words give me comfort and tear me apart at the same time. I grab it from her and set it on the bed for later. I'll read it a thousand times.

I swallow hard. "I have to call him. Or email him. Tell him the truth. He deserves the truth. I did what I thought would be easiest, Shirley. Not what was right," I reply, shaking my head. "I didn't give him the option for fear of him feeling trapped."

Moving fast, I bypass Shirley and head for my open laptop. With his baby in my lap, I tap out a quick email asking him to call me and apologizing for not getting into contact sooner. I don't say anything about Luna or my lies. That's a conversation I need to have in person.

"I told you from day one he was a good guy," Shirley says, both hands on her hips.

Narrowing my eyes, I say, "Please, now you're going to tell me this. You agreed with not telling him about Luna."

"I'd say anything to get my friend back, Malena. You abandoned us here when your mom died."

Closing my eyes, I place a kiss on the baby's head. "I had to. The gossip was easier to control when I came back and she was already here. I didn't have to make up any stories." I send off the email and hold my breath as I watch it leave my outbox. "His sisters," I say.

"They haven't been around here since he left. They cleaned out his house and helped move Mr. Olsen's stuff out after he died, but they're gone, Malena. Without Leif here, they had no reason to hang around." Wincing, I remember discovering Mr. Olsen passed away and I wasn't here to help. I was very pregnant and there was no way I could risk seeing Leif's sisters, so I stayed away. Like a selfish, awful person.

I scroll my cellphone until my finger is hovering over Celia's name. I press the green button without thinking twice. She answers on the third ring, out of breath.

"Hello?"

My breath catches. She must hate me. The bitch she thinks cheated on her brother. "It's Malena, Celia. Hi. How...are you?"

She sighs. "Malena," she says. I hear her swallow. "I'm good. How are you doing? I was sorry to hear about your mother."

My heart trips. "Thank you," I reply, meeting Shirley's eyes. She nods, exaggeratedly, urging me on. "That's sort of why I'm calling, Celia. I just came across a letter she wrote and I was hoping you could tell me the best way to get in touch with Leif." Saying his name out loud slices. It's unfamiliar and that fact makes me break out in a cold sweat. "If you don't mind, telling me, that is. I need to clear something up and fast."

"Malena," Celia whispers. "You don't know?"

"I don't know what?"

She laughs. "Why would you know? You broke his heart and left him. Why would you care?"

"You don't understand. I'm so sorry," I say. "Please. Please, Celia. Tell me." I already know it's not good.

"He was almost killed in an attack off base nine months ago. He's been in a coma every day since, unresponsive. They're pulling life support on Monday. They've done everything they can for him and we can't fight the hospital's attorneys anymore. It's over."

"What?" Half of my brain has processed the tragedy and the other half refuses to accept it as truth. "That can't be. There's no way. Where is he?"

"I won't tell you. You don't deserve it. I saw the photos."

"It wasn't what you think, Celia. I need to see him. His daughter needs to meet him. Please."

"What are you talking about, Malena? I'm at work, and I don't have time for bullshit today."

"It's not bullshit. It's a very long story, but I do have Leif's baby. She's four months old now and looks just like him. He didn't want kids, Celia. You know that. I broke up with him so he didn't have to take on that burden. I did it because I love him. I wanted him to live the life of his choosing and now I find out that not only has he not been living, he's almost dead. Please, if what you say is true it won't hurt for me to visit him, to bring Luna to meet her father before he dies. She deserves that. Please, I'm begging you. I'll do whatever you say."

"You're serious," Celia says. "I can't believe this. The guy in the photos?"

"Was my ex-husband. An ex because I couldn't give him a baby. There was never anything between us after the divorce. I went there to tell him I was pregnant and to…to prove that it was never my fault, or maybe to get closure or something of the sort. I know what the photos made it look like and I'm sorry, but I had to use those to make a break from Leif. I saw it as my only way out. The only way he'd let me go without a fight."

"It never occurred to you to tell him the truth? That he would be happy about having a child with the woman he loves?"

My stomach roils. "No," I say, shaking my head as I wipe tears from my eyes. "He always told me how adamantly against children he was. You have to believe me."

"Eva is going to lose her fucking mind when I tell her this."

I sigh. "Don't tell her. Let me see him first. Where is he?"

She blows out a breath. "He's in Bethesda, Maryland. I'll meet you there otherwise, they won't let you in. How fast can you get there?" I'm already on the computer booking airline tickets when she asks the last question. "You're really going for shock factor, aren't you? I don't know how you were going to keep this secret."

"I have already booked tickets. We'll meet you there at five P.M. Please, just let me visit him before you alert every living relative of Luna. I've kept the secret this long because it means something to me. I want to protect her. I know I was wrong by keeping her from him and you guys, but I need this to be on my terms. Leif told my mother he wanted a family with me. It's what spurred this and why I need to make amends. I can't take back the past, but I can make things right going forward."

"I'll meet you there," Celia says, voice harsh. "Malena?"

"Yeah?"

"Be prepared for the worst. He's not the same person. He looks like he's already gone."

I let out a silent sob, covering my mouth. "I'm so sorry. I'll see you soon."

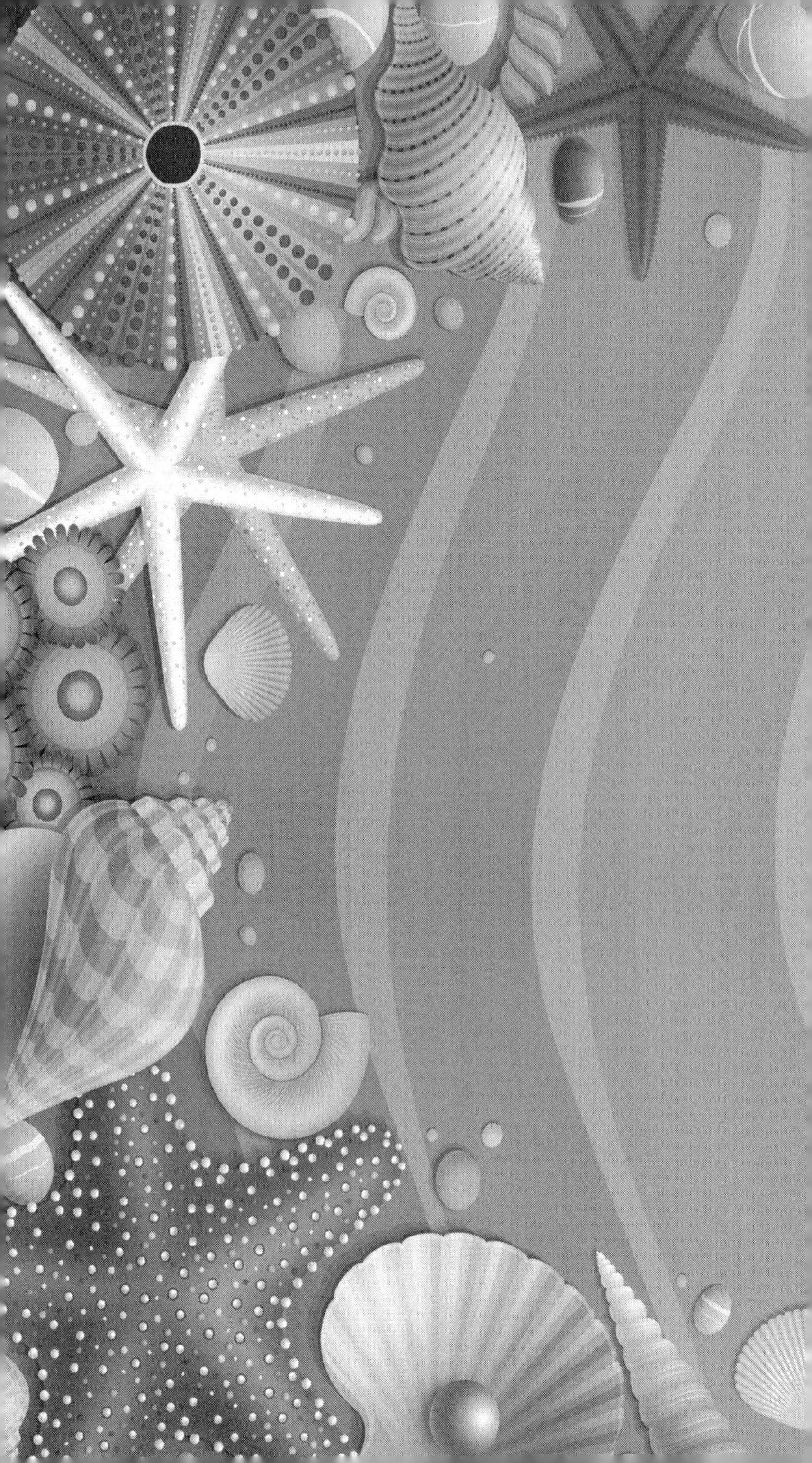

Chapter Seventeen

Malena

I slide Luna's sleeping body into Celia's waiting arms. "Your niece," I say, looking at Celia in her glassy eyes as she runs her hand over Luna's Leif colored hair. "She has his eyes. The exact same shade." Leif's sister has aged since I last saw her. A lot. So much that it pains me to see the severity of the agony she's endured without my knowledge. Pain I should have been sharing.

Celia slides her finger gently over her cheek. I see her falling in love. "She looks just like him," she remarks, unwrapping the blanket to look at her tiny fingers and toes. She rewraps her quickly as the hospital waiting room is freezing. Celia shakes her head. "I didn't believe you. It's a lot to take in, but there's no denying this is Leif's child. He would be so in love with her." A pang of regret hits me square in the chest. "I've arranged for the nurse to take you up to Leif's room. Go by yourself first. I'll stay here with her. Okay?" She meets my gaze, like she's wondering if I'll take the baby from her.

I nod. "That's fine. Here's her diaper bag just in case. She likes it if you hum when she's fussy," I say, gazing at my sleeping daughter adoringly. "You're her aunt, I'm sure you'll have the touch," I add. Celia beams down at the baby.

"This means so much. Having a piece of him. Thank you, Malena," she says, earnestly. "Luna lessens the blow of losing him."

She talks as if he's already gone and it's painful. I haven't had enough time to digest the severity. I glimpse over my shoulder once more before entering the elevator with the nurse, and Celia begins swaying back and forth with Luna. Luna loves that. She'll be fine I think to myself as the elevator begins its climb to Leif's floor. The nurse preps me when we're outside Leif's room. When I enter, I'm hit with a gust of warmer air and the typical antiseptic scent that belongs to hospitals. The man in the bed, hooked up to machines isn't my Leif. Celia was right. He is pale and wasted away to almost nothing.

His lashes flutter as I sit down on the edge of the bed, and take his skeletal hand in mine. The machine that breathes for him is loud and overbearing. Running my thumb across his knuckles, I say, "Sorry I haven't been by yet." The pit in my stomach forces the tears to fall. "I didn't know about the attack. I didn't know a lot of things, Leif."

I squeeze his hand and run my other hand across his pallid forehead. "They say they're taking you off life support because you can't live without it. I can't believe that, though." His hand twitches a bit, but the nurse said that may happen and not to think anything of it. His muscles spasm on their own. I wipe some of my salty grief from my face. "Leif, I came here to say hello and goodbye. I came here to tell you the truth even if you don't hear me, you deserve for me to say it out loud before you go."

Another squeeze of my hand and my heart skips. I can see why his family has fought for his life for this long. "I lied to you when I told you I was in love with another man because it was an easy way to let you go. My love for you is so strong that it can't even be compared to what I felt for Dylan. I visited him to tell him…to tell him…that I was pregnant with your baby. To shove it in his face. I'm sorry you saw the photos and thought something different was going on. I'm sorry I let you believe something else was going on between us. I haven't seen Dylan since that day. I don't even know if you got the email I sent. I assumed you did because you never contacted me. Now I see why," I say, sobbing. "I've only ever been in love with you, Leif."

Leif's monitor beeps and it startles me into a jump. "We have a daughter and she looks just like you," I tell him, stroking his face with my own tear-stained fingers. "She has blonde hair and blue eyes like you. She has my lips and ears. I think she has your appetite." I laugh, a small moment of happiness thinking about Luna's belches after she feeds. "I wish I got to see you hold her. I wish you could see her. What our love created. It's the coolest thing in the entire world. She's a real, live miracle. I think maybe this is why I was granted this miracle," I whisper, looking at the equipment keeping him alive. "She might be a parting gift from the world."

tossing it

I swallow hard, leaning down to press my lips against Leif's forehead. My touch is as light as a feather. His eyelashes flutter. I kiss each closed eye. "I'm going to make sure she grows up and knows how awesome her daddy is, Leif. Don't worry. I got this. I'm going to do right by her…by you. I'll make you proud."

There's light music playing, the radio, I realize and it happens to be the song that was on the jukebox at Bobby's Bar when Leif introduced himself to me. I smile, a sweet memory. The door creaks open and Celia moves into the room with a crying Luna.

"Sorry to interrupt, but I think she's hungry," Celia says, eyes apologetic.

I hold out my hands for Luna and she drops the crying baby into my arms. She soothes right away when she smells me. "Meet your daddy, Luna Love," I coo, bouncing her up and down in my arm, one hand still on Leif.

"I feel like he knows I'm here, Celia," I say.

She shakes her head. "We all feel the same way. You can't argue with tests, though. It's maddening."

"I wasn't supposed to be able to have a baby," I whisper. "We need one more miracle in our corner," I say. Celia sits in the chair next to me. "One more," I plead. I set Luna in the crook of his arm and the sight makes me weep for all of the memories she'll never have with him. Memories I never had with my own father, and ones I did have that are marred by his abandonment. It's not fair. Life is never fair, I remind myself.

Leaning over, I kiss Leif again, lingering longer this time and grab Luna when I stand up. "Let's go," I tell Celia. I hand the baby back now that she's settled and turn to the lumbering man in bed. Celia closes the door again to give me privacy. Leaning over I whisper into his ear. "Love me, Leif. Love me."

A tear falls on his face and it almost looks like it belongs to him and that upsets me even further. "I love you. Forever and always."

I take his hand again, hoping maybe he'll squeeze it, or a muscle spasm will give me a false, warm feeling. "Come back to me. Luna needs a daddy. Please, come back."

He doesn't, though. We leave the hospital with the knowledge that he didn't hear anything I said. That in a few days what little existence he has left, will be extinguished.

Celia is playing with Luna on the hotel bed, a serious game of peekaboo. I'm wistful as I watch them together and I realize this is something to be thankful for. Family coming together in the face of tragedy. The only family I have left.

"Have they tried to take him off life support?" I ask Celia, cradling the hand that Leif held.

She nods. "A few times. It's always been disastrous. These past nine months have been the worst of our lives. I think when Monday rolls around we will be relieved that he will finally be at peace. He'd hate that we haven't let him go yet, but we're stubborn like that."

"Can I be there? When he passes?" I ask, fighting back tears.

tossing it

Celia looks wistfully from me back to the baby. "It would only be fair. You were there when he first started living."

Closing my eyes, I turn away. "I can't believe this happened."

"He killed him," Celia says like it's a consolation. "The guy he's been after all these years. The one he said he'd die trying to kill." Celia laughs. "Never thought that would be funny, but it is now that it's coming true."

It's not funny, but I guess if that's how she's processing who am I to deny her the joke? "I feel like I should have known. Should have felt that something was wrong when he never got in contact with me."

"Eva took over his personal inbox, but everything SEAL related stayed secure." Celia states.

I nod. "You guys have hated me all this time."

She shrugs. "Nothing was what it seems, so it doesn't matter. Eva is on her way here. We have a room next door, and Mom and Dad are in the room next to ours. We might as well pull the plug tomorrow morning instead of Monday while we're all here."

Her no-nonsense talk about the act is jarring and comforting at the same time. They've come to terms with this already whereas I'm just starting to understand what will happen. If anyone has fought for Leif, I know his sisters will have put up the best fight in his honor. "If that's what you want," I agree. "It's so much all at once for me."

She picks up Luna and kisses her belly. "Why the name Luna?" she asks, sliding her gaze to mine.

"Stars," I say, twisting my ring. "The sky."

She nods like she understands. "He told us about the

ring. I wanted to make sure. I love her name. It's perfect." How much did he tell them?

"Thanks," I say. Eva barges in as we have the door propped open for her impending arrival.

"I cannot believe this," she shouts, but then puts a hand over her mouth when she sees Luna wince at the loud screech. "Malena, how could you keep her from us?" she seethes out through clenched teeth.

"I had to keep her from him," I say. It's the only explanation I need. "To give him a life."

"Meanwhile, in actuality, he's been fighting for his life. You should have called us sooner. My God, I've missed so much already," Eva cries, rounding the bed to look at Luna. With a hand on her mouth her eyes water, the same reaction Celia had. "She is his spitting image. Leif looked identical to her as a baby, well, except your features have softened her a bit, made her pretty," Eva amends. "Let me hold her."

Celia delicately places Luna in Eva's arms and it happens again. Someone else falls in love with my baby. With our baby. "She is the most beautiful thing I've ever seen. Did you bring her to see Leif?" Eva asks, and with one phrase I can tell who has done the fighting over these months. Eva. "I bet he loved it," she adds.

Celia looks away, uneasy with her sister's words. "I did," I say. The long story was given and accepted by Eva before she came here, but I wasn't sure how she'd react to actually seeing me after all this time. She's always been the more…complicated sister. "I set her in his arms. He was clutching my hand," I tell her.

Eva's widening gaze flicks to mind. "He grabbed your hand, didn't he?" She's desperate for someone to be on her side. It's easy to sense. "Moved his fingers?"

"A muscle spasm grabbed your hand, not Leif. Don't do this to Malena, too, Eva. This is ending now. We've done all we can do. All you'll do is make this harder on everyone else. Especially Mamma. We're going to do it tomorrow morning while we're all together. Go speak your peace tonight, okay? We just came from the hospital. Our room is next door." Celia takes on an authoritarian voice, one she's had to adapt, I imagine. "Do you understand?"

"I'm about to put the baby to bed," I say. "We can hang out when you get back."

"Great idea, Malena," Celia says.

"She's so precious," Eva says, smiling at the baby. "You're so lucky, Malena. She's perfect."

"She is lucky to have you as an aunt," I reply, trying to bring the mood up. Eva recoils, and I'm reminded of her infertility. "Thank you," I say instead. "She really is beautiful." I don't feel guilty because she does look so much like Leif.

Shaking her head, she hands Luna back to Celia who is reaching for her. "I can't believe I'm going to say goodbye to my brother."

"Not your brother," Celia reminds her. "His body. His mind has been gone for nine months." I think she's trying to make her feel better, saying goodbye easier, but it's making it worse. It's calling her a liar. Eva starts crying and bids us goodbye.

"I'm sorry you had to hear that. It's hard for Eva. I have to be the voice of reason," Celia says, hanging her head guiltily. "I was right there, thinking the best for the first few months. It's been nine. There's no hope, you see? It's futile and she needs to grasp that."

I nod and take the baby from her to nurse her to sleep.

She drifts easily, lashes fanning across her cheek, looking just like her daddy. "I just wish he got to see her," I say aloud.

"Regardless of what he said about wanting kids, that man wanted to be a father. I know it. He would have loved this life with you, Malena. Don't think any different, okay? Let him go knowing he was a good man."

"I know he is a good man. That's the hardest part," I reply, setting Luna into the pack and play in the corner. She coos and turns her head to the side drifting into deep sleep. Watching her, I pray for another miracle, for things to be different.

His mom and dad stop by the room to say hello and see the baby. I think she is the only shining spot in their otherwise bleak lives. A gift Leif gave me that I can share with them. We hug and cry and talk softly. Celia's phone rings a little past midnight. It's Eva.

She's hysterical, a complete and utter disaster. No one can make out what she's repeating over and over.

"I'll watch over the baby, Malena. Please go and talk to her," Celia says, ending the call. "I've said it all before, maybe you can say something I haven't. This is over. It's over." Placing her face in her hands, she shakes her head.

I'm exhausted, but Celia is right and I owe Eva this much. I owe them all. When I get into my rental car, I dial Eva back to tell her I'm coming.

She's still crying—a hysterical squeal, but I hear a hint of laughter as she says. "He's breathing. On his own, he's breathing!" I don't even respond. Tossing the phone into the passenger seat, I race the mile to the hospital, forgetting how I even got there in the first place.

He's breathing.

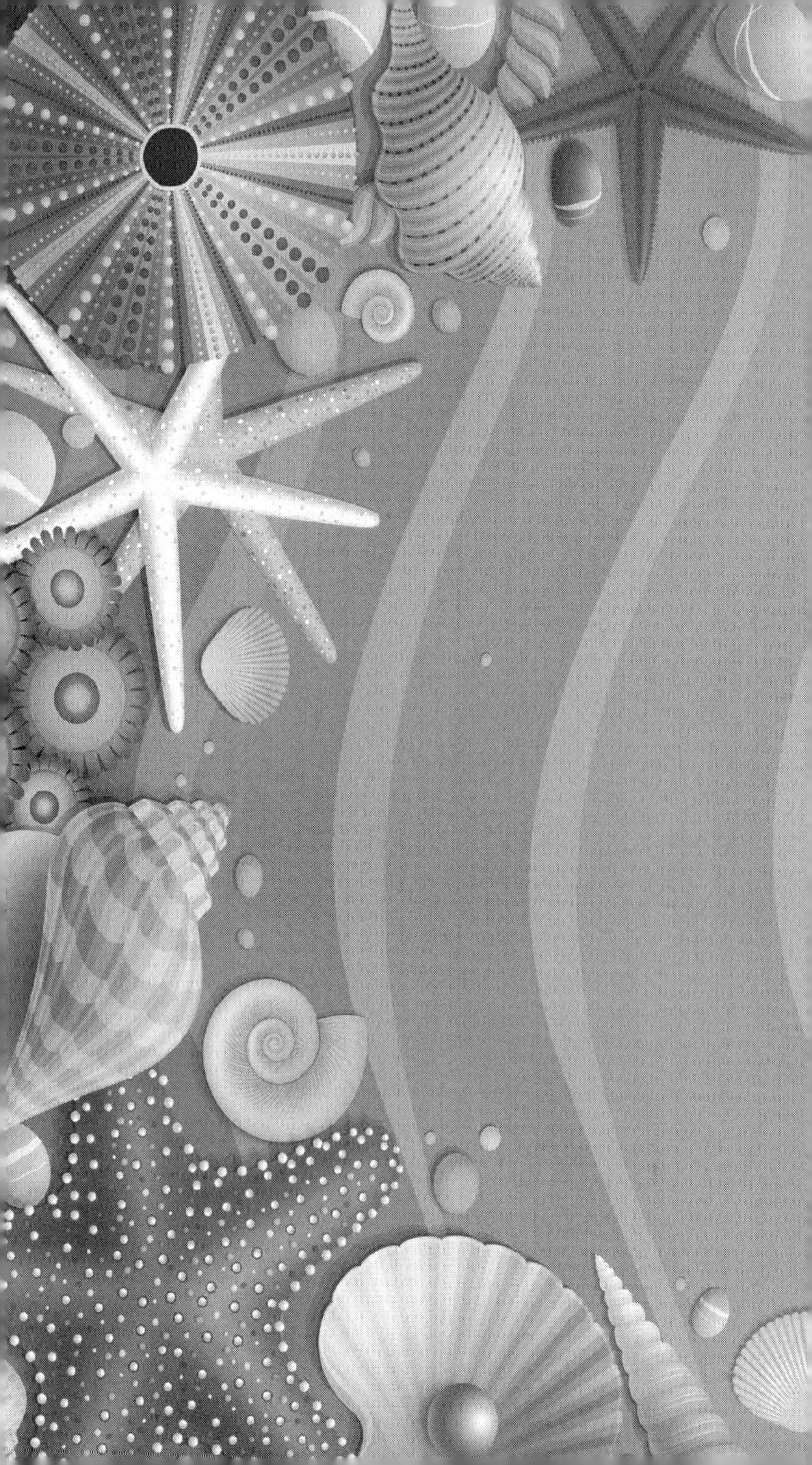

Chapter Eighteen

Malena

There is a crowd of doctors and nurses surrounding Leif's hospital room door when I fall out of the elevator. Eva flies into my arms, wrapping me in a tight hug. "No one believed me. He's going to be okay. I know it."

Her excitement is contagious. I have to remind myself about Celia and her words. She works in the medical field. This is her life most days. Eva is living on a prayer, and even if I want to partake in this particular prayer, I can't. "Tell me everything," I say, pulling back to look at Eva's eyes. "What did the doctor say?"

She shakes her head, an incredulous gleam to her eye. "That he's waking up. Right now. We won't know what we're dealing with until he's completely conscious, but he's breathing. All on his own."

What if that's the only thing he can do on his own. "Let's take it one step at a time." Swallowing, I let my gaze slip to his door. It's poisonous. This hope I feel

tossing it

blooming inside my chest. "Will they talk to me?"

"Yes," Eva counters. "I am responsible for his medical decisions, technically my parents were, but they handed it over to me when they realized I was better equipped to deal with these decisions. I'll tell them you're family." She releases me and bounds over to the nurse who must be in charge and then nods her head my way. I hold up a shaky hand and approach.

With soulful eyes, the nurse takes my hand when I'm standing in front of his room. "It may not be as you hope. As your sister hopes," she says. "This is good news, but it's not a foregone conclusion. Nine months is a long time to be unconscious."

I nod, trying to peek over her shoulder into the room. Eva is already in there, her cell phone pressed to her ear telling the story to whoever she's on the line with. In a rush, Eva squeals, "His eyes are open. They're open."

The next few steps into his room feel leaden—the most difficult steps I've ever taken. If I don't leave this room with the same hope I entered with, I'll never be the same again. The atmosphere has changed, the buzz of energy drives my heart rate up. There's life between these walls that didn't exist mere hours ago. My gaze falls to Leif's face—the gaunt planes sharp, his skin the color of chalk. His lashes are fluttering, and in another step, I'm able to glimpse the ocean blue of his eyes and I close the distance to stand as close as I can to him. He's surrounded by doctors.

Eva's voice prattles on in the background, and the doctors are practically shouting Leif's name at this point, asking if he can hear them. They're checking vitals, with wild, confused gazes. They work with grit and determination. So soft, I can barely hear my own voice, I say, "I need to try something."

Clearing my throat, I say it again, louder this time.

"Who are you?" a doctor asks.

"Malena," I say, my gaze on Leif's face. "Winterset. My last name is Winterset."

Eva chimes in. "She's his baby's mother." *So delicately put, Eva*, I think. "I gave permission for her to be in the room. He'd want her here.

They make room for me on the right side of the bed. I sit, taking his hand. "I need to try something." Leif squeezes my hand. It's no different than before, except now his face is clear of tubes and I'm granted a full view. A chill rises up my spine. He looks so different. Closing my eyes, I envision him the last time I saw him. The last night we spent together in his apartment before he snuck away in the morning and left me with a ring. His wide jaw that ticks when he smiles. His eyes that crinkle in the corner when he laughs. I think of the man he was before when he was in love with me. I recognize I'm feeling so wistful because when and if he wakes up, he might decide he doesn't want me, that my lies were too much to get over. In his ear, I say, "I need to try something right now."

Then, I kiss his closed lips. They're still full, the only things on his face that look the same. I feel his warm breaths push out of his nose, a ragged, out of practice, speed. It reminds me of when Luna took her first breaths. A nurse sets her hand on my shoulder, but I hear someone else say, "Let her. He's responding. He's responding."

I pull my mouth off his and watch his blue eyes search my face. He closes them for another thirty seconds and I think that's it. He's gone, if he was ever really back. Eva sits next to me, one hand squeezing mine like a vise. Turning, I look at her, my gaze teary. That's when I see his parents. They are standing in the back of the room, pain etched across their faces. "I'm so sorry," I say.

"Stop it. This is amazing progress," Eva says.

"Eva," I say, grabbing her hand. "There's a possibility he's not in there. Will never be inside there again. I love this man with everything I have and I have to accept that this shell, this broken shell that housed the perfect man will never be in there again. You have to understand."

Eva looks crestfallen as she pulls her hand out of mine. "You have no right," she counters.

"I have every right. I lived with a woman who wasn't inside of her own head for most of my life. I understand exactly what that means. Grieving a person while they're still alive is torture. It's a technicality. A horrible, disgusting technicality. A beating heart does not mean recognition." I shake my head, memories of my mother flooding my awareness. "Breathing doesn't mean love. It just means life. Life altered. Never the same again."

"You'll give up on him that easily? I should have known better. You ran the first second the going got tough, the very first chance you had to run from him, you did. You used a photo. One that I took, might I add."

My stomach sinks and tears prick my eyes. "You took those photos? You followed me?"

She has the good sense to look guilty. "We protect our own in this family. I'll have you know I followed you because I was worried about you because I'd heard your mom was sick. What I found was anything other than a worried woman."

Wasn't I grateful for those photos? They gave me the opportunity to break it off with Leif in a painless manner. The scapegoat. "I can't believe you would do that, Eva. I've never given you a reason to doubt my loyalties. What you caught was a jaded moment that should have been private."

"I understand that now," she whispers. "I wish I could take it back, I do. You lied to him. To all of us."

I throw my hands up. "No one ever asked if I was married. It was a non-issue. I never loved Dylan. I never loved Dylan." Damn, that feels good to say. "I never loved Dylan," I yell.

Eva stays silent.

"I love Leif. I'll never love anyone other than Leif," I yell. The nurses and doctors turn to my boisterous declaration, trying and failing to pretend they aren't listening to every single word of our conversation.

You could hear a pin drop in this moment. It feels like every person in this room is holding their breath. No one speaks. The monitor beeps, giving a reading of Leif's blood pressure. His heart rate monitor beeps at precise intervals.

Leif groans. And every set of eyes train on him. My own heart rate would set off every monitor on planet earth. He mumbles something, but his throat is dry and his tongue out of practice.

"He's trying to talk," Eva says. "What's he saying?" Our argument is all but forgotten for the moment. That's how it works with family. You move on after fights. You fight for the common good. Our fight turns to the man in the hospital bed.

Disuse has destroyed his voice box. The doctor leans over and narrows his eyes. "What was that?"

Slowly, Leif's blue gaze flicks to meet mine. I'm sure I look like a wild animal—a crazy person without the ability to control her emotions. "Why," he says, broken into two scratchy syllables.

I hold my breath. My heart pounding against my ribcage furiously.

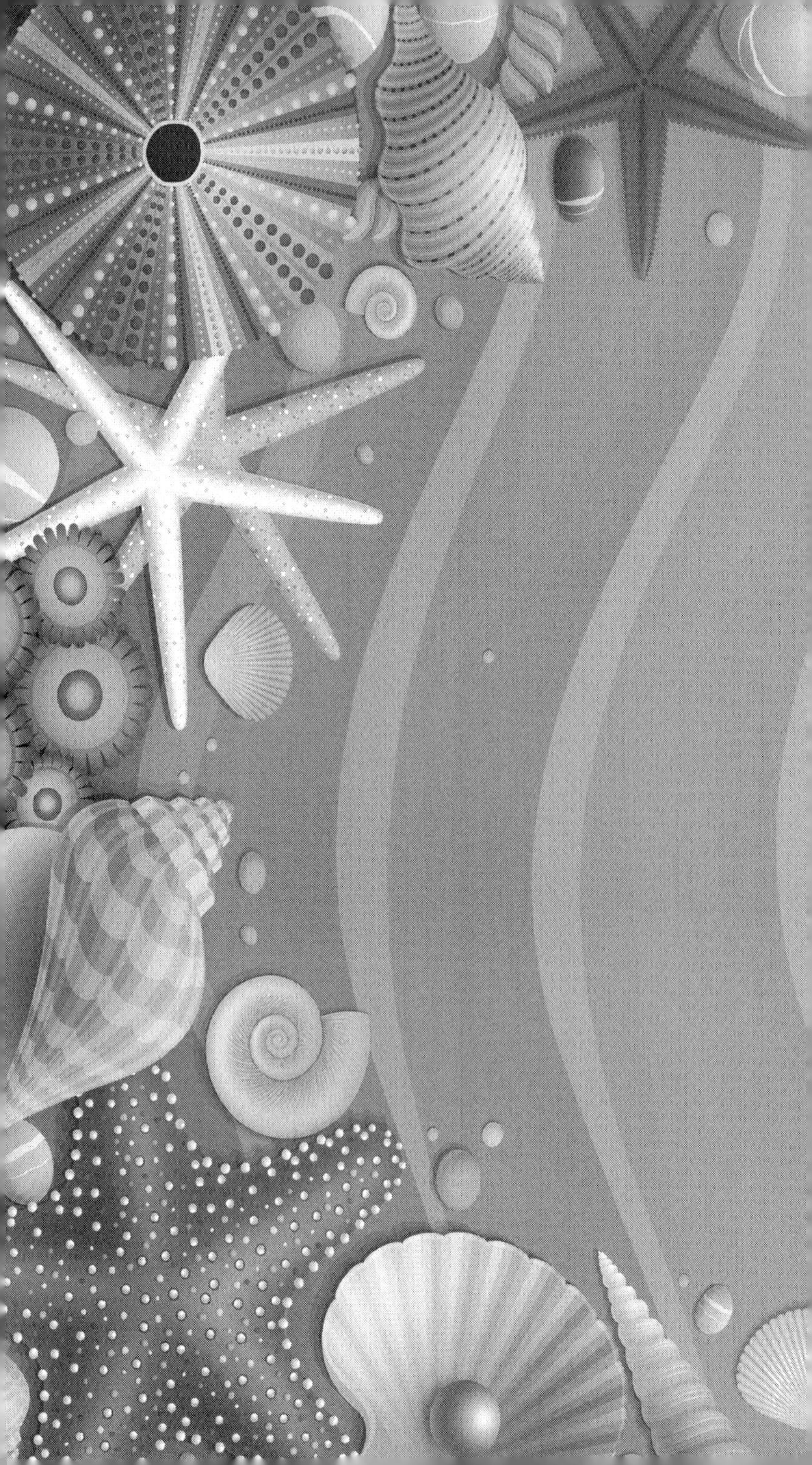

Chapter Nineteen

Leif

I don't wake to true love's kiss. No. The first thing I hear is my sister screeching like a motherfucking wildcat. The next voice is more pleasing, but I can tell she's upset. She talks about not loving Dylan. My brain seems to be a few steps behind. It takes several moments to process what they're talking about and what it means. I seem to be entrenched in some foggy haze. It feels like I'm in a nightmare. One I can't force myself to wake from—knowing all the bad would go away if I could arise from this sleep.

"I never loved Dylan," Malena shouts. The name breaks me from my black prison. Opening my eyes, I'm met with a dull light. Malena. I see the back of her head, her brown hair sleek, with blonde highlights. It's shorter and lighter than it was when I saw her last. When did I see her last? The beeping correlates to a hospital. The dots connect in rapid succession. Malena's hand shakes

tossing it

in mine own. "I never loved Dylan!"

Even in the haze, my recollection is seeping back in. The unexpected gunfight. Aidan. Tacos. Eva messaging me photos. Dylan and Malena. Husband. My leg. The fucking bad guy. My voice doesn't work when I try to open my mouth. A noise I've never heard comes out of me. It's enough to garner stares from those around me. Malena's big brown eyes meet mine and it nearly kills me. Again. I open my mouth, taking more effort than opening a mouth should take.

The word comes out, finally. "Why?"

"Oh, my God. Can you hear me?"

Not going to try to talk again, so I nod once.

"I love you," Malena shouts like she thinks I'm also deaf. "You can hear me."

Eva leans over and meets my gaze with a tearful look. "I can't believe you've been such an asshole," she says.

I grin.

"I was going to kill you tomorrow."

I grin once again.

My mom and dad pace over. How much time has passed? They look older. So much older than the last time I saw them. The worry etched on their faces tells a lifetime of heartache. Mom leans over and hugs me, whispering things in my ear about being so happy I'm okay. How much she loves me. How worried she's been. There's a fear there I've never heard before. Not in a lifetime of deployments and dangerous trips.

"Ai-dan," I croak.

"He's fine. He saved your life," a doctor says. I'm in

a military facility. The uniforms telling me everything I need to know. He leans over me. "You've been gone for nine months, Leif Andersson. In a coma, we have tried everything to get your body to work on its own. I won't give you too many details right now. It must be a lot. You need rest."

Eva groans. "He's had nine months to rest. He needs to meet his daughter!"

Malena's gaze is wild as she turns her focus to Eva and then back to me.

Daughter. Daughter. Daughter. Daughter.

"He's not ready for that, Eva. Shut your mouth for once."

My mom scolds my sister, as my dad hugs me which I think is supposed to distract me from what Eva just said, but it's too late. "Why?" I say once again, touching Malena, my hand brushing her thigh.

"It wasn't what you thought Leif. Get some rest. Like the doctor said. I'll be here when you wake up. I love you," she says, running her hand over my forehead, and into my hair. "We'll all be here when you wake up."

Daughter. Daughter. Daughter. "Daughter," I manage to get out. "Mine?"

Malena cries, her hand covering the lower half of her face. I wish she would move her hand. I want to see her. I haven't seen her in so long, never thought I'd see her again. Against the darkness, her face is like a beacon of light calling me back home. She nods. "Yes. Your daughter. She'll be here when you wake up. I'll explain everything. I'm so sorry," she says, swallowing hard. "I love you. Sleep."

I am tired. Which doesn't make sense, but when I close my eyes briefly it feels like sleep instead of a dark hole, so I let it take me. There isn't blackness this time. I dream of a daughter. A beautiful girl who looks just like the woman I love.

The bed is up and the curtains are drawn. My body isn't mine anymore, my muscles are so atrophied that I can barely sit up on my own. My mother has busied herself about my room. Bringing in flowers and magazines and anything she thinks I might like. My dad strolls around the hospital floor with a cup of coffee in one hand. He pokes his head into the room and looks shocked to see me every single time. Today was the day I was supposed to be pulled off life support and instead, it's the start of my recovery.

"Tell me if you want anything in particular, honey. Anything at all."

"Malena," I rasp, clutching my throat. "I want Malena," I say again, just to prove my fucking voice box I'm the boss. I have a permanent sore throat from the tubes that pumped life into my body all of these months. Sipping water feels like razor blades, and that's what they keep pushing me to do. Drink water, piss a ton.

Mom looks down to the floor. "She will be here shortly, I'm sure."

"Why did that sound like a question? Where is she?"

It's almost noon and Malena hasn't been in to see me yet.

"Leif," Mom croons in that way only a mom can. "Last night was a lot. She's probably sleeping still. If not, she's dealing with the…" Mom pauses. "I'm sure she's busy, honey. What can I get you in the meantime? The physical therapist will be here this afternoon. Celia had to call in a favor as you weren't on the schedule." No one has said the word baby or daughter again since last night. I'm beginning to think I dreamed it. It's why I need Malena. Her words. To tell me if what she said last night is real.

"I need to fix myself," I croak. "I need Malena, Mom."

She nods. "I'll call her now. Stay put," Mom says, then shakes her head. "I'm sorry."

"I'm not paralyzed," I say. "I don't think, anyway. I can't fucking move so maybe I am. Don't apologize. I won't go anywhere," I say, out of breath. It takes so much to get words out. My lungs don't hold as much oxygen as they used to. "Tell her I *need* her," I add. I'm breaking a little more every second her face isn't in my line of vision.

Eva and Celia visited me this morning. They left when the doctors came in to run a myriad of tests on my body and blood. I seem to be doing okay internally, and the fuzzy mental pieces get a little clearer as time passes. They say that's a good sign—that my recovery is miraculous and so sudden that it's hard to medically explain. My sister's fucking ranting could bring anyone back from the grave. Dad is on one of his walks again and I am left alone.

tossing it

There's a walker next to my bed that a nurse brought in for this afternoon's physical therapy session. I eye it like a mortal enemy, one that killed me, but not all the way. Aidan is on his way here, and a few of my teammates are with him. They're the ones that will fill in the blank spaces with regard to attack. I have to piss so I take the urge to try out my legs instead of using the bed urinal. I have to use my arms to scoot my legs to the edge of the bed.

No one could tell me what it would be like to stand up—how my body would react. The act of swinging my legs over the side leaves me breathless. "Fuck, I'm so out of shape," I mutter, then putting both hands on the handles of the walker, I lean my upper body onto the steel frame. A spell of dizziness hits. A string of curse words fly through my brain, my throat too sore to speak them.

"Are you supposed to be up?" Malena says. Finally. Finally.

I turn my head, and there she is. A vision in a long yellow dress, her skin in stark contrast to the light color. I swallow hard and try to shift to get a better view. The afternoon sun lights her face. "You're here."

"I, ah, wasn't sure what to say so I avoided you today," she says. "I was on my way when your mom just called."

"Honesty. I like it," I reply, croaking a little less with every word I say. "How about some more of that?"

She looks down to the floor. When I shuffle, she doesn't hesitate to rush over to help me. "I'll give you honesty if you sit back down."

"If you won't dance with me, I'll find someone who will," I counter, trying on a smile for the first time today.

She's affected by it. Immediately. Her whole demeanor switching into something more familiar. "I'll dance with you. Later."

"I have to take a piss so I can't sit quite yet. I'd like to do it like a man," I explain, nodding to the bathroom attached to my room.

Malena nods. "I'll call a nurse. Can you wait?"

My eyes light. "I can't. Will you help me?"

Her breath catches. "Of course. Is this the first time you've stood up? Walked? If you fall, I'm not sure I can catch you before you hurt yourself. Are you sure you don't want to use the bed urinal?"

I begin shuffling toward the restroom. "I got it, Malena. Even if I fell, I imagine you'd catch me. I'm what? A mere two hundred pounds?" The walker takes most of my weight. My legs are painful as blood rushes in a direction other than horizontal.

"Careful," Malena says, laying both hands on my back. "Your legs are working great, Leif. You don't even need my help right now."

I'd never tell her how much pain I'm in or how much effort I'm putting into looking like a normal human being right now. When we get to the bathroom, Malena meets my gaze, then looks away quickly. "Your ass is hanging out, so I'm going to assume you'll be able to hang it in there and…go?"

I laugh even though it hurts my chest. "I need you to hang it over in the right spot. If I piss all over the floor

tossing it

what will those poor nurses think of the mess?" I tease.

She laughs a short burst, then the smile vanishes from her face. "You're serious?"

"As a heart attack," I say, lips in a firm line.

She lifts the gown tentatively, shaking her head. I shuffle forward a bit, using the walker to get closer to the toilet. "At least one thing looks the same," Malena says, smirking. Using her thumb, she guides my dick up and out. "Okay, shoot," she says.

"I'm getting hard and then I won't be able to piss," I counter, sucking in a relieved breath. It works. Fuck yes.

"Oh my gosh, stop it. Pee, Leif! What if someone comes in?"

"Well, then we close the bathroom door and see just how well my dick works after a year without being inside you."

"Don't do that," Malena says, smile vanishing. "Be serious right now."

"Fine, fine." I concentrate on the white painted, cement block wall and close my eyes and piss. "Shake it," I say when I'm done. "Don't want to drip on the floor."

"Shake it yourself."

"Why aren't you more accommodating in my recovery, huh?"

"Because we need to talk, Leif. I held your dick while you peed. Pretty sure that counts as helpful."

Reaching down, I shake my cock a bit and stand up straighter against my walker. "And seeing as you could have held your own dick, I'd say you're the one not being accommodating. It's been a long time. We have so much to talk about."

Reality stings. She said she loved me, but that doesn't mean she didn't move on without me. "Honesty. You were about to give me more of that," I remind her.

Malena frowns. "Let's get you back to bed."

"I have to sit down for the truth? Yikes."

She bites her lip. "I didn't say it was bad. I'm worried about you. That's all."

"Don't worry about me. Never worry about me. I'll always be okay."

She guides me back into bed and lifts the shoulder of my hospital gown back on my shoulder when it drops off. "You are so weak."

"And frail. What this doesn't do it for you?" I ask, holding my arms out to the sides.

Her eyes smile, then she closes them, blinking away tears. "I thought I lost you. You have no idea what that feels like. You don't get to tell me not to worry. I'll do whatever I want."

I scoot over and pat the spot next to me on the bed. Someone must have walked in the room and then right back out during the bathroom trip because my door is closed now. I bet dad had a disbelieving smile when he watched Malena help me pee. He helped me bathe this morning, wheeling the chair into the large shower stall so I could shower and wash away the months of hospital etched into my skin. The water was hot and I only needed help washing my hair.

Malena sits next to me, tucking her feet underneath her body. "I'm sorry about that," I whisper, as she brings her head against my shoulder. "I'm so sorry about your mom, Malena. My sister told me." Time has changed so many facets of everyone's lives it's hard to make out which way is up. To me, the gunfight feels like yesterday. I'll be catching up on everything and everyone for months.

"Thanks. It's been hard, but I have to believe she's in a better place and she's herself," Malena says. "Everyone at Garden Breeze was amazing, by the way. They took a traumatic situation and made it seem less horrific."

I swallow, the acidic taste in the back of my throat leaving a bit. "Thank God for small miracles," I reply, trying to pull her closer.

"I'm going to start at the photos," she says, sighing. I nod against her head. Then she tells me the story or her mother getting sick and the pregnancy she never thought she'd have. The shock. The terror. The words I said about not having a family. The rules. The words I said about not *wanting* a family. The words *I said*. Malena says things that break my heart. She's been alone in this all of this time.

Dylan was an ex that meant very little to her. She says her pregnancy was the catalyst to finding her strength—realizing she was good enough regardless of what her ex-husband told her, or what anyone else thought about her as a person. She explained to me what she was feeling in the photos that Eva took, and her guess as to what Dylan was feeling in the images, and how it was skewed.

I stay silent as she goes on, her voice a sweet lull that brings me a peace only she is responsible for. "I wanted you to have the life you wanted. When you never responded to my email, I assumed I won—you would stay away from Bronze Bay and never come back. I'd take the repercussions of our love and run because at least I have her. Our daughter. She means everything to me."

"You're breaking my heart," I admit, taking in a large breath that sears. Pressing my lips against her head, I put myself in her shoes and am absolutely horrified. Dying in this bed would have been easier than what she's had to endure on her own.

"After my mom died, she left a note. I just recently found it. She remembered after you visited and wrote it all down. The conversation between you both. How you told her you wanted a family with me. A baby," Malena whispers, meeting my gaze. "Why didn't you tell me that?"

I swallow. "Because you couldn't have kids, Malena. I wanted you in any form I could have you. Even if that meant never having kids. I'd have you. Never for a second think would I be burdened by our child. That's a dream come true. I'm sorry for not telling you. You can't help who you fall in love with. I fell in love with a woman who couldn't have children. Maybe we would have adopted one day. Who knows? She remembered? That's so ironic when you think about all of the things she could have remembered."

She sobs into her fist. "It's a miracle Luna is here. I wish I knew about her letter earlier. Maybe you could have come back to us sooner if I was here."

tossing it

"Luna," I say, testing the name. "That's her name? Our daughter?"

Malena smiles through her tears and nods. "She's beautiful."

My heart races. "Can I meet her now?"

"You're ready?" Malena asks. "It's a lot. All of this."

I nod. "Born ready. No pun intended."

"The act of not wanting kids was pretty convincing," Malena says softly, drifting back to our conversation.

"I think I never wanted them because I hadn't met the right person. Then I met you, and got to know you, and fell in love with you and my desire for you outweighed my desire for a family so I went with it." When she doesn't look at me, I say, "Malena."

She looks at me. "I love you," I confess. "Truly and wholly in every single way it's possible to love another individual. The real kind of love that puts the rest of the world to shame."

Her tear streaked face is unbearably sad. "I said goodbye to you nine months ago in an email and then again yesterday as I cried over your bed."

"Don't say that," I return.

She heaves a sigh and stands from the bed. A coldness replaces her warmth and my stomach pangs in unease. "Here's the thing. I'm going to bring Luna in here to meet you and I want you to have a relationship with her if you want to, but that needs to come first. Before anything between us. You can decide after a bit of time if you're all in, or not. I won't fault you if you decide to walk. I'd never fault you, regardless of what you say you want. We're a package deal, Luna and I, and I need to make sure you're all in, Leif. Luna deserves a father that…stays."

I open my mouth to argue, but she holds up a palm and shakes her head. "Don't say anything. I'll be right back."

"Hey, don't silence me," I shout. The tone of my voice is shockingly loud—demanding. Malena jumps. "If you haven't noticed yet, I'm a fighter. I fight for the things I want. I fight to remedy the things I've fucked up. I may have screwed us up, but I'm prepared to fight for you, for Luna, even if I die trying." Looking around the room, I send a pointed message. "I'm a scrappy motherfucker and I have nothing to lose. Gotta' watch out for men like me, Malena." She sets her hands on her hips, licking her lips. "You need to know right now. That I'm all fucking in. All in. Before I lay eyes on the baby. Before you walk out that door not knowing where I stand, wondering if I'm going to leave you like he did." I shake my head. "I'll never leave you."

Malena cries, a sob escaping her throat.

"I am *all in*," I repeat, grinding my teeth on the last syllable. "There's no wishy-washy shit from me. I know what I want."

Without saying another word, she walks up to my bedside and kisses my lips. Once, a lingering hold with her mouth parted just enough to let me taste her. "I love you, too." Her words heal more than any pills or medicines doctors can prescribe ever will. "So much," she adds.

tossing it

When I've finally worked my arms up and around her waist, she pulls away. "I'll be right back."

While she's gone, I relish the taste of her sweetness on my lips. I'm lost in thought minutes later when Malena comes in carrying our sleeping bundle wrapped in pink blankets. The room tilts, and my stomach feels as if a flock of birds are flapping inside of it. This isn't a moment you can ever prepare yourself for. Definitely not in my circumstance, but not in any circumstance really. Meeting your child for the first time. A human being you helped create. If you're lucky, a tiny, perfect person, made out of love. Without saying a word, Malena leans down and sets the baby into my waiting arms.

At first, I'm shocked at how small she feels, but one look at her face erases everything else. I'm transfixed by her tiny features and golden locks. She looks like something from a storybook. Luna sighs a long sigh and blinks her eyes, fighting to keep them open long enough to see who is holding her. "Hi baby girl," I say when her gaze locks on mine. "I'm your daddy." The word doesn't stick in the back of my throat like a taboo, no, it comes out naturally. The first words I have spoken that don't pain me in any way.

"I don't look like much now, but I'm going to get better and we're going to take on the world together. With your mama," I rasp, looking up at Malena. She has tears pouring down her face. The strongest sense to love and protect rears, stemming from my heart and blooming outward. Everything in my power, and with everything I am, I will protect them. My eyes water, watching the woman I love. "Well done, Malena Winterset," I proclaim. "Job well done."

She laughs through tears. "Yeah," she says, nodding. "I know."

The baby coos and I glance down at her squirming, warm form. "I'm never going to be able to repay you for this, Malena. For her. For giving me this precious gift."

"I think you can," Malena replies. "Get better."

"Then what?"

Folding her arms across her chest, she tilts her head to the side. "Then you come home. To Bronze Bay."

"What after that?" I widen my eyes.

Malena pauses, a comfortable silence, our gazes locked in challenge. "I haven't worked that out yet. Do you have any opinions on the matter?"

I nod. "I never want to be away from you," I say. "Or her." Peeling back the blanket I glimpse tiny fingers and ten little toes. "So that means only one thing."

"It means a few things," Malena teases. "But what did you have in mind specifically?"

"You have to marry me. Obviously. And stay with me forever. And ever."

Malena shakes her head, a smile playing on her lips. "You sound like a crazy person." "A serial killer?"

"No, just crazy. One step at a time. I had to help you pee. Let's work on getting you fully functioning before we talk about life commitments."

"But I am committed to you. To both of you. I want to marry you. I want to spend my life with you and Luna. Almost dying has a way of showing you what's important."

Malena tucks her hair behind her ear and sits next to me on the bed. "She doesn't sleep all night."

"I don't sleep well either. Perfect."

Luna turns her head to glimpse her mom. "I'm moody and my ass has stretch marks now."

Turning my head, I meet her gaze. "You can't scare me off. I love bad moods. And stretch marks."

Malena rolls her eyes. "No one loves stretch marks. Or bitches," she whispers into my ear. A shiver rises up my spine. The combination of the curse word and her breath mingled together is a wild turn on. Maybe my mind feels like only a day has passed, but my dick somehow realizes it's been the better part of a year since it's had any contact with its favorite playmate.

I turn so my lips are almost against hers. "I think I might love a bitch."

The smirk on her face is delicious. I press my lips against hers and say, "And stretch marks."

Kissing her chastely once, I lean away and readjust the baby. Her body is squishy and no matter how I hold her I'm worried I'm not doing it right. "Especially because you got them carrying my child." My child. Mine. I might be a weak bastard, but the inner lion is roaring out in total domination.

Malena stays silent, a serene look on her face. "There are photos of me looking like a blimp. Don't worry. You'll get to see how the stretch marks came to be."

Luna's body tenses and she wails. "Hold her on your shoulder, she might be gassy," Malena says.

I do as I'm told and am shocked at how warm the baby feels against my hospital gown, she is a tiny space heater. The connection I feel with Luna is immediate and the weakness that resides behind that makes me nervous. The desire to get well is now amplified by a million. "You never did answer my question," I say, raising one brow.

"Which one?"

"Will you marry me?" I ask.

She leans away to glimpse my whole face. "Why do you want to marry me?"

"Because I can't live without you."

Malena smirks. "You can."

I shake my head. "I don't want to. Not for another second."

"You're going to have to live without me for work," Malena says.

I nod. "No more deployments. I've paid my dues. Bronze Bay for good."

Raking me and the baby with her gaze, she simply says, "Yes. I'll marry you."

"That was an easy decision. I figured I'd have to do some carnal convincing."

"Don't talk like that while you're holding the baby," she counters. "I didn't need to be convinced because I know what I want. I've known for quite some time actually. Basically, from the second I realized you weren't going to leave me dead in a field with a toe shoved in my vagina."

"Don't talk like that in front of the baby, Malena," I return. "Not a toe. A whole foot. Get it right."

tossing it

She shrugs. "Fine. Sorry. Yes. You need to get better first. Learn more about this little one." She runs her hand over Luna's hair and a tiny sigh escapes. "How did I get so lucky?"

"Luck has little to do with us, Malena. We have anti-luck and destiny on our side."

"Destiny? Isn't that a little…cheesy?" Malena says, wrinkling her forehead. When I frown, she adds, "Anti-luck?"

My arm is tired so I switch Luna to my other shoulder, and can't resist kissing her head. She smells so good. "The only easy thing has been bumping into one another at Bobby's Bar. Everything from there was an uphill battle. That's what you call anti-luck. Destiny because every single thing that goes against medical diagnoses or seems impossible has happened, and we're here—together in this bed. Do you agree?"

"I guess you are right. What if I'd never read that letter? If I hadn't come here. If you hadn't woken up before Monday?" Malena shudders.

"The world can't get rid of me that easily," I say.

"Eva. You owe your life to her stubbornness."

Closing my eyes, I sigh. "I know. She's going to hold it over my head for the rest of my life. I have to get something on her."

Malena laughs. "Siblings. I'll never understand how that works."

"We've gotta' try to give Luna one though."

She looks wistful. "I'm thankful for her, but I'd love that."

"We could just have fun trying too. I'm okay with trying a few times per day." "Get better, Leif," she replies. "We need to get you home and out of this hospital. Can I have her back? I'll take her to Celia."

Furrowing my brow, I say, "I just got her. No one can have her back until I'm good and ready."

Malena crosses her arms and I see the ring on her ring finger. It looks just as beautiful as I thought it would. "I've missed you, Leif." She leans her head back on my shoulder.

Taking her hand in my free one, I spin the ring. "You're my night sky."

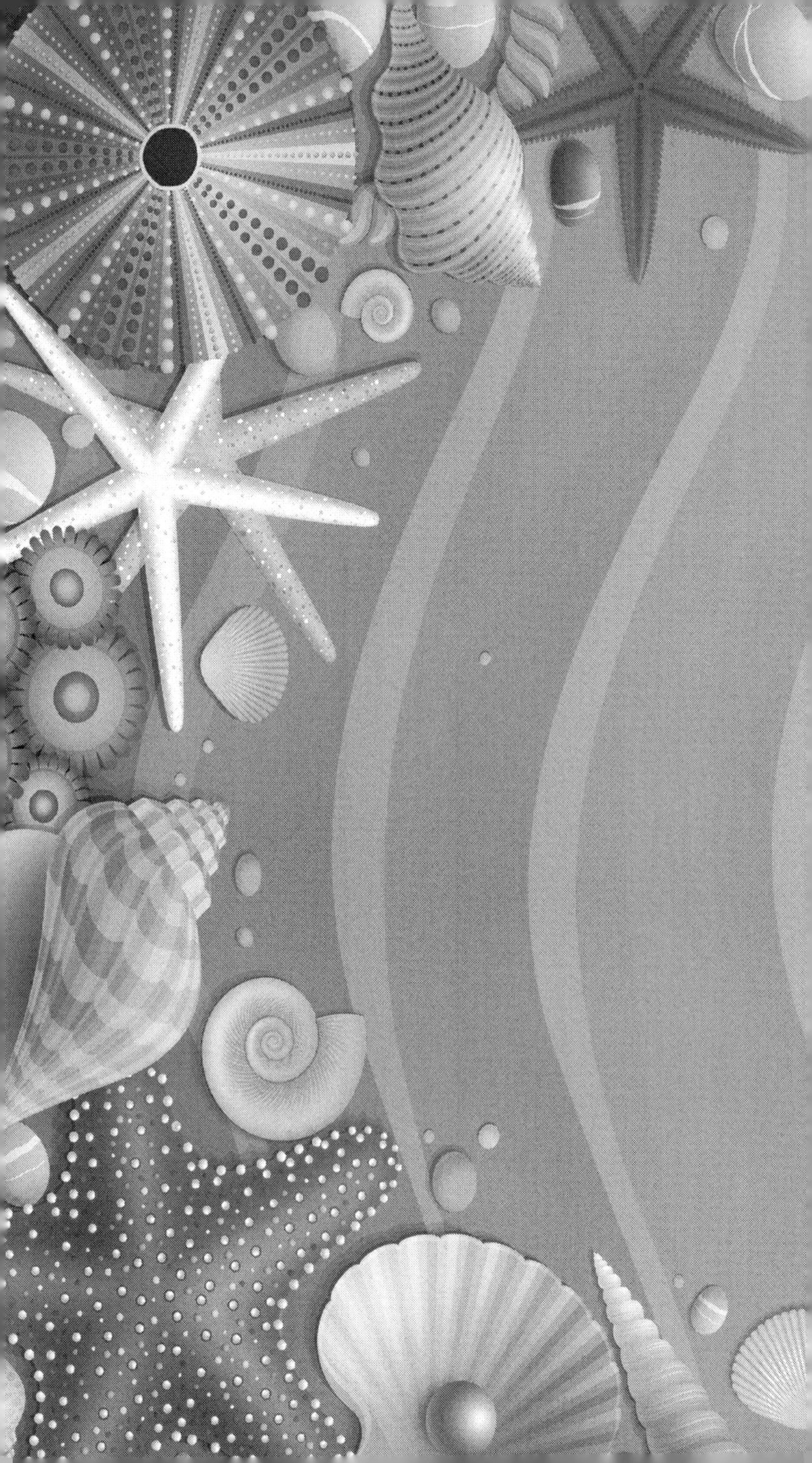

Epilogue

Leif

Three months later . . .

"You had me hanging twinkly, fucking, dangly lights on the deck, Malena. I'm pretty sure if I'm capable of using a step stool, I'm capable of inserting my dick inside you," I say, wiping my brow, a film of sweat threatening to leak down my face. "Come on. I'm cleared for sexual intercourse. You heard the doctor."

Malena gives me a look. One that is meant to defuse the tension, and end the conversation at the exact same time. We got married in the courthouse the second I left the hospital in Bronze Bay. I was transferred there to be closer to her during recovery. It was the first thing I wanted to do. The only thing that mattered on a to-do list so long there's an actual possibility I'll never get it all finished in this lifetime. I guess that's what happens when you're in a coma for nine months.

tossing it

There was no fanfare with our marriage. She wore a white dress that dragged across the ground because it needed to be hemmed. I wore khaki pants and a navy blue button-up shirt. Shirley was our witness and our vows were the most powerful, perfect words I've ever spoken. Vows I'll cherish forever. Promises I'll keep. "We're going to consummate our marriage tonight. I have this planned, remember? Luna is spending the night with Eva. You and I will have the house to ourselves. Let me plan at least one facet of our wedding. You must realize it pains me to organize every trivial detail of other couple's weddings and not be able to control things in my own?"

She tries to scurry by me to head into the house, but I grab her by the waist. "You wanted to get married at the courthouse. That was all you."

"Because I didn't want you to change your mind. I had to trap you," she counters.

"You didn't trap me. I trapped you," I say, glancing at Luna in her playpen. "Because my sperm are like fucking bolts. They sizzle and pop," I whisper into her ear. "Tonight. I won't wait a minute more." "After the party," she says, leaning up and back to accept my kiss. "How are you feeling?" she asks against my lips. "Any pain?"

There's always pain. I don't complain about it too much because I've been fortunate in every other way. My job in Bronze Bay was waiting for me. I have a loving family. A wife. A daughter. All the things I never imagined would make me happiest in life. "I feel great.

Perfect. Ready for tonight. After the party," I deadpan. They cleared me for physical activity today, and sex falls into that category. It didn't matter how much I argued with the doctors, they would smile, and tell me no. One week I tried to convince them intercourse would aide in a quicker recovery. They didn't agree. Fuckers. I still have shrapnel in my body and my leg is fucked up, but I was lucky Aidan saved my ass from total annihilation.

We're having a small intimate gathering to celebrate our wedding. Just a small group of friends and our family. Or rather, my family and Malena's cousin Amber who came into town for the night. Reintegration has been easy. I use the attack as a place to reset. I came back to life and began a new life. Not completely different than my old life, but more important. "Let me get back to it," Malena says, hugging me. "Everyone will be here soon and I want it all to run smoothly." She vanishes into the yard, bustling around the rented tables set with cloths and silverware. Caroline and Shirley are already out there working.

Scooping up Luna, and the rattle she has permanently shoved in her mouth, I head back into the house. We're living in Malena's house. It's farther from the beach, but it feels the most like home.

"Are you hungry?" I ask, bouncing her on my hip. "We've been told to stay out of the way. We should eat." There's a platter of meats and cheeses sitting on the island. I eat a bite and readjust the rest so it's not noticeable. Luna's food is in a container, so I grab it and a spoon, and set her up in her highchair.

tossing it

"The fighter jet is coming to drop a bomb, sweetie," I coo, using a high-pitched voice. "Open up so I can drop it off." She smiles a half tooth, half gummy smile and opens up wide. "And Mommy says you don't eat for her. She needs to drop bombs, doesn't she baby?" I plug the gelatinous wet green beans into her mouth and watch for spill over. "Peaches are for dessert," I say. Luna babbles on, responding in her own language and claps her hands.

"The submarine needs to open the door," I say, opening my own mouth wide. "The divers need to get back in." The baby opens her mouth and makes noises of approval for the sweeter food.

"It's ridiculous, you know? How easily you get her to eat."

I shrug. "I mean we all can't be good at everything," I say.

My sister, Eva rounds a corner. "You aren't good at everything, Leif," she hisses. "You almost get yourself killed. You're like the worst Navy SEAL in history."

Luna laughs, because she always laughs at Eva, and I groan. "Nice to see you too, Sis."

"I brought what you asked, Malena," Eva says, dropping a kiss on my cheek and then pulling a chair in next to the baby. "How is auntie's favorite girl?" Luna slams her hands down on the highchair in glee. "Is daddy giving you a hard time? You want a cookie?"

"No cookies, Eva," Malena and I say at the same time. Then we look at each other and smile. I'm getting the knack of this parenting thing. I mean, I feel like I'm going to war unarmed, but there's a learning curve I'm mastering.

Eva holds up both hands, palms out. "Fine, fine. They're real sticks in the mud. You're spending the night with me tonight. I'll give you cookies later," she whispers loud enough for us to hear.

"There were a few people coming in the side gate. I've got Luna. Go ahead and greet your guests, newlyweds." Eva smiles warmly at Malena. When she turns her gaze to mine, she winks.

Luna cries when I stand up, but Eva distracts her easily with a new toy she pulls out of her purse. It's always equal parts appreciation and guilt when Eva is around Luna. It's so blatantly obvious how wonderful of a mother she would be. She was forced into the capacity of aunt, watching Malena and I hit milestones that she'll never have. She gave up mentally after the last round of IVF failed and she's finally given up emotionally too. Malena says she prays every day that our family and my near death didn't use up all of our miracles and maybe, one day, Eva's dreams will come true. Crazier shit has happened.

I am living breathing proof. As the night wears on Malena transforms from the hostess with the mostess, to my new wife, and as guests trickle out, the longing for her intensifies. If you go by a calendar, it's been way over a year since I've had sex with her. Merely thinking about it makes my dick hard. As people filter out, I wash dishes as I see them pop into the kitchen, so there are no excuses, or things to do when the last person leaves. Nothing to do except her.

tossing it

Eva and Celia left with Luna an hour ago because she was getting tired. It's the first time she's slept away from Malena, and I know she was hesitant to give over control. She wants a night alone with me, though, and we both knew this is how it had to go. This is what family does. And we are indeed, by law, a family. "I'm taking off, bro," Aidan says, getting my attention.

I dry my hands on a dish towel. "See you at work next week, man."

When he sees me watching, he slides his phone back into his pocket. "Back to work so soon?" he says, looking distracted, touching his pocket. Who is he talking to?

"I'm cleared for physical activity. I'm home. Got the girl. I'm ready to tackle anything."

Aidan laughs. "Not quite everything. You need to hit the gym."

"That starts tomorrow, too. Try almost dying and see how much muscle you get to keep," I joke. "It's coming back slowly, but surely. I don't look like a skeleton anymore." Eating normal, square meals fixed that almost immediately, but I'm still a shell of the person I used to be. It'd be a lie if I said I didn't worry about Malena not finding me attractive anymore. The muscles and bulk were my identifier—a huge part of how I viewed myself, and where my self-confidence came from.

"Yeah. I'll be there for you. We'll get you back to normal in no time." Aidan smiles.

"You okay, man? You're acting twitchy and you're not even drinking."

He smirks. "I'm good, man. I'm good. Taking some

time away from the drink, that's all. Working on my abs." He lifts his shirt and flexes.

"You're such a douche canoe. Get out of my house."

"I saved your life. You can't tell me what to do anymore."

"Fair. But it's bro code to tell me what's really going on."

"Woman troubles," he says, jutting his chin up.

Pressing my lips into a firm line, I nod. "Well fuck. That's a bitch." One that I'm out of the loop about. I don't like it at all. Mentally, I add grabbing a beer with my friend to the never-ending to-do list.

"Such a bitch," he replies.

Malena walks into the kitchen carrying a stack of platters. "That's it. We're calling it," she says. "Grab these Aidan." Malena pushes the stack of plates into Aidan's hands. She doesn't think I can carry a stack of glass platters. It's embarrassing. Luckily, Aidan doesn't give me grief, he merely brings them to the sink and turns on the water to begin washing. Good friend mode. Thank fuck. It's almost time I show her how capable I am.

"Tonight was great, right?" I ask, testing the waters.

Wrapping her arms around my waist, she puts her face against my chest. "It was. It was a welcome back party for you, too. We have so much to celebrate. Now I'm ready to celebrate just us two." My dick hardens as I place my chin on the top of her head. "All the stragglers are headed back to the Caroline and Tahoe's Bed and Breakfast."

Aidan coughs. "Platters are clean. I'm leaving before

you guys hump in the kitchen."

I laugh. "Malena wouldn't risk breaking me by humping anywhere except an acceptable, cushioned surface."

"Speak for yourself," Malena says, leaning away to meet my gaze. "Thanks for helping, Aidan," she tosses over her shoulder. "You really kept everything moving along tonight."

"Anything for my favorite couple," he says. Aidan heads to the front door, promising to give me the full scoop on his woman troubles at work on Monday. As I close and lock the door, I'm still trying to process the fact that he cares enough to be bothered by another person. One person. He's the king of letting *everything* roll off his back.

"We're turning a corner. Bronze Bay is good for the soul," I pipe up when Malena closes the sliding door to the deck. She locks it and places the security bar in place. "This place changes lives."

"Ruins them, too, but I won't go down that path tonight when we're on a high," Malena says. The humidity is ratcheted up tonight, leaving a dewy glow on her skin. Her brown eyes flare when they meet mine. "A high that's bound to get better." She walks over to the entertainment system in the living room and turns off the party playlist and selects another one.

She spins when the familiar song starts, gaze locked on mine. Biting her bottom lip, she throws her arms up in the air to sing out the famous first sentence. She's not a small town girl, born and raised in Michigan, though.

She's my girl. My brown eyed, fighter of a woman.

I take her into my arms and lean down to kiss her as she sings the lyrics against my mouth. "You're taking the eleven P.M. train to our bedroom," I say, checking the time. She pulls me down the hallway to our master. Not her mother's old room, and not the newer wing of the house that used to be her room. That's Luna's lair now. We took one of the rooms that has only been used as a guest room. Together we chose what we liked best, mixing and matching our things, and ordering new stuff when we didn't agree. It looks like modern and beachy threw up and the vomit ended up being Leif and Malena Andersson.

"You sick of sleeping in the other room?" Malena asks, dragging her lips across the neck of my shirt.

"If you're asking if I've missed sleeping with you, the answer is kind of. Having a big bed to myself is pretty ace after the twin bed at the hospital, if you're asking if I missed fucking you, in our room, in our bed, then the answer is fuck yes. Every second you were in here and I was down the hall, I thought about creeping in."

"Two days. It's only been two days since you got home and we got married," she says, laughing. Even as she jokes her hands glide under my shirt, taking it up. I pull it over my head to help her. Her fingers splayed on my chest, I hold my breath. Her hands are reverent.

"Two days too long," I counter. "I was starting to think you were avoiding me."

She turns her confused gaze up to meet mine. "Why in the world would you think that? It's been just as hard for me, Leif."

"I don't look like I used to," I admit.

She winces, raising one brow. "I love the way you look. I'll love any way you look. That has no hand in my libido. I'm madly in love with you. That erases any preconceived notions the world has with regards to looks and expectations."

"But I do look different compared to before."

"I'm in love with this," Malena says, putting her hand on my chest. "And what's inside your mind," she adds. Sliding her hand down my body, she grabs my package. "This too. It still looks and feels the same to me. You are my wildest dream made real." She shakes her head. "Don't ever think you're not everything to me. You're perfect."

I should correct her, but my ego won't let me. She's stroked every part of my subconscious that needs reassurance. The only thing on my mind now is connection. In every way possible. "You know that saying, you never know what you have until it's gone?" I say, watching her hands as Malena familiarizes herself with my torso, arms, and neck.

"Yeah," she replies, distractedly, rounding my back to take stock of every new scar. "I can't believe how many holes you have all over your body." Her declaration is absentminded, she doesn't expect a response. The scars aren't something I mind if she doesn't.

"I think that saying is bullshit," I say. She sits on the bed in front of me and pulls the slinky, form-hugging dress over her body. Swallowing hard, I watch her, let my gaze flutter to all of my favorite features. She is a vision, a dream woman. A visceral creation that steals my breath.

"Bullshit how?" she says, tilting her head to the side.

"People need to appreciate what they have when they have it so it never leaves," I explain. "Only weak people need to lose something to appreciate it." I clear my throat.

She looks thoughtful as she reaches behind her body to unfasten her bra.

"Not weak," she says. "Maybe they aren't sure what they have? Maybe they don't understand what losing it will feel like. Not everyone can be certain of something so important, so quickly." Malena shakes her head. "Our love isn't typical, Leif. You're the one who pointed that out to me."

"Fair point," I say, unbuttoning my jeans. They fall to the floor and I step out of them. Malena stands, sliding her panties down mimicking my move. She takes my hand in hers and picks up my left hand to admire my new piece of jewelry. "Tell me something," I say.

When she releases my hand, I pull her naked skin against mine and delight in the practically foreign feeling. "Why do I feel like this isn't going to be a question I want to answer?"

"Why did you really go see your ex-husband?" My question causes her to stiffen in my arms. She relaxes a moment later, but I can tell I've surprised her. "It's just something that's bothered me. That's all."

"When I walked in the auto shop, his wife and little girl greeted me. She was pregnant. It was so odd. The reason I went there, to get closure, to speak my peace, seemed like utter nonsense when I realized he was happily procreating elsewhere. I don't think he ever loved me. Not the way you love me. I know I didn't love him the way I was supposed to. I'd call it luck that I didn't get pregnant, but honestly, I'll use your word and call it destiny. I wasn't supposed to be with him. I was supposed to be with you."

"That makes sense. Sometimes I wonder why you didn't tell me, and then other times I'm glad you didn't because things might have ended up differently had it came up."

"I should have told you," Malena whispers. "I was too afraid of losing the only good thing I've had in my life."

My chest burns with adoration. Taking her face in my hands, I kiss her. I back her up to the bed and follow her down trying desperately not to disconnect our lips. Her love tastes like honesty. The truths are so loud that they block out anything that might cloud this moment. I kiss her until her breathing speeds, and she's raising her hips seeking me out. "You're so fucking beautiful," I murmur against her lips. Her eyes open and I'm greeted with a hint of mischief. "I'm not going to last five seconds."

She laughs, tips up her chin, and waits for my kiss. "Are you saying you didn't know how much you missed sex until we didn't have it?"

I kiss her neck, her collarbone, tracing my lips down her chest and the hollow between her breasts, dragging my fingers over her nipples as I move. "No, I'm quite aware of what I've missed." I continue my assault down her stomach and kiss between her legs. My fingers slip into her wet folds and her moan lights the air.

"This feels better than in my dreams." I lick her clit until she's bucking against me, surging toward orgasm, her breathing speeding. Then I stop, wipe my mouth against her inner thigh, and press my lips against hers.

"That wasn't nice," she says, wrapping her legs around my waist.

I grunt. "Trying to level the playing field a little." Lining up my dick to her wet pussy, every muscle in my body tenses. "When I make love to my wife, she needs to come."

Her panting turns ragged, as she lifts her hips farther, urging me inside. I close my eyes and drive into her. The familiar inhuman feeling of her core gripping me sends a rack of chills down my spine, an awareness that trumps every pain.

Finally. Finally. I'm home.

Malena runs her hands up the sides of my face, resting her forehead against mine, gaze locked on mine. We find our rhythm, together. A year of time has nothing on the fluidity of our chemistry—our connection. She's in my head, in my rapidly beating heart. Her hands slide down my back and pull on my ass. The pace quickens, as do her moans so I know it won't be much longer. Giving myself over to just feel it is easy now.

Tucking my face into her neck, I breathe in her skin. It's her. Everything about this woman—my wife, that I'll never get enough of. "I'm coming," Malena says, sighing out and clenching my glutes tighter.

tossing it

"Me too," I say against her pulse, pressing a kiss there, and then deciding to suck a little instead. We come at the same time, releasing a years' worth of pent-up emotions, or lack thereof.

"That was worth the wait," Malena pants, not releasing her grip.

"Let's never wait that long again, though. Don't get any crazy ideas," I say.

"Agreed," she replies, searching for my lips.

She kisses me, raising her hips to feel our connection. "I love you so much. You're my favorite person in the entire world."

"You're my favorite person in the entire universe," I reply, jutting deeply inside her.

Her reply is that smile.

No one tells you how to love a universe. It's so big and awe-inspiring that contentment comes from merely existing inside of its wonder. I'll spend my life loving in this most impossible way.

She's my miracle. My constant. She is devotion unfiltered and in high def stereo. The words she spoke and thought I never heard ricochet through my mind.

Love me, Leif. Love me.

And so I will. For the rest of time.

International Bestselling Author
RACHEL ROBINSON

Rachel Robinson grew up in a small, quiet town full of loud talkers. Her words were always only loud on paper. She has been writing stories and creating characters for as long as she can remember. After living on the west coast for many years, she now resides in Virginia with her husband and two children.

racheljrobinson.com
Facebook: racheljeanrobinson
Twitter: @rachelgrobinson

Printed in Great Britain
by Amazon